The Gunnersbury Gang

Martyn MacDonald Adams

Caffee

With thanks to the kind and friendly members of the Godalming Writers Group and especially Alan Barker.

Illustrations

Philip Wills

Edited By

Alan Barker

ISBN: 978-1-7396924-4-5

Published by MMA Associates

Dedications

I would like to thank everyone at Scratchers, London Songwriters, Godalming Writers Group, and to all the staff and instructors at Arvon.

1

Helen Meets Caffee

She bit her lip, not knowing what to do next.

Despite the morning rush hour being long gone, Piccadilly Circus was still a frenzied place with people going in and out of the underground station, hurrying to work, rushing to the shops, or just sauntering along to see the sights of London. No one gave the teenage girl, a scruffy waif in green anorak and jeans, a second glance.

No one that is, save for one who was watching her carefully from a distance.

She grimaced. The thirst and hunger were stronger now, but not yet as strong as the pain of her isolation. That had been growing steadily since even before she had arrived at London Kings Cross the previous day. Fleeing had been a stupid thing to do, but it was born of out of despair and she couldn't think of an alternative.

She remembered she had been running for what seemed like ages before she had found herself outside the railway station at Doncaster, her home town. Her only concern then had been to get away as far, and as quickly as she could. So, she bought a ticket and caught the first train to the city of opportunity. People can get lost in London and start again. Right?

Sleep must have overcome her during the journey as most of it was a blank. The gentle rhythm of wheels on rails must have calmed her enough so that she fell asleep. After arriving at London, she had gravitated to the Piccadilly Circus Underground Station with no plan and no clear understanding as to why. So now what?

Stupid! Stupid! Stupid!

How much food could she have bought with that rail fare?

But staying there would have been stupid too. Even more so.

Feeling faint, she walked around the curved edge of the wall to one of the exit tunnels and leaned against the tiles. They were dirty, but so was her torn anorak. Subconsciously her head moved away from the grime. There was no need to smear the stuff, whatever it was, onto her hair. She didn't *want* help, but she knew she needed it.

Were they watching her through the cameras?

Hunger gripped her again and she slid to the floor, eyes squeezed shut, almost curling into a foetal position and she cried silently. Now she had run away she had no idea what to do next.

She couldn't go back. Not now.

"Christ! You're a state, aintchya?"

Still facing the floor, fearful of what was coming next, Helen opened her eyes and wiped away a tear with a sleeve. It left a faint line of dirt on her cheek.

Standing between her and the striding shoes of commuters bustling past were two enormous pink- and white-striped platform clogs occupied by little, naked feet. The clogs looked at least one size too large for those feet. The toenails were painted the same shade of pink. Around one of the ankles were three pink and turquoise plastic bangles.

She moved her eyes up taking in the spindly legs, slightly knobbly knees and impossibly short, pink mini skirt. They skipped past the bare midriff and finally finished at a thin pink and yellow top that covered an almost-flat chest.

The girl was noisily champing on gum. "What's your name, love?"

Two enormous plastic earrings, that matched the rings on her ankles, bracketed an elfin face under short, bleached hair. Her eyeshadow was pastel blue. A pink strap for a small pink- and yellow-striped bag was slung over one shoulder. It must have held a music player of some description because thin white wires led up to each ear. Her thin frame made her look about fifteen or sixteen but something about her eyes said she was a lot, lot older.

"Helen," she whispered.

"You don't look like a Helen. I knew a Helen once. She was fat. She would've 'ad you for breakfast," the girl in pink beamed.

Helen didn't have the strength to smile back. Being accosted by a prostitute didn't appeal.

"And her breath smelt of garlic. She married a chef. *She* landed on her feet. Life can be so surprising, can't it? I bet you're hungry, aintchya? Here..." She handed over a half-empty drink carton and watched as Helen hesitated, took it, then greedily sucked from the straw.

"Thanks," croaked Helen. She tried to hand the empty carton back.

"No fanks. My name's Caffee. Need a crash pad?" The elfin face was still smiling, the mouth still champing.

Helen frowned then caught the sickly-sweet smell of the gum as the girl bent down and asked again, slowly, "Dew... yew... need... a... place to crash?"

Helen hesitated a moment then nodded once.

"Right. I thought so. I gotta go fishin' first. Stand up and don't move." The girl in clogs clumped off down the tunnel toward the stone stairway leading up to the street above. After a short pause she turned sharply back and bumped into a large, middle-aged man wearing a long coat over a three-piece suit and carrying a briefcase.

Caffee was knocked violently against the wall. She cried out. The man stopped and apologised. He offered to help but Caffee insisted she was alright and angrily waved him away. Holding her leg and wincing with pain she limped back toward Helen while the man shrugged and ran up the stairs two at a time, eager not to be associated with a girl of dubious character and to forget the incident while trying his hardest not to give the girl a second thought.

"Are you hurt?" asked Helen.

"What? Fuck no! Here's your ticket." Caffee squinted at it before handing it over. "It's a good 'un. All zones. Result!" She punched the air and wiggled her skinny derriere. "Can I suss 'em or what? Hey? Ready? F'low me!" And she walked into the station showing no signs of her earlier collision.

She headed straight for the ticket barriers pausing only to make sure her new-found friend was following before she went through.

As the two waited on the train platform, Caffee, still chomping on her chewing gum, turned and examined Helen's face.

"You ain't such a minger," she declared. "I bet if we got some cloves for yuh…" she leant forward and sniffed, "… and if you had a shower, you'd clean up a real treat. Yeh?" She grinned.

Helen attempted a smile. "Do you have any more to drink?"

"Nah. Wait 'til we get home. Mam'll fix us up."

"Where are we going?"

"Home. It's not a real home-home, like. More like a doss-house. But it's a good 'un as digs go. The landlord lives in South Africa and doesn't know we live there. He thinks a little old biddy has it but she pegged out over a year ago, so we got it rent free for a while. You on drugs?" Caffee abruptly grabbed each of Helen's arms in turn and pushed the sleeves up looking for tell-tales.

5

"No."

"Course not! Silly me." She stood back. "But you must be shit at blowin', if you're so hungry."

"Pardon?"

"Never mind, luv. No need to play with dicks anymore. You've landed on your feet, you 'ave. Wotchya running from? Pimp? Ploppers? Boyfriend? Girlfriend?"

"I... I'm sorry, I don't know..."

She asked again, slowly, "What... are... you... running from?"

"I... I ran away from home."

"Yeh? When?"

"Yesterday."

"Yeh? Yeh?" Her eyes narrowed. "OK. I believe yuh." Leaving no doubt that she didn't believe her at all. "Dew like the Bay City Rollers?"

"What?"

"Bay City Rollers? About a hundred years old? Classicuddle music? Yeh?"

Helen shook her head.

Caffee sighed. "Never mind. Stay close," and turned her player up.

At that point a warm wind blew across the platform and shortly thereafter the train arrived amidst a descending fanfare of electric motors. The doors opened with a hiss and 'shunk' sound, and after the shuffling horde of passengers had exited the carriages, the two boarded.

After just one change of station the two eventually got off at Gunnersbury. Mercifully for Helen, it was only a short, if almost suicidal, dash across a busy main road to a side street. Another short walk and they arrived at a rather impressive red-brick house among a row of impressive red-brick houses.

The windows were clean, but the frames were clearly rotten and the beading was coming away in places. Grey-brown net curtains prevented anyone from seeing inside. The front lawn had been concreted over some time ago, but now it was weathered and dusty grey with weeds growing out of long cracks. A frail wooden fence on one side was broken and ready to collapse. A step led up to the porch and a heavy black door.

Caffee took out a front-door key, pushed it into the lock and turned it before opening the door. She pushed it wide and entered calling out, "Mam! 'Ere's a lost kitten. Will she do?" Helen followed timidly not knowing what to expect and ready to make a break for it as soon as something didn't seem right.

The house was even larger inside than it appeared from the front. In the hallway the floorboards creaked and it smelled vaguely of damp wood, polish, beer, and lilac. As Helen gently pushed at the front door behind her, the door to the living room opened and a tall, gaunt, grey-haired man regarded the newcomer.

Helen tensed up.

The man threw out his hand and in a deep theatrical voice boomed... "Good-morrow, gentle mistress. Where away? Tell me, sweet Kate, and tell me truly, hast thou beheld a fresher gentlewoman? Such war of white and..." he hesitated, leant forward and squinted closely at Helen "... grey within her cheeks. What stars do spangle heaven above with such beauty as those two eyes become that heavenly face? Fair lovely maid, once more good day to thee. Sweet Kate, embrace her for her beauty's sake."

"Fuck off, you perve! Her name's Helen, and *I* found her!" She turned to explain. "Don't mind this old git. He finks he's an actor – but he's harmless. Voice like a foghorn though – aintchya, Dad!"

The man made himself taller. "To you, your father should be as a God! One that composed your beauties, yea, and one to whom you are but as a form in wax by him imprinted, and within his power to leave the figure or disfigure it."

"Don't you fretten me, you old git! Or I'll cut your nadgers off!" Caffee's hand grasped at something in her purse.

Helen did a quick double take. In that split second the frail elfin girl in oversized clogs had changed to an angry viper about to strike.

The man looked shocked. "But I am not threatening thee, my child..."

"Good. Fuck off, then! She's mine. Come on, Helen." She grabbed at the green anorak and pulled her friend through to the kitchen where a large, probably Jamaican, woman in a bright floral dress and apron stood drying her hands.

"Hi Mam! Look what I brought home."

"Well, hello dear, and what is your name?"

"Her name's Helen."

"Hello, Helen. Are you hungry? You look like you need something. Would you like a cup of tea, now?" She grinned broadly and gave Caffee a welcoming hug.

Helen couldn't help but smile back. She nodded. There was something instinctive about Mam that made her feel safe and welcome.

"And I bet you'd like a sandwich too. Set yourselves down now, and I'll make you both a sandwich. I'll put the kettle on."

Caffee dragged her new friend through the kitchen to the dining room and they sat down at a large wooden table. Made of rough wood it had six place settings, but every chair was different and every setting had a different type of doily. None of the knives and forks matched. In the centre was a broken menorah with only places for five candles. Two used candles were stuck in the middle.

Helen, confused by the name 'Mam', asked quietly, "Is she your mum?"

Caffee threw her head back and burst out laughing. "No! No, she ain't my mum. We all call her Mam though, coz she runs the place, see? And before you ask, the old git ain't my dad, neither. None of us is related. Fank God!"

Three cups of tea and two cheese and pickle sandwiches later, Helen was feeling a lot better. Caffee had asked her a few simple questions about where she came from and why she'd run away. Helen had tried to avoid answering and when pressed only answered vaguely. Mam then interrupted and suggested that if Helen wanted to keep her life private, well that was fine – provided that no-one got hurt because of it.

"She can sleep in my room. Is that okay, Mam?"

"Yes, Cathy. That's fine."

"Okay." She stuck her face into Helen's – nose to

nose. "You don't snore, do you?"

Helen, eyes wide, slowly shook her head. "I don't think so."

"Well, if you wake up on the landing with a black eye, you'll know otherwise. Yeh?" She turned to face Mam. "We need to use the barf-room so that Smelly 'ere can have a shower." She turned back to Helen. "First, I'll introduce you to the others." She grabbed Helen's sleeve and dragged her into the living room.

The floorboards creaked as they entered.

It was a large room with stained, half-drawn velvet curtains at the bay window and several armchairs. Nothing matched. Each chair was a different style and colour. One large, green, three-seat sofa, complete with one leather, one red, and one blue pillow. The pillows were, needless to say, all different designs. They were strewn about and a small mahogany coffee table stood in the middle – and one of its legs had been replaced with one made of pine. At one side was a dark chest of drawers beside an oak display cabinet with wine glasses and bottles of various drinks. One of the cabinet's legs was standing on an upside-down mug. In the middle of the room were two mats. One apparently modern, the other old and ornately patterned – where it wasn't worn through.

Three men sat watching a football match on a large TV. The sound was down very low, but a text commentary was displayed underneath the picture.

"Hello everyone. This lost kitten here is called Helen. She's staying with me. You've met Norman already. What's your name, Norm?" Caffee pointed to the largest armchair, the leather one with wings on each side in which sat the tall, gaunt gentleman who had greeted them earlier.

He stood up and addressed the girls. "Ah, but how sweet a thing it is to look into happiness through mine own eyes. My name, fair maid, is Norman Winchester Haine Le Burgulian. At your service." He bowed with a flourish before sitting down with a thump.

"He's harmless but speaks funny." She pointed to the next one, an unshaven, scruffy man in his mid-twenties reclining on the sofa. "That's Colin. Or sometimes Dave, Steve, Barry, or Garry depending on who's asking. Don't trust him with anything, coz he ain't trustworthy. Are you, Trouble?"

He stuck up a hand and waved, his eyes remained glued to the football game, but otherwise ignored the pair.

"My first night here he pinched all me knickers and Mam had to brain him before he gave 'em back. But we've come to an understanding now. Ain't we, Trouble?"

He glanced at the pair and nodded slowly before returning his attention to the TV.

"I got my own back. It was February, see. We were all freezin', so a dose of Rohypnol and a bottle of water and I'd frozen his todger to the lamp-post outside. Poor thing. Took him several days before he could wank without screaming – but we've got mutual respect now. He leaves me and my stuff alone. Ain't that right, Trouble?"

He winced, crossed his legs and nodded.

"One may speak daggers to her – but dare use none!" Norman smiled meaningfully at Helen.

"And this last one is Adrian." She pointed to the third man. "This one's as weird as a fish in a hammock drinking a custard pina colada, this one. Don't let his uncombed hair and insane grin fool you. This one is not only *completely* bonkers but has a dark and sinister history that I've yet to figure out. But I'll get there."

At the time, no one knew how dark his story, and how intertwined with Norman's, it was. And no one would even conceive that it could involve the government.

2
The Family

Wiry, unkempt hair, and also scruffy but in his early thirties, the man waved sheepishly. Helen noticed the buttons on his checked shirt were buttoned in the wrong holes.

"But he's probably harmless because of his insanity. Aintchya, Ade?"

He smiled and waved back, stuck his tongue out, feigned surprise at its sudden appearance, and then pushed it back in with his fingers before looking sideways at the ceiling and grabbing at his right earlobe.

"He knows he's insane though. Which is a good thing. Norman claims it's because he's so intelligent he's off the scale and halfway down the other side. Colin thinks he's omelette froth. Where's Barry, Ade?"

Adrian put a finger to his lips before an almost incoherent stream of words came tumbling out as if streaming straight from his consciousness.

"If he isn't snoring snores, he's in a higher plane of existing existence, which I strongly doubt because existences don't stack, unless the denizen of the deep dark dungeon isn't a figment, whereupon we can guess that the dancing dead are down there dancing in the baking basement. Is there a baser basement to the base basement, I wonder?" He looked down at the floor, gripped the sofa fiercely as if afraid to fall off, and stared intently at the carpet.

"See? Completely bonkers. The wheel turns, but the hamster's down the pub and completely shit-faced. Take my advice, Helen, never, ever ask him or Norman to choose from a menu."

"He's in his room," offered Colin, pointing up to the ceiling. "Probably asleep or looking at his comics."

"Thanks. Me, Mam, and Barry are the only normal ones here. Oh, and Barry has a bit of a hearing impediment. He's a bit deaf in one ear. Remember that. Come on, we'll leave these weirdos to their football. F'low me!"

Again, Caffee grabbed Helen's anorak by the sleeve and led her through, then out the living room. As she clunked up the stairs she called out "Time to ditch your whiffiness, gel! I'll lend you my bathrobe and you can have a bath an' a shower. You'd best do both and scrub up proper-like."

They arrived at the bathroom door.

"We got hot water at the moment, so you're lucky. And wash your hair coz, given 'arf a chance, Mam will pounce and be checking it for livestock.

"There ain't no girly smellies apart from mine. I like strawberry. You can borrow that if you want, or some lavender, but not too much of that. Mam likes lavender. Other than that, we got about seven hundredweight of industrial strength deodorant for men which Colin nicked. Poor sod is under the delusion that it makes him attractive to women. Personally, I think it's reject spray paint without the paint. Mam thinks it's insect repellent, and Norman thinks it's a fire hazard."

Caffee eyed Helen up and down.

"I suggest, if those are your only cloves, that you wash your pants in the shower at the same time, and then dry 'em using the hair dryer. *Don't* do your jeans, yeh? They'll stay wet all night and, in the morning, they'll be so fuckin' tight you won't be able to get 'em off. You'll have to pee with 'em still on and then your legs'll go all purply." She thought for a moment. "Which is why I wear a skirt. Anyway, we'll get you cloved up proper, tomorrow. And don't touch my stuff!"

She stood by the bathroom door and held it open for the new girl, her face turning serious.

"Finally, house rules. Don't nick nothing from us. No trading sexual favours with one another, that includes freebie blows, massages, or anything like that – especially with Colin. Don't believe anything – especially if it's from Colin. No tantrums, violence, or shouting – unless it's with Colin. Don't do drugs – unless you need to knobble Colin. No flashing – *especially* at Colin." She leant forward and whispered conspiratorially... "Although if you catch one of Barry's dangler, see if you can get a picture of it on your phone, okay?" She giggled, then composed herself and said aloud, "Break a rule and you're out. Savvy? Tonight, you get free. Tomorrow, we talk about rent. Okay? Have a nice bath, and try not to use *all* the hot water. Any questions?"

Helen shook her head once.

"And lock the door. And try to pee in the bowl. Us girls have a reputation to keep. Oh, and I forgot, if you get a boyfriend do your humping at his place, okay? The banging embarrasses Mam... and everyone else, in fact. Unless he's a fuckin' musician, in which case you'll have to do it in his van, so make sure the springs ain't rusty coz they can break at just the wrong fuckin' moment... probably. Oh, and make sure he's got a decent mattress in the back, otherwise you'll get bruises and stink of oil, and it takes fuckin' ages to get it out of your hair. And make sure he ain't already married with a kid, neither. Musician is Latin for bastard, all right? See yuh later."

Helen took stock as Caffee's enormous shoes clumped away along the bare floorboards.

She sighed and wondered if this was to be her next home after all. Unless 'rent' meant something else.

After an extended stay in the bathroom, Helen emerged looking and feeling much better. Despite what Caffee had said there was a good selection of shampoos and conditioners, mostly in small hotel-sized bottles. So, now her brown hair had been very carefully cleaned, blow dried, and brushed. Colour had returned to her, now almost-rosy, cheeks. Feeling much more confident she went downstairs to the living room and found everyone enjoying a glass of wine – except Colin who held a can of beer.

She couldn't help but smile at Colin.

Adrian was busy licking the outside of his wine glass and mumbling something to himself about not knowing whether he was on the inside or the outside. He deduced that if he was inside then the universe was made of wine, which in turn implied a cosmic vineyard somewhere. It was quite probable that the creator of said universe spent a lot of his, or its, time drunk, and thus it was likely to be French, or Italian, too. So, did the God of the English only speak French or Italian? And what happened when this god hiccoughed?

Caffee was spread out on a pile of cushions and beckoned to Helen by patting a bean bag beside her. Norman handed her a large glass of red as she sat down.

"Good wine is a good familiar creature if it be well used," he smiled. "A bird in the hand is..."

"...is going to shit up your shirtsleeve!" interrupted Caffee.

Helen thanked him, not really sure if she wanted it and not really sure what he meant by other 'uses' he had for the wine.

Caffee introduced her to Barry, a somewhat large, short haired, ebony man in his early to mid-thirties. He wore a dark woolly pullover with frayed sleeves that looked at least a size too small. He smiled broadly at her, a gentle and genuine smile which seemed to light up the room. He raised his glass in a toast to their new guest. She couldn't help but respond likewise.

"I like wine. It looks like blackcurrant juice, but it isn't," Barry explained in his deep, clear voice. Helen nodded in agreement as he continued. "I like blackcurrant juice. Mam buys me blackcurrant juice. Sometimes I pretend it's wine. It looks like wine, but it isn't."

Colin changed the channel on the TV with a remote.

"We got a guest tonight. Be polite. Switch the box off." Caffee looked at the young man and inclined her head meaningfully towards the new girl.

"The scores will be up in a minute."

"Give us the fuckin' remote," she sighed and held out her hand.

Colin made no move.

"Switch it off or give us the fuckin' remote! There's a reason why they make those things long and thin with rounded corners, you know? If you don't pass it over, I'll shove it... I'll show you a new place where you can keep it warm and safe."

She paused, then wagged a finger. "It's a place where the sun don't shine but brings tears to your eyes. I'm warning you!"

Colin reluctantly switched the TV off but kept hold of the remote.

Caffee sipped at her glass. "Sorry, Helen. Sometimes civility has to be taught through diplomatic negotiation."

Colin ignored the episode and returned to the subject they'd been discussing just before Helen's entrance. "I still say they're a bleeding stupid bunch of wank..." He glanced at Mam before continuing, "...idiots. It's all bleedin' stupid. I heard from a mate of mine that *all* our imports come from *abroad*. I mean, honestly, who thought that one up? Our fff... stupid politicians, I reckon."

Norman nodded in sozzled agreement. "Politics. A word from ancient Greek. It means 'many parasites'. And then there's 'political', a word which means 'many tickles'. They make you laugh. So fitting, I'm thinking."

"It doesn't take a genius like Alfred Einstein to figure it out, for Christ's sake. Forget to pay a stupid parking fine and the police are on you like a ton of shi..." He saw Mam frowning "...sugar. So, I reckon they should be in charge of rounding up all those immegal illigrants instead." He hiccoughed and giggled.

"Is that not what they do at this very moment?"

"Yeh. Right. But if they gave them fucking parking tickets instead, I bet they'd all be out of the bloody country by now. What this country needs... what this country needs is more out-of-work potty-lishan... poli-ticians."

"So that they might understand the plight of the unemployed?"

"What? Naaah, numpty. We just need to put more potty..." Colin sighed and gathered what few wits that remained, "...politicians out of work, is all. Fff... king money grabbers, the lot of 'em. It's not as if they do anything, is it?"

Mam had grown bored with the subject and suggested that Colin explain his latest money-making idea to Helen. She wanted to know what the new girl thought of it.

Colin sat forward, sobering up. "You come from up North, right?"

Helen nodded hesitantly.

"Do you know how to train racing pigeons?"

She shook her head.

"Do you know *anything* about... about racing pigeons?"

She shook her head.

"Do you know anyone who wants to *buy* racing pigeons?"

Again, she shook her head.

"Uh. Oh, well." He slumped back, disappointed,

hiccoughed and burped at the same time, making his eyes water.

"Go on, tell the girl about your latest crazy idea. Let's hear it proper, now. Tell it proper," Mam cajoled.

Colin sighed, then sat forward again.

"Well, I got this idea. Pigeons like birdseed, yeh? So, I convert the loft into a racin' pigeon factory. You make a door at one side of the roof, with a ledge. It's a win... window really. Just inside is a tray of birdseed. A wild pigeon flies along, sees the ledge and lands on it. Then it sees the... the birdseed just inside and goes in to get some. Then wham!" He clapped his hands making Helen jump. "A little device springs out and wraps a little weight around its legs and opens up a drop hole. So, the bird goes mental like and flaps its wings, but the weight is just enough to keep it stuck in the hole. It flaps like crazy until it's exhausted, then it falls into a box to the bottom. But there it gets all the birdseed it wants, and maybe a little steroid, and has a chance to rest for an hour or two.

"Meanwhile the box is being slowly winched up a ramp until it reaches the top. Another small weight is added to the bird's legs and then the bottom opens up and the bird has to keep flapping until it's exhausted again. This is repeated several times because pigeons are stupid, but it's good training, yeh? By the end of the process that is going to be one super strong bird. And the beauty of it is that all you need to run it is some birdseed."

He sat back, obviously pleased with his brilliant idea.

"With all these wild pigeons in London, that could be a very profitable business. It's my Automated Racin' Pigeon Training Factory. And it's humane too. It could make us a fortune. It turns wild pigeons into a valuable commodity. Wild pigeons are vermin, right? Everyone is happy. We could box 'em and flog 'em up North to pigeon racers. We could have Formula One Pigeon Races. What do you think?"

Norman mumbled. "This fellow pecks up wit, as pigeons pease, and utters it again when God doth please," and raised his glass.

Caffee asked, "What about the old ones that die of stress, then?"

Colin thought for a moment. "Pigeon pie?"

The room burst into a lively discussion for several minutes on the merits and problems of building and running such a factory, and what the recipe for pigeon pie was. Caffee suggested that it could be marketed as a wild pigeon keep-fit and leisure centre, but Mam wouldn't hear any of it. The thought of pigeon droppings and dead birds in the loft left her cold.

Norman was no longer misquoting Shakespeare but rather discussing seriously as to how the quality of Christmas turkey could benefit from an automated exercise turkey factory.

In the end, the problem of cleaning out the bird poop won the day, and the idea was put on hold. Mam rose to make dinner and the conversation turned to the neighbours and which wives were rumoured as being swapped with whom, or sometimes what. Then it turned to the dustmen, then the merits of big wheels on cars (and roller skates – Caffee's idea), and finally how to train squirrels to be ninja assassins using an automated factory built into the loft and using acorns to lure them in.

Helen relaxed. At times she even found herself laughing. This was the most fun she'd had for a long time. She mainly listened, but every now and then she made the odd sensible suggestion or observation – but she giggled at some of the most ludicrous ideas. More than once she caught sight of Colin looking at her, but that was also because she couldn't stop herself from glancing at him.

At one point everyone went quiet as Adrian started mumbling.

"Old pen materials are useful from the dropped manna into our manor, be so cheap to be free and if honed and combed and sliced and diced and split 'til fit they'd be novelty copies of the ancient blot makers. But soft they'd be too, but not, tis true, true duck, but yet maybe with coarse hemp be of use somewhere as unworthy pillowed packing. Say you all 'tis a fair idea for the embryonic corporation conceptualised just here?"

He grinned and looked sideways up at the ceiling.

"Bravo!" boomed Norman and applauded.

"Almost poetic that was," mused Caffee and everyone politely agreed, unsure as to what exactly they'd agreed upon. Then they continuing their discussion that soon turned to automatically training armies of roller-skated ninja squirrels and the recipe for squirrel pie – until Mam's voice called out from the dining room that dinner was ready.

"What we got? Does anyone know?" asked Colin.

"Beef boggy-non, I fink," said Caffee.

"I am a great eater of beef, and I believe that does harm to my wit," said Norman then aside to Helen he explained. "I think she means beef bourguignon."

Something nagged at Helen's subconscious. Adrian's short monologue didn't have the *feel* of being *completely* random nonsense. And also, what kind of dark and sinister past could this wiry young man with a scrambled brain possibly have? Nowhere near as dark as hers, surely.

3
The Hunt

"You mean, John Hughes?"

"It was bloody gruesome."

Two men sat in a shadowy corner of the small pub tucked away in a Doncaster side street. There were no wooden beams or horse brasses but lots of printed adverts framed as if they were works of art. There were faded adverts for butter, cigarettes, beer, petrol, girdles, and anything else that was either out of date or not considered fashionable or 'green' anymore.

The man in the black leather jacket, a tall man with a hard, angular face, nodded in response to the sergeant's news. There were few other customers but these two must have been regulars for they were relaxed in each other's company. Earlier they had been chatting and laughing amongst themselves. The sergeant and the man in the jacket always sat at the farthest, darkest corner. Now they spoke quietly and called it 'discretion'.

Jacket's eyes narrowed. "So, I heard... stuffed down his throat?"

"Yeh. He was already suffocating when they cut it off. He died from blood loss, but he must have been gasping first. Not quick. Poor sod. Blood everywhere."

"Suffocating?"

"Steel hook in his back. Hung from the ceiling. Internal bleeding. Drowning in his own blood. Christ knows how they got it into him."

Jacket grimaced. There was a pause while they sipped at their coffee, then, "John wasn't a fragile man. They must have been right beefy to overcome him. Did he have bruises? Was he knocked about? What do they think?" He leant forward and stared into the sergeant's eyes. "Have I got to worry about another fucking foreign crew invading my patch?"

Sergeant Middleton justified his unofficial relationship with the local crook on the basis that it was better to deal with one local gang, and sometimes get them to help keep the peace, than fight several warring factions. Besides, there were a few other benefits to be had this way. Everyone wins.

"Not sure. Could be a warning, a message, or it could be a serial killer."

"Eh? A serial killer? Here? Are you kidding me?"

"Nay. We got this tart and a few of her buddies down from Manchester to help out with the investigation. All hands to the pump and all that. The bloody newspapers made this a headline so some poncy politician kicks arse. She reckons it might not be a message, it might be a serial killer."

"Looks like a fucking message to me."

"Aye, but he did have form, didn't he? Bit of a perve, that one. Spiteful one, I heard."

Jacket thought for a moment. He had always disliked Hughes. Loud mouth, muscles like tree trunks and the intelligence of a rabid bull. "Only with girls." He paused then conceded, "Once or twice with boys, but we stopped that. He liked his knife, he did, and he had a bit of a mouth."

The sergeant put his hands around the coffee, it

was cooling far too quickly. As he glanced around the reflection of a flashing one-armed bandit caught his eye and he had to force himself to look away.

"She has her theories, this tart. We have ours. She reckons it's similar to the bodies we found on the dump. Remember them? Two young fellers with their dicks hacked off and left with the garden refuse. One earlier this year and one last year. We never did find a proper motive for those two. This one is different. I reckon it could be a new crowd trying to make an impression. It's not quite the same MO as the others. Either way, it's got top priority. We've got nearly thirty officers chasing up leads now. And that could go up."

"Looks to me like I got to see to another fucking mess. Nothing from immigration?"

Sergeant Middleton thought back to the two earlier murders. At the time there was little that Forensics could offer his team, but extensive questioning had turned up several suspects. There were a few acquaintances and ex-girlfriends with form, one of which they had in common, but that one was as non-violent as they came. It was more likely that the origin lay somewhere with the dodgy drug dealings that both lads were involved in.

At about the same time there had been several more conventional deaths, which *were* clearly gang related. In Middleton's view, if youngsters were involved then, in the end, it always boiled down to drugs. He'd been actively involved in both investigations and at the time that had been his view.

To the force it was statistics that counted. How it appeared to the public took priority above all else. It would look bad if gang warfare was breaking out under their noses, therefore it was easier to lump all the unknown murders together with known gang hits.

But recently the crime statistics *had* jumped badly. Over time, and with the help of the jacketed man sitting in front of him, the numbers were now back under control... although the real cost had almost certainly been more bodies. But Jacket was experienced at covering up that sort of thing. If a person was reported as missing then the police strongly suggested that they had fled the area. They certainly didn't want to find too many murdered corpses in their patch. Budgets were tight enough.

After that recent episode he knew Jacket was feeling nervous about other groups moving onto his turf. It was bad for business, especially now that this bitch from Manchester was looking the place over, particularly into places she was unwelcome. Serial killers were rare. But serial killers made headlines.

Sergeant Middleton had to be sure. "Those two... the ones with their dicks chopped off... I know I've asked you before, but...?"

"Nay, Middy. Like I told you. Not us. None of mine did those, and anyway, it's not my style, you know that. So, you've got nowt from immigration or anything?"

The sergeant was satisfied with that answer. Most probably the castrator had been from outside. Then, with any good luck, he had become a victim himself. Besides, Jacket was right, those two earlier murders weren't his style. He, or his colleagues, would never be so sloppy as to leave them in the dump like that.

Underneath it all, Middleton had respect for

Jacket. He was a pro. He could be approached and he was always reasonable — until he lost his temper or felt threatened.

"Nay. Nowt on the radar. Could be a crowd pushed out from t' South moving North, or maybe down from further up. Maybe they thought they'd scare the locals, a warning, like." He laughed but Jacket didn't laugh back. "What was he to you, anyway?"

"Oh, we did a bit of business with him. Nothing major. A bit of muscle when needed, that's all. He's related to one of my boys though — Donny? You know Donny? Most upset, he is. I'm worried about this. It's out of order. What leads have you got?"

"So far, we've got eight sets of DNA. Five male and three female, but it's a public place. I reckon we could easily find several more. We've got prints and partials from dozens of sources, but most are smudged. Blood on the scene from several other sources too — Christ knows why. Looking at the way the vic was strung up I reckon we're looking at a couple of males, at least. Probably young, fit and not frightened of a bit of butchery, either."

There was a short pause before the sergeant continued. "I might be able to help, though. Interested?"

Jacket nodded. "Yeh? If this *is* a new crew, I want them out. We both want them out. It could turn nasty if we wait too long. I guess you don't want another fucking war on your doorstep either."

The sergeant shook his head. The political fallout from the last one had been bad enough. "I've been put in charge of collating all the video and photographic evidence. It's all passing over my desk." He smiled wryly. "Would any of that be of any use to you?"

Jacket nodded. "Aye. Oh, aye. That might do nice, like. When could you get it to me?"

"We got to coordinate this though. Don't go off half-cocked or we're both in the shitter."

Jacket nodded again. Despite disliking the older police sergeant, he had some respect for his word. This one had been around a while and he had never broken a promise. Nothing bad had stuck to the dirty old git... yet. "No problem, Middy. It works both ways, as always. You scratch my back and I'll be a good boy. Anyway, whoever did this must be one kind of a cunt. We both want them off the streets before it gets worse. It can *only* get worse. Right?"

"Right. Most of the CCTV from traffic is being downloaded as we speak. I can get the railways and one or two of the local businesses to you by lunchtime tomorrow. The rest over the next few days."

"How?"

"I'll copy it onto those little memory sticks. I'll go to lunch at Geoff's Greasy — you know the place — and leave them in a folded newspaper. One of your boys can pick it up after I leave. Okay?"

Jacket nodded. "I know the place, at the end of the High Street. Aye, sounds good. You won't get caught?"

"I will if you spread the stuff around. You promise to keep this quiet?"

"Utmost discretion, pal. Top secret. You have my word. I'll only pass it on to one other."

"Who?"

"Never you mind. The less you know the better but I'll be reet careful, like. You're precious to me, Middy, you know that? Are you sure you've got your end covered?"

"Aye. They're too busy organising at the moment. The bitch wants everything changed around. If there's a problem, I'll back off. You know me, I'm careful."

Careful when he wants to be, thought Jacket. When he sees a chance to get laid for free, then he sees himself as some sort of bloody hero. Still...

"Aye. Very much appreciated. And what can I do in return?" He knew there would be a price. Nevertheless, an insider like Middy was gold, and he never asked for something which couldn't easily be supplied.

The sergeant grinned. "Well, I wondered, for a start, if I might borrow one of the girls for a night or two?"

Jacket nodded. He'd expected that. "You get me that stuff and you can fuck yourself blind, mate. On me."

"Nothing illegal though..."

"Nay, of course not. The one I'm thinking of keeps crying, but she'll get over it. Or you can pick your own. No problem." He sat back and sipped at his coffee, feeling a little generous to the old letch.

The sergeant nodded and raised his own in a toast. "To keeping them fuckers off our turf."

Jacket raised his cup. "Aye. To keeping the fuckers out."

Like the two men, both of the cups were cold.

4
The Morning

Helen woke early in the morning and listened, half asleep, to people moving about the house and getting ready for work. She couldn't be sure what time it was, but it must have been early. She could tell that they were trying to be quiet, but the old wooden floors and the enthusiastic plumbing made that impossible. For now the runaway felt warm, comfortable, and, for the first time in a while, safe. So, she kept her eyes closed and allowed herself to drift off again.

She awoke sometime later and yawned. Her memory of the previous days came back slowly. She was lying on the floor of Caffee's bedroom in a sleeping bag on top of an older sleeping bag on top of some old blankets and towels. There were cushions between her and the cold wall by her side. It was surprisingly comfortable, but they had yet to find a proper bed for her. Squinting over her shoulder she saw Caffee's bed, strewn with cuddly white, pink, and pale blue bears and some plastic horses. No Caffee, though.

At the far end of the room a dirty shower curtain hung from a bent rail. That made do as Caffee's wardrobe. She had donated her 'dresser', a large cardboard box, to Helen but as yet it only held one pair of jeans, one dirty green anorak, a pullover, a top, and a pair of mud-stained shoes — each with its own little white lace-topped sock.

She remembered the previous night when they'd had lentil soup followed by the beef, a mixed salad with continental dressing, sausages and rolls for dinner. It was an impressive spread. After that the dishwasher had refused to cooperate so she and Mam washed the dishes by hand while Barry made them all hot chocolate.

Now she smelt toast and this was just too much. Unzipping the sleeping bag, quickly got dressed and after a short visit to the bathroom, almost fell downstairs in her haste.

"Good morning, honey bunch. Would you like some toast, there?" beamed Mam.

Barry was busy at the sink enthusiastically scouring a pan. Beads of sweat on his forehead.

"Yes, please. Thank you."

"I'll make you some fresh, girl. You set yourself down, now."

Helen went through to the dining room. The table had yet to be cleared. There was a not-quite finished bowl of cereal, a couple of mugs, and some plates.

She heard Barry rinsing the pan, then Mam's voice. "Have you finished the pan, son?"

"Yes, Mam. Look, it is all bright and shiny now."

"Goodness... Barry?"

"Yes, Mam?"

"Was that a non-stick pan?"

There was a short silence followed by a sigh.

"I think it best if you went to work now, Barry."

"Yes, Mam. Sorry, Mam."

A dark shadow flashed by the kitchen window followed by a thud and a groan from outside.

"That will be Adrian. Sometimes he forgets when he's upstairs," explained Mam, opening the kitchen door. "Are you hurt, Adrian? You silly boy, come in here and get some toast, now."

He groaned again. He'd landed on a strategically placed mattress underneath his bedroom window for just such occasions. It was full of holes, damp from the weather, and stained from its dubious history — but still soft enough to break his fall.

He staggered in with a hand to his head, mumbling. "Bouncy, bouncy. Silly billy wildly mildly slightly plummeted to the bruising place again, again. And then. Must remember to remember else dismember. Need digital memory, not a not knot but a string on a finger not a ram — that's too horny with kicky legs and hairy ankles. Is a body bruise count a constant for some of us?" He staggered to the dining room and sat at the table then put his head flat against the top before examining his reflection in a spoon. "Oh no. I'm bent again," he muttered.

"Are you really insane?" Helen was still unsure if it was some sort of joke.

He sat up and looked at her. She tried, but it was difficult to keep track of his stream of thought.

"And what lies outside? Why? The rest of the world by its own admission. But I claim to be amongst the few in this landless land. What no one knows is if everyone else is out, then what else is it they're in, instead? Madness, sadness, and badness? Oh, woe is them, they're lost, but I *know* where I am. Like my favourite singer tells me, I am Aladdin

Sane."

He grinned and looked up at the ceiling, apparently very happy with his answer and already recovered from his fall.

Helen smiled back weakly. It definitely was *an* answer, she thought.

Probably.

She debated whether to help clear the dishes, but she was hungry and so waited patiently for the toast. Adrian replaced the side of his head against the table and continued examining his reflection in the spoon.

The front door opened followed by a rustling and then closed with a bang. A familiar clumping sound approached them from the hall then Caffee exploded into the kitchen with a lot of huffing and puffing and four bags of groceries. The waif dropped them gently onto the kitchen floor.

"I saw Barry beaming outside. He said he cleaned up another pan."

"Oh, yes. He did at that."

"Did you let him clean another non-stick one?"

"Yes, honey bunch. I'm sorry. He so loves cleaning them, you know? He tries *so* hard. I haven't the heart to stop him."

"I'll have to get Colin to nick a few more. Either that or I could spray some of the old ones black and let him clean them."

"Did you get the white rolls, darlin'?"

"Yes, Mam."

"Did you get the mint sauce?"

"Yes, Mam. And the jam, and the milk, and the butter, and the ganotchy, and the fussily. Any chance of a cuppa?"

"You set yourself down, girl. I'm making tea and toast for Helen and Adrian. Would you like some toast?"

"No, fanks. Just a cuppa will do nicely. Hiya, Helen!" Caffee entered the dining room and flopped onto a chair with a sigh and an 'Oooh...'

"Hello."

Mam could be heard rummaging through the bags, then she called out, "Did you remember the coleslaw?"

"Oh, fuck!" Caffee buried her face in her hands and called out, "Sorry, Mam. I forgot."

"Oh, that's alright, girl. I can pick some up on my way home from work."

Caffee sighed and looked at Adrian's head lying on the table facing away from her. She idly picked up a fork and stroked Adrian's ear with it. "So, what do you fink? You wanna stay? Yeh?"

Helen nodded, captivated by the cutlery in Caffee's hand.

Adrian scratched his ear but not before Caffee had snatched the fork out of his reach. Then she absently dipped it in the milk in a used cereal bowl behind Adrian's head.

"Good. Then we got to sort out rent. Everyone contributes. It's a rule. Barry and Norman work at the council and pay us when they get paid. Me and Colin pay on account coz' we don't have regular jobs. Adrian gets a special pension from the government because they're the cunts that screwed up his mind. Mam works part-time at the old peoples' home, but she always does the housework and dinners and stuff — so she's exempt. I take it you ain't got a job, right?"

Helen nodded then, slightly confused, shook it. "I don't have a job," she clarified, still not taking her eyes off the fork.

"Can you sign on?"

Helen remained silent, not wanting to answer that one.

Caffee delicately scooped up some soggy Cornflakes. "Doesn't matter. Do you like cakes?"

Helen nodded.

She carefully raised the fork with its mushy load. "Good. Coz there's going to be a part-time job going in the bakery down the road tomorrow. That okay for yuh?"

Helen nodded again.

She moved the fork over Adrian's prone head. "Good. And once we've had our tea, we're goin' shopping. I take it you got no other cloves on you. How much cash you got?"

Helen cautiously reached into her jeans — her eyes still fixated on the laden fork.

"Don't be bashful, I don't nick from friends... or even Colin... well, not that often, anyway," she added, then turned the fork over.

The sodden Cornflakes landed in Adrian's ear. He froze, eyes and mouth opened into circles of shock before he yelped and shot to his feet. "Cold! Cold! My ear! Cold! My ear! It's drowning!" He stuck a finger in and pulled out the mash and stared at it with horror before sticking it under Caffee's nose. "See? Bits falling off! Oh, Mam, quick. Where's the duct tape?" He ran out the room and they heard his footsteps beat a frantic rhythm upstairs to the bathroom.

Mam entered the room with a tray. "*Now* what have you done to our poor Adrian, you wicked, wicked girl?"

The tray held four mugs of tea, three small plates of toast, three knives and a new jar of jam. She placed it on the table, crossed her arms under her ample bosom and looked sternly down at the little girl in pink.

Caffee was grinning. "I just put some Cornflakes in his ear. He was in a coma, like. I thought he needed livening up."

Helen valiantly prevented herself from giggling out loud by biting her lip and looking down at the floor, but her shuddering shoulders gave the game away.

"You are a naughty girl, Cathy! You know he doesn't see the world as we do. He doesn't understand things in the same way as us. Helen, you must keep an eye on this one. She's a scamp! Be a dear and go upstairs and tell Adrian what our naughty girl did to him, would you now?"

Helen nodded and left the table, barely managing to suppress the sniggering. When she got to the bathroom Adrian was holding his ear between his fingers, glancing in the mirror and then turning his head away quickly.

"My ear's hiding! I can't see into it," he whined. "It's embarrassed!"

Helen explained Caffee's prank, and then, after a little calming, he relaxed. She cleaned his ear with a tissue before reassuring him and leading him downstairs again.

Adrian sat at the dining table, saw the plate of toast and pointed to his cup of tea and beamed. "Raise a tea toast to the tasty toasted toast tasting testers. If they got in a jam, then that's a sweet icky licky sticky place to be, and we'd have none. But we do. So, toast — Ouch! But when the hot tea's less, less coldish anyway." He sniffed cautiously at his cup of tea and nursed a burnt finger.

"That's true," said Helen, and showed Caffee the five-pound note, fifty and two ten pence pieces she had extracted from her pocket.

"What? You understood all that?"

"Yes. Bits."

Caffee looked at Adrian then back at Helen. "What's he say, then?"

"He said we should salute the people that first tested toast, otherwise there'd be no such thing."

"Bleeding 'ell! You talk Ade? Can you understand everything he says?"

Helen shook her head. "Only bits."

"I didn't think *any* bits of his ever made any sense. Learn something new every day. Anyway, you've not got enough dosh so I'll sub you and you can pay me back later. Yeh?"

"Today is a day of significance," declared Adrian. "Today my ear got its own breakfast!"

Mam looked disapprovingly at Caffee, who raised her eyebrows questioningly. Helen giggled and thought to herself that this place seemed to be the perfect place to settle.

Sadly, that was not to be.

5
Shopping

Helen shivered. She felt damp.

The Chiswick High Road was pretty busy with shoppers and traffic. The weather had turned sultry with low clouds turning everything damp and grey. It wasn't actually raining but the roads were still wet from last night's downpour, and there were long puddles in the gutter. Cars and trucks were swishing by, overtaking and just missing each other before suddenly stopping, then swishing off again.

Walking on the pavement consisted of dodging people, dogs on leads, tots on leads, push chairs, and splashing puddles. Signposts were another hazard. The local council seemed addicted to placing them wherever there was an opportunity to give an unwary pedestrian a smart smack on the nose.

Caffee had dragged Helen in and out of a few charity shops and she'd bought several items of clothing for her new friend but Helen had the distinct feeling they had acquired more clothes than had been paid for.

None of these, except the generic underwear, were particularly to Helen's taste. She was now starting to feel foot sore and tired. Furthermore, she was building up a whole new set of mixed feelings about the entire situation, including the domestic arrangements, and felt uncomfortable with some of them.

But she was more than thankful for the rescue, no

matter how temporary, and very grateful for the offer of a place to stay. In fact, it was almost as if some maternal deity was looking after her – which didn't make any sense after what she'd done before coming south to London. She'd been given food and a warm place to stay. 'Rent' had simply meant that, after all. Nothing more sinister. Now she was being bought clothes and, so far, none of this was costing her a penny, so she was reluctant to complain.

Nevertheless, she felt the need to browse on her own, for herself and in her own way. After knowing Caffee for such a short time, Helen wanted time to be alone – to spend some time in quiet reflection. To do that she needed to break away, get away from the skinny girl's awful accent and overpowering attitude.

But it was more complicated than that; she also felt a kinship with the skinny girl. She guessed it was like having an older, overbearing sister. Caffee had a refreshing, if somewhat blunt, attitude to life. The loud semi-dressed waif found humour in almost everything. Helen could not. But above all, when it came down to it, she knew beggars couldn't be choosers and at this moment she was definitely a beggar. For the time being she knew she had to content herself with knowing that soon, once she'd got on her feet, she'd be able to strike out and be independent. Until then, she'd have to put up with her new-found friend.

Besides, despite the problems, Caffee did make her laugh. And that was very important to Helen. Crucial, in fact.

She'd just have to wait and see how things turned out. She'd keep her eyes open and wait for her opportunity to move on, but her immediate priority was her hair – she needed to keep it dry. Washing with soap and conditioner and then immediately brushing it was okay, but wetting it with simple water and letting it dry led to it exploding into a puffy rat's nest of a hairball. An unkempt, untameable frizz of knots and tangles. She absolutely hated that.

Caffee had zoomed ahead to her favourite second-hand shop. They often sold white clothes and white shoes there. Apparently, the owner had a 'thing' for 'purity' – 'purity' being defined as anything white. The whiter, the purer. The front of the shop was dedicated to new stock with long white satin slips, white lacy lingerie, and white wedding dresses – or, as Norman once put it 'Bridal garments of broadcast chastity for the vicar, the photo album, and the gullible.'

At least two of the white wedding dresses had been resized for mothers-to-be, so endorsing Norman's definition.

The further the merchandise was from the window, the more colourful and less pristine it became. White nearest the window, cream a little further back, pastel shades behind that, and so on.

Caffee had her own 'thing' for pastel pinks and blues. A comprehensive private collection of dyes, spray cans and marker pens ensured a continual supply to her growing wardrobe – provided the raw material was cheap and adaptable, or nickable. The girl was adept at trimming skirts and tops with the use of scissors and then, with Mam's help, the subsequent repairs.

The skinny Londoner had just wrestled a heavy pink and white floral nightdress from an elderly lady who was even shorter than herself, and was wondering what kind of woman would wear such a tent when she noticed that Helen wasn't with her. Glancing out the window she saw her talking to a young, clean-cut stud. She frowned. Despite the cold, Helen was stroking a lock of her hair, gently swaying from side to side, and gazing dreamily into the stud's eyes. Caffee was about to replace the nightdress on its upholstered hanger when she noticed the leaflets in his hand.

Cursing, she threw the garment over the head of the old lady, grabbed the bags of shopping, and stormed outside.

"... so, you see our Lord Jesus Christ died for your sins. It was His unbounded love for us all that brings us together into a brotherhood of love and caring..."

Helen seemed to be listening intently. Whether she was attracted to him or to his words Caffee couldn't tell, but she had her suspicions. It didn't make a difference, anyhow. Helen was *her* territory.

"Hello, mush! You believe in God then?" Caffee put on her innocent face.

"Hello. Is this a friend...?"

Caffee took immediate control. "Yup! She's wiv me. And *I* think you really love your God, am I right?"

The young man smiled. "Our Lord welcomes all those of faith into His heart."

Caffee had been here many times before. "So let me get this straight. You reckon God made the universe, yeh?"

"God made all things..."

"So, he's not of this Earth. He's an alien. He must

be. He's from another universe, right?"

"Well, I wouldn't..."

"So, let's not call God a 'Him' coz it's an 'it'. It ain't human, is it? Can't be. It's an alien. Humans don't create universes. And there ain't no 'She' Gods neither, so if he's got a todger it'd be useless and that proves it – unless you've seen it. So, God is an 'it', yeh?"

"I wouldn't..."

"Well, it ain't human because it created the universe and everything in it. *We* can't. It's not a fing us humans do – create universes. Simple, yeh?"

Anger was erupting from somewhere deep within the girl. She put the shopping down on the pavement and crossed her arms.

"And then, after 'it' created this universe, 'it' waited thousands and thousands of years before 'it' *then* decides to come down and tell some semi-literate flea-bitten bronze-age nomads all about itself. Yeh? Is that right?"

The young man stood paralysed as the girl's voice got louder.

"Then this *thing* makes a young girl preggers without *her* having any say in the matter. Nowadays, we call that *rape* – but the fucking alien didn't give a toss about what *we* would think of it, did it? Oh, no. Then she gave birth to a half-alien cross-breed kid you called Jesus. Right? Yeh?"

"Erm. Let me call for..." The young man turned away, desperately searching the street for a colleague to rescue him.

"Now, wait a moment you cock-head! *You*

entrapped my friend here, so *you* take responsibility for your cock'n'bullshit myth!" She stepped forward and poked him in the ribs. "A bunch of tribal bronze-age goat-herds dreamt up some cock'n'bull creation stories and you..." (*poke*) "fell..." (*poke*) "for 'em..." (*poke*) "...didn't you. I bet every Sunday you an' all your mates get together and try praying – because telepathy to an alien works, doesn't it? Do you get any answers back? Hey? I hope not, coz voices in your head is *proof* that you're bonkers. Are you bonkers? Hey?" (*poke*) "Believing in an extra-terrestrial alien, a half-breed zombie and sending telepathetic messages? Very rational, I *don't* think!"

She paused, picked up her shopping bags then, with her head to one side, she dared him to respond before continuing.

"Don't pass this puerile shit on to me or my mates, Mister Shit-for-brains. Try picking on some other morons. Now *FUCK OFF*!" Caffee grabbed Helen by the arm. "F'low me!" she commanded and dragged her away.

After a fast two-minute walk Caffee seemed to calm down and released Helen's sleeve. After another minute she stopped and looked back at Helen.

"Sorry 'bout that."

"You seemed very angry..."

"Yeh. Fucking smarmy gits think they know it all... until you start asking 'em questions. They're like strawberry yogurt on a bed of dog poo."

She paused and decided an explanation was required. "A priest kept touching me up when I was a kid. No matter who I told no-one would fuckin' believe me. I even got smacked about for being disrespectful. Fuckin' wankers!" She pulled Helen to one side away from the edge of the road just as a car splashed through a puddle.

"So much for the 'Wrath of God' and 'Come Unto Me All Ye Little Children' crap. Fuckin' pervs, the lot of 'em. So, I read the bits of the Bible they don't like to preach in church. Then I thought about it and realised what a load of bullshit it all is. God kills thousands of women and children all over the place, drowns nearly everyone, doesn't give a *piss* about women's rights. He even sets bears to killing kids because some wanker is bald, and yet not *once* offers to teach anyone about washing their hands and staying clean! Basic hygiene is all it is and it ain't mentioned in the Bible. Then there's that God Raped Me and made Me Pregnant' story which we're all supposed to believe. Fuckin' hell!"

Helen nodded slowly with the best 'I understand face' she could muster. Caffee's anger was readily apparent but abating quickly. Caffee never stayed angry for long.

"I dated a feller once who was a 'Born Again'. The wanker wouldn't shag coz we weren't married. Then I learnt he wouldn't marry me coz I kept asking questions. I made him feel uncomfortable in front of his friends." Caffee stopped, her eyes seemed to glaze over, and she looked into the distance. "Blasphemy they called it. Curiosity is blasphemy to those wankers."

"You loved him...?"

"Loved him? Nah! Don't be fuckin' stupid. He had a good job, his own flat, a car, and a body like Adonis. He didn't get drunk and hated football. He kept himself clean and had a lunch box the size of a Routemaster! You don't think I'd go out with a wanker like that otherwise, do you?"

They burst out laughing.

"That's the thing with men, there's always *something* wrong. He was so good I reckon he was gay, anyway."

She looked around for a cafe or burger bar to sit down, have a pot of tea, and review what they'd acquired so far.

Nevertheless, the memories had triggered something within Caffee. The anger had evaporated quickly but behind her eyes something else remained. Something lost. Every now and then she went quiet and looked out the cafe window gazing at nothing in particular. Helen noticed that sometimes, at times like this, she aged a good five years.

"Does Colin have a girlfriend?" ventured Helen.

"Wot? Colin? You fancy Mister Wankalot?" Caffee looked surprised.

"Not really. Well... not much. No. I was just... wondering."

"Fuckin' hell! That'll make his day. What do you see in him? It can't be his smelly socks."

Helen shrugged, embarrassed, wishing she hadn't mentioned anything. "I don't know. He makes me laugh."

"Yeh. That's about the only thing he can do. Make women laugh. Especially when he's naked."

There was a short pause, then Caffee continued. "It's the one thing I do feel sorry for him for – he has absolutely *no* luck with the girls. The last one he fancied he bought a Valentine's rose. Took it to her house and handed it over with a poem he'd memorised off the interweb. Just as she took it from him her pet dog leapt up and ate it. Colin, quite naturally, got a bit upset and punched it one in the head. She screamed and at that moment her pimp came to the door and brained him. The pimp was a surprise. When it comes to girls, not very lucky is our Colin."

"Oh."

"Besides, he's a wanker." There was a short, awkward pause. "You got any boyfriends?"

Helen shook her head. "I did, but not for long. I had to dump them." Then decided to change the subject. "What happened with the priest?"

Caffee shook her head. "Let's just say we both had ourselves a learning experience. He learnt not to fiddle, and I learnt how to make a grown man squeal falsetto. Come on, let's see what else we got."

Helen sympathised. She also knew how to make men squeal falsetto but had yet to master it without making a mess. She also hoped that Colin would continue to make her laugh – she was sure that *that* mess would upset Mam.

6
The Kidnap Request

The entrance to the offices of the Royal Navy Support Executive (just off Whitehall) is unsigned and nondescript. Very few passers-by even notice the old wooden door set into the cold grey concrete of the government offices.

Inside is a small, but plush, reception area very much in the style of a small, old hotel. There is a dark mahogany reception desk complete with a brass bell and visitors' book. Scattered around are several Victorian chairs, a coffee table, and a leather settee. The chairs and settee have obviously been reupholstered many times over the years. The area could comfortably accommodate up to ten people, but today there's only one man sitting on the settee patiently waiting to be admitted.

The room smells of polished wood and brass. On the walls are pictures of battleships and moustachioed naval officers, most dating from the early twentieth century when the Royal Navy was at the peak of its power.

On the far side of the reception is a heavy mahogany door that leads to offices. It looks normal enough but is in fact armoured. It can also be locked electronically from a remote security centre. Discreetly positioned TV cameras in the ceiling observe everything.

The reception area is staffed by a receptionist and a full-time door attendant. The former is always young and on temporary secondment from one of the various security agencies. The latter is invariably a middle-aged retired naval NCO, now working for the agency. Both wear simple two-piece lounge suits.

Today, a phone on the reception desk buzzes and the young man at the desk picks it up, listens for a moment, then simply replies, "Certainly, sir," before replacing the handset. He looked at the lone visitor.

"You can go through now, sir."

The man, immaculately dressed in a dark blue suit, white shirt and blue tie, nodded, grabbed his coat and leather briefcase and strode to the rear door. He was sorely tempted to salute, or at least look for a salute to respond to, but all were wearing civilian clothes. This was something he hadn't grown accustomed to... yet.

The older attendant opened the door for him. "Room one-one-two on the first floor," he said and smiled. "It's signed, 'Doctor Fitzgerald'."

"Thank you."

The man walked through the door into a hallway of completely different decor and atmosphere. He stopped, checked that the door behind him had been closed, and then took out a silver-handled comb and ran it through his hair, though it was neat enough already. He looked around to get his bearings.

The harsh strip lighting in the hall made these cold, pale blue walls appear even colder. A few prints of more modern naval vessels seemed to be carelessly hung and all were slightly askew one way or another. The thin carpet beneath his feet was highly patterned, again, much as one would find in an older hotel. The hallways had been maintained, but there was no sign of it having received any loving care. The corners had been chipped and badly repaired many times. Here and there one could see the lighter undercoat beneath the flaking and fading paintwork.

He examined the comb and smiled to himself before blowing on it and re-reading the engraving, 'For S.E. RN, Love J.L. XX', then ran his thumb over the letters before carefully tucking it away in his inside pocket. Ignoring the lift, he headed for the staircase. In his experience lifts were always too slow and claustrophobic. He ran up three steps at a time before taking the short walk along the corridor and knocking on a door signed, 'Dr. J. G. E. Fitzgerald PhD, MD, BPharm, RN – Director Medical Liaison'.

"Come in."

He opened the door and stepped into the office. "Lieutenant Commander Evans reporting."

"Yes. Yes, do come in." The older man stood, and they shook hands across the desk. Again, no salute was needed.

The doctor was shorter than the officer expected, with dark-rimmed glasses and remarkably curly hair below a bald, almost shiny pate. "You can put your coat down there." He pointed to a second chair.

The officer laid his coat and briefcase in the second chair and sat. The office wasn't large or ornate. To Evans, a stickler for neatness, it looked untidy. Medical books, reference books, papers and folders lined cheap pine shelving to each side. A printer stood on its own stand and there was a computer occupying one side of the desk. A white lab coat and an overcoat hung on a coat stand beside the door.

Something about this unusual assignment made him feel wary, and nothing about Fitzgerald made that feeling go away.

"Good trip?"

"Yes, fine. Thank you."

The distance between the two was palpable. There was nothing else to say between the two strangers, so Fitzgerald got down to business and passed a couple of folders over to the Lieutenant Commander.

"I'd like you to pick up a gentleman by the name of Adrian Channel. We understand he's living in London. Probably the west end of Chiswick or Gunnersbury way. He may be living with an ex-marine named Norman Leicester."

"What for?"

"We need him to come in for an examination."

Evans nodded, opened the folder marked 'Adrian Channel' and flicked through a few pages. It was a couple of minutes before he looked up again. "Why don't you simply telephone and ask this gentleman to come in?"

"We're pretty sure he won't comply."

"Oh?" He flicked through the pages of the dossier. "He was attached to the MWC at Collingwood? And Portsmouth?"

"Yes. For a while."

"A Field Liaison Officer. With several commendations. Why do you think he wouldn't comply?"

Fitzgerald cleared his throat. "That's classified, I'm afraid."

"He's a civilian now. Has been for..." Evans flicked back to the front of the folder "...more than five years. He was discharged as medically, mentally, unfit." He looked up. "Obviously not a terrorist, or a danger to security is he, otherwise you'd get the police to bring him in. What's the catch? Why is this a Navy matter?"

"That's classified, I'm afraid."

"Then read me in. You're keeping something from me. What is it? Is it something to do with this Leicester chap? Who is he?" He turned to the second folder.

Fitzgerald scratched his nose, thought for a moment and came to a decision. "It's delicate. Leicester is ex-SBS."

The officer paused, looked up and stared coldly at Fitzgerald for a moment before answering. "Special forces? I'll need a team then."

"Sorry. We can't budget for that."

"So... you want me to kidnap a mentally deranged civvy from an ex-SBS officer, exact address unknown, for no explicit reason and with no budget. They're civilians now, they have rights you know?" Evans sat back and waited a while, then, "Come on, tell me the story. The whole story. If you want this done, I'll need to know."

Fitzgerald nodded, coming to terms with the fact that this officer was probably correct. Anyway, there was no way he could keep this from him in the long run. He was right, he did need to know. But the last thing Fitzgerald wanted was too many people knowing the full history of the affair but, all credit to him, this officer had picked up on it very quickly. He seemed a bright enough chap, albeit somewhat arrogant. Excluding him from the full knowledge of the situation would only create more problems later and Lord knows there had been enough of those already. He took off his glasses and scratched his head.

"Five years ago, we – and the Americans – mounted several covert operations into Iran. We aimed to pick up a few engineers, chaps that weren't political but probably knew a few details about their support for terrorist cells."

Evans kept a straight face.

"We did four ops. Two succeeded, one was aborted, and one got into trouble. Captain Leicester's group. We had to get them out and our field liaison officer managed it, but only by some brilliant manoeuvring. Not only did he turn a potential disaster into a complete success, we even managed to pick up the secondary target. That liaison officer was Adrian Channel."

Evans considered asking for the mission report, but then decided against it.

"But...?" he prompted.

"At the time Channel and the three other operators were on... stimulants. IQ drugs, if you like. It helped to keep them focused and aware of everything that was happening. All the operations lasted less than ninety minutes, except Channel's. Because of the complications that operation lasted nearly seventeen hours. I understand Channel dosed himself up so he could get his team out of trouble. It affected him. We don't know what went wrong, or why, but subsequently he had a bad reaction to the overdose."

"So, what happened next?"

Fitzgerald replaced his glasses. "We admitted Channel to hospital, of course. He was severely impaired at this point. Almost autistic, apparently. He couldn't walk or talk properly, symptoms of dysphasia, no signs of... anyway, we needed to know what went wrong, and how to put it right. The medical team decided they needed a biopsy, a tissue sample from Channel to see what exactly had happened to him.

"Unknown to us, Leicester's group had already arrived back in the UK from theatre and decided to thank Channel personally. Then some bloody fool let them in and explained the procedure, in detail would you believe, to Leicester. So, naturally, they kidnapped him. 'Never leave a man behind' they said, as if *we* were the enemy."

Evans waited silently for Fitzgerald to finish.

"SO15, the police if you like, were tasked to retrieve Channel but his rescuers threatened to reveal the situation to the newspapers. Well, we weren't going to allow *that* to happen. We managed to muzzle them all, except for Leicester. A few of the team were transferred back to the marines, some left the service of their own accord. We tried to get Leicester for a Court Martial, a CMP in fact, but he would have none of it and went underground. By that time my predecessor had had enough and decided to let it go at that. Budget constraints and whatnot. We managed a dishonourable discharge for Leicester but agreed a small disability pension for Channel – we're not animals after all. That last decision was fortunate, now we know roughly where they are at any time."

"Why do you want him back?"

"We have a new drug ready for human trials. But we still don't know what went wrong with Channel. We don't even know if he managed a recovery or not. We want him back. It's important."

"You want to dig around inside his brain?"

Fitzgerald sighed. "Look, lives are at stake here. Servicemen in the field. Our own intelligence officers. We want to know if it was a genetic reaction that we can account for, or if the overdose did something unexpected. We *need* to know. We need to know if it's permanent. You can understand that, can't you?"

"Yes. Yes, of course. I just want to be clear."

"Can you get him for us?"

"Have you been in contact with him?"

"No. No, we didn't want to forewarn Channel, or Leicester. They'll disappear again – if they're still together."

Evans nodded. This didn't seem to be half as bad as he thought. Moreover, he had the element of surprise on his side. This looked quite doable and, better yet, he got to remain in England for this one.

"Yes. I think I can manage that. What's the time limit?"

"We have a few weeks. The earlier the better, of course. I needn't emphasise we want Channel undamaged. Leicester... well pretty much the opposite, really. If he's out of the picture that would be... helpful. Let me make it clear though, I am not suggesting you do anything to him. We don't want anything to blow up in our faces, so try to keep this discreet. We just want Channel, here, in one piece. If Leicester is still in the picture, then maybe he could be... dissuaded... to interfere. Or better yet, left out of the picture altogether. Do you think you can manage that?"

Evans nodded. "Yes. How much freedom do I have?"

"Complete freedom, provided you stay in touch and use your common sense. Don't be doing anything extravagant. Besides, we don't have the budget. Discuss this with no-one outside my team and retrieve him in a timely manner. How long do you think it will take you?"

Evans shrugged. "If all goes well, I might be able to pick him up a couple of days after I've ascertained his address. It doesn't sound too difficult, save for Leicester who is a wildcard. I'd need a few things though, some sedatives to keep him quiet. Is that possible? It's not going to affect him, is it?"

"No. No, I shouldn't think so. My people will set you up. You'll find the Post Office where Channel's pension is picked up in the folder. You should be able to trace him from there."

Evans nodded. He knew that already. "You have nothing more up to date on this Leicester chap?"

"No. I'm afraid not. The department has left them alone since the affair. Anything else?"

Evans shook his head.

Fitzgerald stood, smiled, and outstretched his hand. "Splendid. Let me introduce you to the rest of my team."

7
An Evening

The film had finished. The muscular hero with the handsome semi-shaven square jaw had saved the world yet again. He had single-handedly killed all the terrorists, destroyed half a city, and won the beautiful – and surprisingly athletic – girl. All assisted, no doubt, by his perfectly aligned white teeth and unnaturally alluring smile.

Norman had successfully predicted the first romantic meeting, the subsequent disillusionment, and the capture – where the chief baddy explains the plot for the benefit of the audience. Then came the amazingly clever escape, the subsequent car chase, and the screaming – but quick – death of each of the bad guy's many muscular men. Finally came the inevitable fist fight between the hero and the antagonist before the baddy's spectacular, and gruesome, demise. The film finished with the romantic embrace between the two lovers-to-be followed by the fade out to the credits.

Colin's unsubtle additions to the heroic and romantic speeches with his unique range of timely hiccoughs and fart impressions had Helen, Caffee, and Barry in fits, and yet they only seemed to add to the quality of the production.

It passed the time in any case.

"It's amazing how the most handsome of actors are usually quite gay," stated Norman as they watched the incredibly long list of people, companies, and hangers-on that had contributed to the film − or, perhaps for a fee and a mention, had not complicated its production.

"He ain't gay."

"He *is* a good actor, is he not?" Norman smiled. "Despite the form."

"I like that bit that was *just* like real life," Caffee sighed as the fifteen-minute-long credit sequence crept up the screen. She reached over and turned the TV off.

"What part was that? The part where he chopped the terrorist into pieces with the helicopter blades?" Colin suggested.

"Yeh, that happens in Gunnersbury most Friday nights, dunnit. Can't move for bleeding 'elicopters everywhere. Bleeding nuisance, they are."

"The part where he tapped the guard on the shoulder and then bit his nose off?"

"Nope. Although I have seen that happen down by the Kings Arms more than once."

"The part where he got shot in the shoulder, but sewed it up with needle and thread, and cured himself within minutes?" Norman offered.

"Nope, not that neither. That's a skill most people in Gunnersbury's got. It just needs plenty of practice."

Norman thought for a second. "How about the ubiquitous gun delusion? You know, where the baddies shoot at our hero and miss, but yet the returned fire always strikes true?"

"Nooo..." Caffee answered, uncertain if she understood the man.

60

Colin suggested, "Then they run out of bullets so there's a fisticuffs fight, and he just about clobbers the leader who, despite being an office worker and very old, is an expert in martial arts?"

"No. Although that was surprising for such an ugly old git."

Helen offered, "What about the part where she has a salad in that romantic restaurant, but she doesn't get any green bits stuck in her teeth?"

Caffee guffawed at that. "Oh, *right*! Yeh, I been there alright. Real romantic, like. Nah, not that one – but a lot, lot closer."

Norman dived in again. "Perhaps the part where he and the girl danced the tango. No toes were trodden upon, no ankles were kicked, and no steps were stumbled even though the two had never even met before?"

"Nah. Anyway – where the fuck do people dance the tango, anyways? Not around 'ere, unless some old biddy smoked some of Colin's wacky baccy."

Mam tried her luck. "Oh, his bedroom was a mess but the living room – it was so immaculate, wasn't it, girl? And all those paintings, now. I have never seen pictures like those before. I bet there wasn't a cobweb or dust anywhere. And it was so big. Who cleaned it for him? Do all the people really have such large apartments in America? Oh, it was *so* silly."

Caffee grinned but shook her head.

Barry tried his hand. "The bit where she held the white bird, but it didn't poop in her hand." He laughed and the others joined in.

"Nah – best one yet, though, Barry."

"What then?"

"The bit at the start where she's waiting by the bus stop and three come at once."

"Oh yeh. *That* ruined it for me."

"True. True. No needed bus has ever travelled the streets alone. And yet, as music be the food of love, shall we now enjoy a little background music?"

"Aw fuck, Norm! Classicuddle music? Better than Colin's crap rap, I suppose. Okay," she sighed. "Put that one on I like."

"And pray, which one might that one be?"

"I don't know. It had violins in it," Caffee suggested, trying to be helpful. She crawled over to a box of CDs beside Norman's leg and flicked through them. "We got Mooze-art, Beet-oven, Choppin', Batch, T-check-ovski, Bra-harms, and Verdi."

Norman sighed. "I don't suppose you'll ever learn to pronounce their names, on intention if not of ignorance. How about a Vivaldi?"

"Nah, I got enough wine, fanks. Fuck it. Let's try 'A Neck Liner' – I think that's the one I liked before."

"'A Neck Liner'?"

"Yeh. It's got them violins in it – like *you* like, me tosher. Put that on."

Norman shook his head, confused.

"It's by Mooze-art – you know the one."

"Ohhh..." The penny dropped. "Eine Kleiner." He extracted a CD and placed it in the player then turned the volume right down knowing that music with violins was not something he dare play too loud. He idly wondered if Mozart could ever have composed hip-hop, and if he had what it would have sounded like.

"Would anyone fancy a game of cards?"

"Poker?" suggested Caffee.

"Strip poker?" offered Colin.

"Whist?" proposed Norman.

"Snap?" asked Barry.

"Strip poker?" offered Colin again.

They fell silent for a while. "A board game?"

The silence continued until Mam spoke up. "I caught my Mrs Sweeney kissing the toilet paper today."

"What? Yuck!"

"Hush your mouth, girl. She always washes her face, puts her makeup on then kisses a clean sheet of tissue paper. I asked her why she did that and she said that her mother taught her to always kiss the toilet paper goodbye. It made her lips softer."

"Did it?"

"I do *not* know, child. I have never kissed the woman to find out. It must work though. She's eighty-seven years old and has been married three times, and from what she tells me I think she still is."

"Still is what? Married?"

"Yes. Three times. Yesterday the funeral director came to the home to discuss something with the lady in the office. Mrs Sweeney caught him on the way out and suggested he should stay the night. Grabbed him by his coat, she did. Oh, she's a naughty woman, that one. Full of laughs though, full of laughs. She refuses to go to her friend's funerals. She says that it wouldn't be worth the bus fare coming back."

"Sounds like a character."

"She says that all her old friends are now in heaven and thinking she must be in the other place by now. Mr Tappenden proposed to her a few months back. He got all excited. But then she forgot which of the men had proposed and one of her husbands came to visit – at least I *think* it was one of her husbands. He was younger than her. She wasn't too sure, either. Or which one. Her memory is quite terrible. But they had a wonderful day together and that's what really counts, isn't it?"

"Wot about Mister Tappenden?"

"Oh, he doesn't know. He says he's going to propose again, as soon as he can get out of bed and get into hers. He's a naughty one too. He's a few years younger than her and his ambition is to be her toy boy. I don't know what they're going to play with though."

"All the world's a stage, and all the men and women merely players. They have their exits and their entrances, and one man in his time makes many farts," sighed Norman.

"You and your bleedin' Shakespeare. I don't know how you manage to remember it all so accurately."

"'Tis but a gift," grinned Norman.

"How do you tis-but?" asked Barry.

Mam continued her story. "I was a little disturbed by Mrs Grangermouth yesterday. She told me how, years ago, her husband was unemployed. He never went to work. She worked at a law company as a secretary. But one day she came home early and found him in bed with a neighbour. She was most upset."

"Male or female?" enquired Caffee.

Mam looked puzzled, then ignored her. "She said she didn't do anything. Not for weeks. Then one day her house burnt down. They found two bodies in the ashes. She said that she was lucky with the insurance, too. It set her up for the rest of her life." Mam stopped and bit her lip. "Then she said a most peculiar thing. She said... she said... 'The insurance man wasn't all that handsome, but he was a very understanding, and helpful man'."

"Yeh?"

"Then she said something else that made me think."

"Yeh? Like what?"

"She said that she had never believed in being unfaithful until then." Mam looked at Norman. "You don't think...?"

Norman shrugged. "Sigh no more, lady, sigh no more. Men were deceivers ever. One foot in the mouth and one in the mire. To one thing constant never."

Mam looked blankly at Norman for a few seconds then turned to Colin. "Tell us about your latest project, Colin."

Colin raised an eyebrow. "Nah. It's too early yet."

"Awww – come on. They're good they are." Caffee nudged him with a foot.

"Well... I thought as how car engines have silencers... and old men fart a lot... and it gets cold in winter... so, I thought about adapting drinking straws. You make a really long one, shove it up a trouser leg and into your arse. The heat from your farts keeps your leg warm too."

Colin looked at Helen, who was listening attentively.

"It, erm... it works like this..."

At which point Mam decided to leave the room and make them all a cup of tea.

Unknown to all of them, while they watching the film, things were starting to happen in shady places and a hunter was being recruited to hunt one of them.

8
The Hunter

His first name was Terry, and he liked to think that people associated the name with the phrase 'The Terrier', or even better, 'The Terror' – but that was as far as his creativity went. He was hunting for the murderer, or murderers, of John Hughes.

The rented apartment was dark, damp, and smelled of mildew but he paid no attention to that. He sat on the one wooden chair by the dining table in his jeans and dirty raincoat, which he never cleaned. The view in the window was of a brick wall just feet away, not that he noticed or cared. It was just a place to live and live cheaply.

His client, known as Jacket, had given him a new laptop, stolen only a week before from a warehouse. It was both a tool of his trade and also served as the deposit on this job. He'd been given some memory sticks and some money too. Apparently, this new job was an important one so he was taking it seriously.

The memory sticks were stacked to one side, each had a number and he'd made corresponding notes in a notebook. He had listed the numbers, the video file names, the observations, and from them he'd diligently calculated the timings between the recorded events. He liked to be methodical.

Had Terry remained an auditor in his previous life he would have been good at it and probably be living in comfort in a semi-detached with a mortgage. He'd ruined all that after being caught and then doing time for embezzlement. The punishment had taught him just one lesson – don't get caught.

As he couldn't find employment after the conviction so his new career was investigating, tracing, and hunting people for the more criminally inclined citizens in his area. Sometimes his targets were fraudsters trying to get one over on the local money shark. More often they were drug addicts unable to fund their habit. Once in a while they were men or women, young or old, running from heartless pimps. Whatever the reason, he didn't care.

After they had been found, 'exacting the price', or 'applying the consequences' was normally handled by the client. Sometimes he'd employ some local muscle to do the job on his clients' behalf but sometimes, for an extra fee, he'd handle them himself. Particularly if they were soft targets like women or drug-addled teens. In any case, the results of his work rarely left his prey in one piece.

Terry felt no empathy when finding defaulters. It made him feel useful, important even. A growing bank balance was further testimony to his success. Six months ago, he'd acquired a pistol with a suppressor and although it hadn't been used yet, it was something he was looking forward to. Simply having it gave him 'cred', gravitas. He felt like one of those secret agents in the films. Most important, it gave him the one thing he desired the most, self-respect.

This was to be one of those jobs with potential. This time even the physical bit had been handed to him. Not only did this mean more money, more respect, but better yet, maybe even a chance to use the gun for real. It would show the world he really *was* somebody.

He'd been told that the murderers of John Hughes were probably just a small group of males, probably foreign. They were most likely members of a gang looking to muscle into this patch of Doncaster. So, he was looking through the video files for a car with fresh, maybe nervous, faces in the right place at the right time.

However, no matter how hard he tried he couldn't make any of the footage fit the likely scenario. There were several possible suspects but somehow none seemed right. He sat back and frowned. The police were looking for the obvious too. He was competing with their forensics teams, expertise, and equipment. Would they get to the murderers before him? From what he'd been told, they were not making any progress either. He had to think laterally.

What if it wasn't a foreign gang? What if they didn't arrive by car? What if they were already in the old factory when the deed was done?

They'd kill the man then, without any transport - they'd have to get away on foot. He checked the map again. They'd run north, keeping in the shadows and in the small parks right up until they reached the railway. There would be no footage of them until they reached the station, but there, when they arrived, they would have been running. Breathless.

The time of death was reported to be about seven thirty in the evening. Quite early really. If they ran to the railway station after that it would be just before eight o'clock when they arrived. He checked the train timetable. There was a London bound train at just gone eight o'clock.

He checked his notebook and selected a memory stick from the stack, delicately ejecting the one he'd been watching before and replacing it with the new one. He selected a video and skipped through it until he reached ten to eight. Then he scanned slowly. There were quite a few people milling about the forecourt. Several he discounted quickly. The old, the obviously relaxed students. He looked for men, possibly a group. There were several candidates, all currently being checked out by the police, no doubt. But none appeared to be nervous or tired from running.

He noticed a girl. She was only in a few clips but here, outside the forecourt, was clearing mud from the bottom of her shoes. Scraping them on a concrete step. Had she just run across fields? She had no case, or bag. He looked closer at the screen, squinting in its light, and examined her expression. The girl seemed to be nervous, but she wasn't glancing around, she was keeping her head down. She didn't seem to be out of breath, but then how could one really tell? He checked her from other angles. This one was the only, very faint, credible candidate. He sat back and double-checked his reasoning. Without anything else, this had to be the one.

The girl, in her late teens or early twenties, wore a dirty green anorak and jeans.

Was she deliberately avoiding the cameras? Where were her accomplices? She had to have at least one. Maybe they'd split up? From the warehouse she had gone north to the station, maybe the others went south?

He thought of checking the CCTV footage around the factory from that time, but that's what he had already been doing and that's what the police were doing with far more eyes – and no doubt they were doing it much faster. And yet, according to what he'd been told, they were still none the wiser. They had nothing.

He went back to the girl. The female was definitely alone. He watched the silent footage in detail again and was surprised to see that early on she seemed undecided, unsure of her destination. She checked the small bundle of notes in her pocket, so she couldn't have known how much she had. Furthermore, she seemed not to know how much the fare was. This was a last-minute decision. Then he realised that she must have made her mind up at the same time as a railway announcement. There was no audio but he could see some of the faces around her perk up and react accordingly.

He changed the recording to one close to the cashiers. When she got to the ticket office the picture of her face was much clearer. Also, the picture of the notes she gave to the cashier was quite clear too. He smiled, he knew how much she paid, so he knew her destination.

He took out a mobile phone and selected a number.

"Hello. It's Terry. Tell your source I want the footage from London Kings Cross railway station from nine forty in the evening of the night in question... Yes... And tell him to call me back. We need some files to disappear."

"You have a lead?"

"Yeh. A girl. A teenager or early twenties."

"A girl?"

"Yeh. A girl."

"Really? Are you certain?"

"Yeh. I'm certain."

"Okay, get the bitch! I want you to bring her to me. Can you do that? I need to find out what's going on."

"Yeh. Yeh. I'll bring her to you."

He hung up and smiled. The hunt was on, and he was going to London.

9
The Letter

It was Colin who first noticed Norman's dark mood early one morning when he dashed downstairs and snatched his mobile from the settee. Colin saw Norman's face but didn't say anything because he was about to visit a friend regarding a business matter. As a rule, he avoided asking people why they looked moody because, from Colin's experience, all too often he was at least part of the cause. Anyway, today he had his own problems.

He slipped out the front door quietly, making sure it didn't slam before checking up and down the street for any 'undesirable encounters'. Then, with his hood up and head down, strode away.

When Barry saw Norman's face his approach was the complete opposite. He immediately asked Norman what was wrong but was met with a blank stare for a few moments before he was handed an open envelope. Barry extracted the letter and tried to read it, his lips mouthing each word in turn so Norman explained its meaning. Barry left the room with moist eyes and biting his lip.

Later that evening the atmosphere at mealtime was subdued although Caffee and Helen were happily chatting amongst themselves and didn't notice the mood for a while. Even Adrian picked up on it and seemed quieter than usual. When they had all finished the meal, but before they left the table, Mam stood up and addressed them.

"I have some bad news." She held up the letter that Norman had passed to her earlier. "We are being evicted." She slowly looked around at the others. "This is a letter from a lawyer. They tell us we are here illegally, and that we must leave."

"Who ratted us?" Colin was quietly relieved it wasn't his fault this time, but he also appreciated the food, the lack of housework, and the company. Finding new digs was not part of his plan. He was sure that whoever gave the game away wasn't any of his contacts. No one that he did business with knew where he lived. At least, he hoped that was the case.

"It doesn't say. But we all knew this time would come," she sighed.

Norman muttered under his breath. "You take my life when you take the place whereby, I live."

Caffee's response was a little more abrupt. "Fuck!"

"It is an ill wind that..."

"...that always comes in a shit-brown envelope," she snapped back.

"We have been given fourteen days to depart." Mam lay the letter on the table for all to see.

"How much is in the kitty?"

"Enough for next week's food. Maybe a bit more for the lottery."

"We might win?" ventured Barry.

"This ain't good. Not for any of us." Caffee pointed to each in turn starting with Helen. "She's a dodgy runaway who doesn't want to be found. Ade will be sent to a dodgy institution where they won't understand him. Colin is just dodgy and will need a new hideout. Norman talks funny but I suppose the council *might* give him a place or he'll have to live on the street. Barry, you've been picked on and bullied in every place you've been at, so you don't want to move either. Yeh? And Mam...?"

"I do not want to leave. I like it here." Tears started welling up in her eyes. "I do not have anywhere else to go." She turned away from them. "I just do not want to leave," she whispered and left the room.

There was a moment's silence before Adrian mumbled towards the ceiling. "And the moving, moving is the resulting result of a lack of fiscal financial monetary money funds which the far too little baby feline, but wishing that it were a line, unlike a fishing line which felines like because of fishy, fishy food, like to fees, isn't stuffed full of. So, we're going to be left leaving like how leaving leaves us, unless we..." he paused, slowly lowered his gaze and stared into Caffee's right eye. In an uncharacteristically sober voice, he said, "...rob the bank."

The audience got goosebumps.

"What's he on about?" Colin frowned.

Caffee and Adrian's eyes were locked together. A silent battle of wills, a hidden message, a silent conversation.

"I don't fink we're ready to do that, Adrian."

Helen looked worried. "Should I start to look for another place to stay?"

"With what you earn, luv? You could just about afford a semi-detached cardboard box."

"Will I have to live in the streets again?" murmured Barry.

Caffee sighed. "This is so *shit!*" She leaned forward across the table to Adrian. "Esher?" she whispered.

Adrian touched his nose. His tongue fell out and, a little surprised, he pushed it back in before grinning at the ceiling again.

"They won't do it," she said.

"Them's that won't, will lack of fiscal financial monetary money funds which the far too little baby feline isn't stuffed full of so they will be left leaving like how leaving leaves left for the streets in the streets of London. A song I like. Cry for the crying, cryers who cry to cry off when it isn't necessarily so. Necessarily necessary so it is. So, it is."

"What?" Caffee wrinkled her nose in confusion.

Adrian sighed and left the table.

"What was that about? I wish he would speak fucking English just for once." Colin was busy trying think of any place he could hole up.

"He wants us to rob a bank?" asked Helen.

"Though his be madness, yet there is method in't," Norman misquoted.

"What's that stuff about Esher?" Colin asked. "It's a nob's town, innit? Full of rich-types and BMWs."

Caffee shuffled awkwardly on her seat. "What if...?" She paused.

"What if what?"

"What if we did have a foolproof plan to rob a bank?"

"Don't be fucking stupid."

Barry shook his head. "I am not a bank robber."

"No." Caffee stared intently at her fingernails. "But seriously. It can be done."

Colin again. "It'd have to be some bloody foolproof plan like *I've* never heard of."

Barry shook his head. "I do not want to rob people."

Colin sat back. "So, are we going to be all tooled up with guns and stuff? Burst into Barclays and shoot people? For fuck's sake, we ain't crims. Not *real* crims, anyway." Colin thought a bit more. "Not *all* of us... Not *all* the time, anyway."

Caffee shuffled uncomfortably. "No. Nothing like that. We break into the bank after dark. It's a smash and grab, really."

Barry was still shaking his head. "Mam won't like it. She'd tell me off."

Colin held up his hand. "Hold on a mo' though. Think about it. If we get caught, and we're penniless and homeless, the judge isn't going to give us more than a few years in an open nick, isn't he? We're social victims, right? Open nicks are a breeze. We'll be out paroling around before you'd know it, provided there were no shooters involved." He was thinking hard. "And then afterwards they got to find us all digs, ain't they? And they got to get us jobs before we rescindivate. We got to be re-introgated into society." He waited for a response. "Fuck it! It's a win-win, ain't it?"

Barry shook his head. "We would all have criminal records."

"Oh yeh, right! Which means what exactly? It would jeopardize your careering up the executive ladder within the council's refuse department? No

77

more business trips to the Bahamas? Fuck 'em! Anyway, we'd all be fucking heroes after what the banks did to the economy." Colin grinned at Caffee. "We'd only be taking back what we're owed. It all depends on the plan though. And the take. How much do you reckon? You say it's easy?"

"It's do-able."

"Poverty is but the parent of revolution and crime," whispered Norman. "It's been a while. Methinks I am ready for a little excitement." He smiled. "Nothing ventured..."

"...saves on bus fares?" Caffee raised her eyebrows.

"And what about Helen? She's the quiet one." Colin grinned across to the quiet one.

Helen shrugged. "I don't know. I want a place to stay."

Norman was grinning. "Oh, we few. We happy few. We band of brothers..."

"I'm a girl, you wanker! Or ain't you noticed?" Caffee raised her eyes. "And this is *my* op – alright? Savvy?"

"I savvy." Norman fell silent, thoughtful.

Colin muttered, "Too many crooks spoil..."

"...piss about. So, *I'm* in charge of this, okay?"

Barry was still worried. "Mam would not like it. If Mam won't do it, I won't do it. It is wrong."

At which point Mam reappeared at the door with a cup of tea in her hand. "And do you think I wouldn't, boy? It was a bank who took away my home, you know? I want to hear this plan of yours, girl. I want to know how you think we can get away with such a thing." No one had seen Mam react like this before.

"Mam...?"

"Hush your mouth now, Barry. Let the girl speak. Desperate times calls for desperate measures, there."

"Mam, it's a sin."

"If it is a sin then the plan would not be good. But if the Lord truly loves us, then maybe, just maybe He's given us a good plan. The Bible itself says 'Sell that ye have and give alms. For where your treasure is, there will your heart be also.' Are not the money lenders the vassals of Satan? Maybe this is the Good Lord's way of helping us when we need help the most. Help to take from the devil's servants. Maybe He's finally answering my prayers, giving us a sign when we are at our lowest ebb. A test of our faith. Provided that we hurt no-one, and that all we take is the devil's ill-gotten gains. Let us at least listen to the girl. Besides, He sent me a sign, and now I think I understand it." She nodded gravely.

"What sort of sign?"

"Never you mind, girl. What the Good Lord says to me, He says in His own special way."

At that point Adrian staggered into the dining room holding a large thick plate of metal about a foot square. Helen and Norman made a grab for the dishes just before Adrian dropped it in the centre of the table with a resounding *ka-dunk*!

"Adrian! What are you doing, boy?" Mam was startled but Adrian smiled, tugged an ear, spun around in a circle and sat in his chair looking awfully pleased with himself before looking up at the ceiling.

She shook her head sadly. "Caffee, your idea. Is it just a dream girl? Now tell us, how can we, all of us here, rob a bank and hope to get away with it?"

Caffee had popped another chewing gum in her mouth and started champing the life out of it. "Basically, it's straightforward. One night we break into the bank, open the safe, take the money, and then leg it."

Adrian extracted a small glass bottle from his pocket.

Colin's face fell. "That's it? That's your plan? That's your great, wonderful plan?"

"Nah. There's a lot more to it. We'll need a lorry, a van, ladders, blocks of wood, sheet plastic, a small alarm clock, a paintball gun, and a wet suit – or long woolly coat," she grinned. "And it depends on Helen's ability to dance 'n' shoot in the rain."

"What?" Colin frowned, baffled again.

"You really *do* have a plan?" asked Norman.

"Fuckin' right, we do! And most of the stuff we need we have already stashed away, too."

From his small bottle Adrian extracted a small tube holding grey, sparkly powder and placed it in the middle of the metal plate. He delicately, and with much concentration, replaced the top on the bottle and returned it to his shirt pocket.

"How do we get into the safe then?" asked Colin, eyes on the tube. "We don't know the combination and those motherfuckers are big and heavy."

"Easy," said Caffee champing on her gum.

Adrian struck a match and all eyes flicked toward him. Adrian and matches were not a good combination. Norman went to reach for it, fearful Adrian would set his eyebrows alight, when Adrian reached forward, and the match touched the powder.

There was a hiss, a crackle then a brilliant flare shot up from the tube, temporarily blinding everyone. In a moment the flare suddenly became even brighter. Everyone stood and backed away from, what was now, an inferno knocking their chairs over and shielding their eyes from the intense glare. Adrian squealed in delight while Barry shot out the door.

The fire quickly rose up to head height, spitting sparks like a demented, over-powered firework.

"Adrian! What have you *done!*" Mam grabbed his arm and dragged him away. Norman tried to get to the flame to bat it with his hand, but the temperature was far too high, the incandescent light turning everything in the room a vivid monochrome and making their shadows dance on the walls like black demons. Norman threw his glass of wine at it, but it had no effect. The wine vapourised before it even got to the flame which was now growing taller and filling the room with acrid smoke and a choking, metallic stench.

Helen, coughing, ran from the room into the living room. Mam dragged Adrian out to the kitchen and Norman reluctantly followed vainly batting at the air. Caffee, grinning from ear to ear, casually followed Helen, dabbing her eyes with a flowery, pink handkerchief.

Barry re-appeared with a fire extinguisher, ran into the dining room and started putting the fire out – or at least he tried to, but the flame died of its own accord and fizzled out as quickly as it had flared up leaving smoke and smuts floating in the air.

"Shouldn't we call the fire brigade?" yelled Helen.

"Nah. Fire's out now." Caffee champed on her gum and coughed.

Barry called out, "It's okay. It's okay. It's all out. We're safe. We're safe."

"For goodness' sake, open the windows and let the smoke out." Mam, Norman, Barry, and Kathy ran around the house opening the windows and the back door. The cold breeze entered the house quickly cooling everything down, but no one noticed the cold when, finally, all eyes settled on Adrian.

"What the *fuck did* you do that for?" Colin bunched his fists.

"Adrian. My Adrian. Are you trying to burn the house down, now? Whatever got into you, boy?"

Adrian just grinned, looked sideways up at the ceiling and pointed back to the dining room.

Waving their hands back and forth to waft the smoke and smell from the room they re-entered the room one by one. The metal plate still lay on the table but in the centre was a neat round hole. Barry, Norman, and Colin approached, leaned across the table and slowly looked down from above. The hole went right through the plate, through the table and had scorched a hole in the carpet and floorboards beneath. Little wisps of smoke rose from the charred carpet. They felt the heat rising from the still-hot plate.

A section of burnt plaster from the ceiling fell onto Colin's head.

"And that's how we get into the safe!" declared Caffee, leaning against the wall with her arms crossed. "Easy as a piddle in a puddle."

10
Contact

Lieutenant Commander Stephen Evans telephoned the manager at the Gunnersbury Post Office. He explained, very politely, that one 'Adrian Channel', ex-Navy, had been invalided out of the service and ever since had been given a Navy disability pension. Evans would like to identify the person picking up the money and check that there was no fraud taking place. Would it be alright to visit?

Suzanne Whitehouse, (almost) happily married with three grown children, was an experienced manager with over twelve years' experience. She replaced the telephone thoughtfully. At first doubtful she checked the information Evans had provided with the police and a few hours later they rang back to confirm his identity.

When he arrived, Suzanne took an instant liking to the handsome naval officer and agreed to help. More than once she caught herself running her fingers through her hair and giggling at his slightest joke. In the back of her mind, and not knowing why, she had a vague feeling of guilt but the officer's visit was a new and very unusual event.

She explained that the gentleman that signed for the money was a tall man in his mid-fifties, registered as being the legal guardian to Adrian and an authorised signatory to the account. The address given on the form was one ostensibly in

Gunnersbury. Evans guessed that the house didn't exist.

Recently the tall man had been accompanied by a younger black man, probably in his early thirties, but he was quiet and never spoke. She remembered them well because they always wore overalls and smelt musty and unclean – as if they needed a good scrubbing. They would arrive mid-afternoon every Friday and empty the account. It wasn't much, she thought, not for a pension. Evans agreed, it was a pittance considering what the man had been through.

They decided that the next time the two arrived she would call Evans on his mobile, and they swapped numbers.

That Friday Evans was standing across the road from the Post Office, unaware that Norman and Barry had left work early that day and were already inside. He answered the call just as Leicester and his friend were leaving. The ex-SBS officer must have heard the phone's ring tone, even over the traffic, because he glanced at Evans. Evans cursed himself for being so stupid and turned away, but still, in his most polite voice, thanked the manager for the information. Even over the phone he could sense her running her fingers through her hair.

Evans held back, watching in shop window reflections, then followed the two men to their house. He took great care not to get too close now Leicester had seen him. As they walked, he evaluated the older man. Time had definitely taken its toll. It looked like he'd let himself go a little. There were signs of a paunch, thinning hair, and none of the expected confidence in his stride. If anything, he detected a slight stoop. His hair was a lot greyer than in the photos and from the quick eye contact, none of the original fire he had detected in the man's file remained. Civilian life did that to warriors.

They must have walked well over a mile through the busy London streets before they turned into a side road. Evans sped up and stopped at a corner to watch Leicester let himself and his friend in the front door of a house. He had the address now. Next, he needed to confirm that Adrian Channel lived there. He turned to call the office with the update.

Norman entered the house behind Barry, removed his coat and hung it on the broken brass hook taking care not to snag the worn lining. As he went to close the front door the memory of a man hurriedly turning his back to him in the High Street made him pause. He peered around the edge of the door and looked down the street. There he was again, in the reflection of a window at the end of the street. He was making a phone call and started wandering away.

Norman quietly closed the front door and frowned.

Damn! They were back. He needed a plan.

11
The Plan

Everyone was gathered in the living room to listen to Caffee's plan. The area to one side of the TV had been cleared for a flattened cardboard box resting on the back of a chair and against the wall making do as a notice board. Anyone looking at Caffee would not have said she was nervous, and she certainly wouldn't have admitted it. She was noisily chomping on her chewing gum and in her hands was a broken pool cue she intended to use as a pointer, or maybe as a pain-providing, attention-keeping device.

Helen observed what looked like a spot of dried blood on the broken end but elected not to comment. Various bits of paper were stuck on the notice board, some with pictures others with writing. The Blu-Tac was somewhat aromatic and looked suspiciously pink.

"Okayyyyyy..." She whacked the whiteboard and glanced around the room. Something about Caffee's stance, and probably her threatening expression, commanded their attention. The only discernible noise in the room was Caffee's jaws. "Here's the detailed plan. It's detailed right? It's got details in it so don't worry if it doesn't stick. Bits may change after this discussion so keep your questions 'til later. Right? Unnerstood?"

Everyone nodded.

"The bank we're going for is in Esher, the one near the crossroads. It'll have the weekend takings from a lot of the shops in it. I did look at the others, but this one is the one. It's an old building and both of those facts is important. Furthermore, this is Esher where there are a not a few rich people and loads of Arab types living there. But basically, I reckon on a take of about fifty grubbies to a plum which works out at about nine to eighteen grand each, give or take. Enough to see us alright for the next six months – no prob."

Caffee saw the puzzled expressions on everyone's face. She sighed.

"What? Jeezus! Grubbies, yeh? That's about fifty to one hundred thousand pounds. Do you understand now? Jeez..."

She whacked the board again. "We do the job early on a Saturday night. The passing traffic creates enough noise to cover any noise we make. It's too dark and cold for people to get curious, and too early for people to figure out what we're up to, but being a Saturday night, the police will already be busy with the night clubs in Kingston.

"Now, I've sussed out the place and it ain't spectac'lar." She slapped a hand-drawn diagram with her stick. "There are three video cameras in the foyer linked to a secure recording machine in a locked cupboard. There are five infra-red motion detectors and at least two fire detectors scattered across the ceiling. These systems are independent of each other. The motion detectors are connected to an alarm system which has a bell on the outside wall and an automatic dialler to the telephone system and they've added the radio telephone as part of a security upgrade. The radiotelephone is only used in emergencies for outgoing automated calls. The landlines are also used by the national computer centre for incoming calls. Each branch is called automatically about twice a night by their central computer and all the internal systems is checked – it's especially meant for the hole in the wall cash machine in case it runs out of notes or gets nicked. For that reason, we're leaving it alone. It's not worth it."

Barry put his hand up.

"Not now, Barry. Later."

"How do you know all this?"

"Look, Barry. I know. Okay? Leave the questions 'til later."

Barry put his hand up again. Caffee walked over to him, brandishing her stick and stuck her face into his. She whispered, "What is it... you don't fuckin' understand... about the word '*later*'?"

"I just wondered..."

Mam grabbed his knee and shushed him. He fell silent.

"Fanks, Mam. Let me continue...

"The fire system, as I said, is older and completely independent. The smoke detectors are connected to a sprinkler system built by TCS, so this has about eight to twelve minutes of sprinkler water in a separate pressurised water tank upstairs. There's a separate fire bell on the outside wall as well.

"There is another bell on the West wall high-up. This is connected to the automatic dialler. If this one goes off – we leg it. But it shouldn't."

She whacked a picture of a large safe. "The safe is a large, old, stand-alone Dewy Commercial Two-

Forty. It stands in its own little room on the ground floor. It's about two metres tall, and is just over a metre wide and just over a metre deep. If you opened the door, you could just about stand inside. It has metal shelves on all three walls. The walls are made of solid, high quality, toughened steel about two inches thick all round and it weighs well over two tons and stands on a solid concrete base. The shelves are just tin and easily detachable.

"To open the door requires two sets of keys, a three number combination and it's on a timer too. The door is flush to the front of the safe, about three inches thick, and there are six mild steel rods that lock inside the front wall of the safe when the door is closed and locked. There's a big spoke wheel on the front which you have to spin to wind the steel rods in or out when opening or closing the safe.

"It's as tight as an 'amster's bum. So, we're going to melt it with Adrian's magic powder."

Barry put his hand up. Caffee's eyes narrowed but Mam pulled it down and shook her head.

"Okayyyyy. Inventory. We'll need the following..." She slapped the extensive list, handwritten on the inside of two cornflake packets. It was long.

"Now tell me, seriously, without taking your eyes off mine, how many heaters are there in our dining room? Can any of you remember? Can you remember exactly what colour they are and what size they are? If you work at an office, would you know exactly how many heaters there are in your office and exactly what they look like?"

Pause...

"No. I think not. So, with that in mind, here's the

plan and timings."

Caffee went to one of the more densely printed pages and scanned it before continuing.

"Phase 1: Saturday in the morning. The Tragic 'orse."

"Trojan Horse," muttered Norman, hoping that a poke-in-the-eye wasn't headed his way.

"Let's hope so, okay? Barry, 'elen, Mam, and Norman all enter the bank. Barry and Mam create a little diversion while Norman puts down his 'briefcase' against the outside wall. In fact, he'll slide a smoke pot down between the heater and the wall. You will be on CCTV but you'll be in disguise. The radio-controlled smoke pot is just a couple of centimetres wide – nothing hi-tech. Colin can knock that up easy coz he made that fuckin' radio control truck. Remember that? Yeh?"

Colin nodded cautiously.

"After the pot is attached behind the heater and it looks okay, then you all leave quietly. I needn't remind any of you that no one is to look directly at a camera and everyone is to change their appearance beforehand. Okay?"

Barry put his hand up, but Mam promptly brought it down again.

Caffee scanned the papers again before continuing.

"Phase 2: Saturday mid-afternoon. Bell muffling."

"Using a customised ladder. Colin and Norman will be dressed up like window cleaners outside the bank. They'll extend the ladder to about eleven feet and lean it 'accidentally' against the higher of the two

91

outside alarm bells. At the top of the ladder is a short three-eighths drill – whatever the fuck that is! Then, with a discreet flick on a hidden trigger, it'll drill a hole in the bell case. Colin can rig that up. Then they move the ladder over and 'accidentally' lean the other side of the ladder on the bell. This time the nozzle of insulating foam is injected into the hole in the bell and we discreetly squirt and fill it up. This foam crap goes hard after a few minutes, so provided we squirt enough into it it'll be all gummed up. Remember it's dark at four o'clock so no one should notice.

"After gumming up the first bell, we then lower the ladder, check the drill and the spray. Then we do the same thing on the lower bell. So now both bells are gummed up with foam and silent and no one's the wiser. Yeh? We've got to practise doing this without looking up at the bells and making it obvious what we're doing. I'll be there watching from across the road. After you've finished you can both pootle off for a pint down the pub." She grinned around the room. "Everyone happy so far?"

Norman was nodding. Colin was frowning. Barry went to put his hand up then glanced at Mam but she shook her head.

"Good."

Caffee scanned the sheets on the board again.

Norman's face remained impassive. Caffee's accent was still there but somehow, it wasn't as abrasive as it normally was. Was her accent fake? Did he detect some hidden middle-class background there? He couldn't be sure.

"Phase 3: Saturday evening early. Preventing

calls."

"Colin turns up in the workman's outfit, opens the green telephone box in the street – I'll show you where later – and he cuts *all* the telephone lines. We ain't got the expertise to know which is which – but it doesn't matter. It's a commercial area so no-one will be using it – except maybe a restaurant or two who won't get any last-minute bookings. Oh, well. Boohoo."

"Phase 4: Saturday evening. Insertion."

Colin stuck his hand up and Caffee casually whacked it with the stick.

"Ow!"

"This is the tricky bit that we've got to rehearse and get absolutely right. Time is of the essence here. Our white truck drives into Esher from Claremont Lane straight across the crossroads and parks beside the bank in Church Street." She whacked a large-scale, hand-drawn map.

"It pulls right up on the kerb beside the bank – except that the white truck isn't white. We've plastered the back with thin plastic polythene sheets to make it look dark and replaced the tarpaulin sides with ones of a different colour. The false set of plates will be for a different dark truck, and will be stuck on top of the plates for the white truck. Geddit?"

She looked around for a response but just saw blank expressions.

"The truck pulls into Church Street, and pulls right up onto the kerb so that the right side of the truck is flush, almost touching the wall of the bank. As soon as it stops Colin will check around to see all is okay and then press the remote control on the smoke pot which, if you remember, is behind the heater inside the bank. This will cause the fire alarm to go off – but remember it's been muffled, and the sprinklers will go off. Everyone is wearing bovver boots – including Mam. Helen is dressed in her frogman outfit and is wearing a balaclava, a thick woolly pullover, thick woolly stockings and woolly mittens. As we pull up Mam and Colin will pour two buckets of cold water over her and make sure she's absolutely saturated and wet all over. Yeh? She'll then put on her safety glasses."

"While all this is happening Barry, Norman, and Colin will open the side of the truck against the wall and raise a pre-cut centre section of the tarpaulin. Then we place a floorboard to make a short tunnel from the side of the truck to the second window by the bank. Make a note, Norm, we'll have to make sure the ramp can handle the height difference. Meanwhile, Colin will be outside the truck and making sure that the smoke pot has gone off and it's pouring water inside.

"Once we have the short tunnel connected from the truck to the window, you wait for my 'Go' signal then you break the window to the bank and completely remove it into the truck, but we keep the outside of the window frame in place because that's attached to the window alarm – so the window frame *must* stay shut. Just the glass and the middle of the window is removed and we have to make sure that any glass is brushed inside the bank onto the carpet. That's why we have bovver boots, so the broken glass and about two inches of water won't be a problem.

"We'll time this to happen as the traffic lights change because it gets really noisy as the cars pass.

Also, it explains why the truck is parked so tight against the wall – to let cars pass.

"Inside the bank the smoke will have made sure that the sprinklers will be on full blast. The cloud of water will prevent the motion detectors detecting any motion coz infrared doesn't travel through water – that's why you've been wetted, Helen. You'll step through the short tunnel between the truck and the window taking your broom handle with the greasy paint pads on each end inside the office. Using the ends of your broom pole you paint the motion detectors, the video cameras and the fire detectors too – just in case. Or maybe we use a paintball gun – we ain't decided.

"You should be pretty safe though, as you'll be wet all over and even your eyes are behind safety glasses so you won't have an infrared sigana... signanatu... whatever. I'm just playing safe you understand, yeh? You must make sure that the detectors are well and truly painted though.

"Fuck!" She took a breath, then checked with the papers on the board before continuing.

"The time is now about ten to eight. We've had twenty minutes for this phase and that should be plenty. Helen, Colin, Norman and I will now be inside the bank, in the dark. The carryall bags with all the kit will be thrown in."

"Phase Five: Saturday night eight o'clock. Execution."

Barry's mouth dropped open, but Mam reassured him with a pat on the arm. "Hush, boy. Let the girl have her say."

Norman sat forword. "Caffee? I cannot believe

95

you came up with all this on your own."

She laughed. "Me? Nah. Wish! Just sit back and listen. Everything has been thought through in detail, yeh?"

"Apparently so." He sat back, steepling his fingers thoughtfully. This planning was very unlike Caffee, although she clearly enjoyed being in charge of it.

"Okayyyy..." Caffee sighed deeply, slapped the bank diagram with her cue stick, then continued. "We are now inside the bank foyer with Mam outside and we should be secure inside. Helen will have to take off the wet woolly stuff, pack it along with the smoke pot – and help herself to a flask of hot soup. Meanwhile, the rest of us will spray paint the windows black from the inside to reduce the likelihood of anyone spotting the flames later on. We'll also scatter some light sticks around. They work quite happily under water. Then we'll unpack the jimmy bars and pry our way into the back offices. If we have a problem, we've got enough spare powder from Adrian to make short work of any locks and we've got the bank's own fire extinguishers in case Colin gets carried away. Yeh?

"Once in the back room we cover the radio telephone with a metal box – just in case. That'll prevent any signal from getting out. We don't tamper with it because there's no need. We then break open the door to the safe room and we'll have to get stuff to stand on so that we can look down onto the top of the safe from above. Colin uses flower pots to make a crater-type shape on the front of the safe above the door and then places a measured amount of powder on it. Norman and I will be opening the windows at the back as we'll need the fresh air later, and the smoke will need a way out. We also make sure the back fire escape door is open in case we need to leg it.

"Colin then burns through the top of the safe with the molten metal pouring over the front of the door. He'll keep using measured amounts until we've made a small hole. We can use a carbon dry-oxide fire extinguisher to prevent fires inside the safe.

"He then makes another hole so we have one above the door and a large one at the top at the middle."

Barry shuffled in his seat, raised his arm, looked at Mam's scowl of disapproval, and then dropped it again.

"Phase Six: Nine o'clock. Lolly time."

Barry perked up but made no sound.

"Once we have two holes, we use the webcam on a stick poked inside the safe to watch and guide a vacuum cleaner as we vacuum up the money. We'll have dropped light sticks into the safe beforehand. If the vacuum cleaner doesn't work, we use the litter grabber to pick stuff up and drop it into a bag."

A quick glance at the board, then she continued...

"Phase 7: Saturday night ten o'clock approx. Extraction, and retire."

"When the safe is empty we literally throw everything into the truck, run up the ramp and close the door and replace the dummy window in the 'ole, so it's not too obvious we've broken in. Then we drive off.

"Barry drives us up Church Street, turns left into Lammas Lane then west again into West End Lane until we get to just before Portsmouth Road. If there's no traffic there, we all leap out, take off the dark tarpaulin and drop the rolled up white tarpaulin back down again. We also peel off the plastic on the back. Helen will pull off the false number plates. We throw the lot into plastic bags and put them into the truck. We then pile into the lorry – which is now white – and head back to where we can dump stuff. We then drive back here to drop off the truck and pick up Ade. We casually transfer all our stuff to the mini-van. Then, we all drive off up north for our getaway.

"We stay in the holiday cottage for a week, then move to a second holiday cottage for another week. We do this for a month or so. After one month, with no leads, the ploppers will start running the investigation down."

Caffee slapped the board one final time. "And that's it! Now... questions?"

There was an intake of breath all round.

Colin stuck his hand up. "Shooters. I think we should have a gun just in case..."

"No guns." Caffee shook her head. "It's a requirement. Anyway, mister dick-for-brains, it was you who said we'd be rescindivicated if we didn't use guns."

"Ay? I know where I can get one, cheap like. Just in case..."

"No guns, Colin. Ain't necessary."

"I disagree. What if some crooks try to nick our nickins? We'd need protection. I think..."

Norman's voice boomed. "Young man, do you know what a gun *is*?"

"Yeh. Of course, I bloody…"

"I doubt it. You sound like a yank. A gun is a *tool*. It's a tool designed to maim and kill. Is it your *intention* to maim and kill?"

"What? No… but…"

"Then, if you have no intention to maim, cripple or murder, you have no need of a tool to do the job for you. Right?"

"But what if…?"

Norman sat forward pointing a finger menacingly at the would-be gangster. His voice took on darker tone. "Trust me. One mistake with a gun, just one, can ruin your life forever. Understand? There will be *no* guns!"

They locked eyes.

The following silence made that decision final. Then Norman relaxed and sat back.

Finally, Colin, still a little shaken, got the courage to make a comment. "What about the paintball guns?"

Caffee answered. "Paintball guns are tools designed to bruise and embarrass in psycho-delic colour. Ain't the same."

Mam was nodding to herself. "It *was* a sign. It was a sign from the Good Lord. When that mouse stole the bacon rind and got clean away, it was a sign. Oh Lord, I knew it was a sign." She closed her eyes and crossed herself. "Then I dropped the toast, but it landed butter side up so it was alright. *Then* I knew. He was telling me. He was telling me not to worry about making a mistake. He would be there for me." She crossed herself again and finished on a whisper.

"Praise the Lord."

Norman asked, "How do we pay for the holiday cottages?"

"Colin?"

There was a pause while Colin pulled himself out of his sulk. It wasn't going to be the same without a gun. If he was going to be a bank robber then a gun would have added extra street cred.

"I know someone who hires a few out," he mumbled. "This time of year is all quiet, so we can use them without suss. I have addresses."

"I am impressed. You seem to be a man with connections."

Colin perked up a little and examined the older man's face. Norman really did seem impressed.

Norman then enquired, "And how, pray sir, do we obtain the truck?"

"No praying needed. I've nick... lift... uhm... borrowed trucks from... I know where to get a truck, alright?"

Norman nodded. "It seems we have serendipity on our side. Now whether it be bestial oblivion, or some craven scruple of thinking too precisely on the event, a thought which, quartered, hath but one part wisdom." Norman went quiet and thoughtful.

"What?" Caffee's face screwed up in confusion.

But Colin decided to ignore Norman's babbling. "Where are we gonna get all this other stuff? You've got webcams on sticks, carbon dioxide fire extinguishers, smoke pots, sheet plastic, and fuck knows what else. We've only got about twenty quid and ten days to pull this off."

"Who is Sarah Dipperty?" asked Barry, finally able to get his question in.

"Hush your mouth," whispered Mam.

"Humm..." Caffee shuffled a little on her feet. "Well... most of the stuff is already got. It's in a garage." She smiled weakly waiting for the inevitable interrogation.

"You've been planning this for some time, girl?" Mam raised her eyebrows questioningly.

"No. Not me. I knew this feller..." Caffee couldn't look Mam in the eye and concentrated on a stain on the carpet. "It was his idea."

"And he and you were going to rob this bank?"

"Humm... yeh. Might have..."

"Who is Sarah Dipperty?" pressed Barry.

"And how come you know so much about it?"

"Humm... 'e wrote it all down in English so I could understand it. I memorised it. It's a good plan. It was like a hobby... like... sort of."

Colin asked, "You dated a bank robber?"

"Nah. Nothing like that. He's just a friend." She couldn't help but glance sideways at Adrian who took this as a sign to speak out.

"I saw this a rank bank prank with funny honey money which is economic energy uneconomically inergetically lying dormant like a dormouse in a box with locks that rocks that we need to live but they only take to give to their part owners who already have enough but they always want..."

"Shut up!" Colin pointed to Adrian accusingly. "*You* planned this?"

Caffee surreptitiously shook her head trying to tell

Adrian to be quiet but all eyes were now on him.

"You planned a bank robbery, Adrian?" Mam was wide-eyed.

Adrian grabbed his right ear, closed his eyes and started rocking back and forth.

"He is upset," said Barry.

"He's a messenger of The Lord," whispered Mam.

"He's a fucking genius," mused Colin.

No one noticed Norman silently nodding in agreement. He knew it was Adrian some time ago. It was Adrian's 'thing'.

They all turned back toward Caffee. Colin asked, "But how do you expect us to remember all of those details? We're bound to fuck up and get caught."

Caffee put her hands on her hips and frowned. She had expected the plan to be dismissed as absurd and Mam to have exploded with anger about it all being evil, deceitful, and sinful. Instead, the feeling she was getting from everyone was that they all wanted to do it. They weren't arguing with the idea – they were looking for faults in the plan.

"Ade wrote a large document on a laptop. Everything itemised. Each step has a fallback position. Few bits of kit are *absolutely* necessary. No one has to do anything difficult. We can cut and run at any time. You've only heard the plan, not the other bits like what we do if something goes wrong. Each bit has conatin... conantin... conatingen'encies. I will have a checklist and a phone. I'll be there co-ordinating everyone so no one forgets what to do."

"And you understood that free... him?"

"Ade writ it... writted it... wroten it all down in

102

English. Proper like. He don't waffle on paper."

"But what about fingerprints and DNA? They're going to catch us, you know."

"Nah. All taken care of. We wear gloves and I get to carry in a load more spare DNA to keep the fuzzies occupied. Also, only one or two of us are on the register and the place will be covered in water. Besides, my job is to clean up just before we leg it."

"How long have you been planning this, girl?"

"Humm... ever since Ade showed me his plan. Over a year ago."

"You've been planning this for a year?"

"Mmm. More or less." Caffee nodded. "But I never thought we'd actually *do* it. I just liked pretending we might, you know, be rich one day. Like in them films, you know? With them helicopters and them dancing the tango." She bit her lip.

There was a moment's thoughtful silence before Norman asked, "This is all very well but you're forgetting one thing. We will have lost this house, our heavenly abode, even before we return."

Adrian perked up and mumbled again. "Not so the loss but better made by a better maid service needs this old cold house with a mouse they'll do so they'll pain-ly pay to paintly re-rate and decorate and repair and fix for the new occupying occupants once we've rightly left, or left rightly, whichever is rightly left right, before we return, as the new with our honey money rent and then there we'll still be here." He grinned. "But richer."

"What?"

Helen answered. "I think he said that after we

103

leave the landlord will fix this place up and we might be able to rent it back with the loot."

Adrian touched his nose, blinked several times, bounced a little in his chair and grinned sideways at the ceiling.

"Who is Sarah Dipperty?" asked Barry.

Norman stayed quiet. No one asked him for his opinion, but if they had they would have been surprised at his answer. He knew Adrian better than anyone. He had every confidence in the young man and his planning. His life had once depended on Adrian's planning, but under very, very different circumstances when Adrian was a different person.

"Jeezus!" Colin muttered to himself under his breath. "It's like being in half of Ocean's Eleven, but there's only seven of us brain farts and the criminal mastermind is a fucking dingus!"

Mam picked up her handbag and hit him on the head with it.

12
A Private Discussion

The TV had finished and everyone was preparing for bed. Norman and Colin were in the living room, Mam and Barry were in the kitchen tidying up.

"Barry?"

"Yes, Mam?"

"Have you set the mousetraps, boy?"

"Yes, Mam." Barry pointed to the two black humane mousetraps. She had originally used the sprung type but seeing the dead mice broke Barry's heart. So, now they caught the mice in humane traps and every morning Barry would take them to the end of the street and release them into someone else's garden.

He yawned.

Mam turned from the refrigerator and held out a tub of butter. "What have you been using as bait, boy? Have you been using this butter?"

Barry nodded.

"And what else have you been using?"

Barry went to the cereal cupboard and brought down the small open packet of muesli.

"Oh no, Barry. Barry my boy. You've been feeding them mices with extra vitamins, haven't you?"

Barry's expression was blank.

"No, no, Barry my dear boy. Look here, you've been feeding them with all this health food and this omega three butter which is supposed to be good for the brain. You've been feeding them with brain food, now. Oh Barry, no wonder we have so many mices in here. They keep finding their way back!"

"I do take them all the way to the end of the street, Mam."

"Yes, yes, I know. You drop them in Mrs Willis' garden, ever since she shouted at you. But you have been feeding them brain food. They must be more intelligent than us by now... Oh Barry, my boy. They'll have made a path straight from Mrs Willis' garden to our kitchen, I have no doubt. Look here now, we feed them with scraps of animal fat. Like this bacon rind here. It saves us money, you know?"

"You said bacon fat was unhealthy."

"It *is*, Honeybunch. It is. For us. But we feed it to the mices now, you see? They don't become so healthy and clever then. Besides, they don't live long enough to have cholester-oil."

"But I like mice..."

"Awww..." Mam stopped and sighed. Barry was showing signs of real concern. "Bacon rind is bad for us, but it is good for catching the mices. They like bacon rind."

"Better than omega butter?"

"Yes. No. Well, giving them brains is not a kind thing. It is bad for them mices. We don't give them expensive omega butter or the added vitamins, you know? If they get too clever the cats can't catch them, now can they?"

Barry's confusion grew. He frowned.

"...and you like cats, don't you, dear?"

"I like cats."

"Well, there you are then. Think of the cats, boy. They can't catch the mices if they're too clever, now can they? We'll bait the traps with the bacon rind from now on. Yes?"

"But what if we fed cats the omega butter?"

"Cats don't like butter... well..."

"We could feed them both omega butter and muesli."

Mam sighed. "Cats don't like muesli. So, we don't feed any of it to them. They can look after themselves. No more muesli or omega butter now. We'll trap the mice with the bacon rind."

"But I like mice."

Colin poked his head around the door. "Bacon is from pigs," he grinned.

Barry perked up. "I like pigs."

"Hush your mouth! You are not helping you wicked boy! Go in the front room and stay there."

"What size feet you got, Barry? I got a nice pair of..."

"Off with you now!" Mam flicked a tea towel at him.

Barry was so confused. How could Colin be wicked by stating the obvious? Everyone knew that bacon came from pigs. So how could making mice intelligent be bad for cats? It must be good for mice. But feeding mice with bad food was good? But the cats caught and ate the mice. Naughty cats. Would they get brainy by eating the omega-fed mice?

The world was something he would never understand so he resigned himself to just do as he was told and hoped he got it right.

Colin returned to the living room.

"'Ere Norm. Can I have a word?" Norman was slightly worse for wear having had a few glasses of cheap wine. He was about ready to turn in.

"If it's about guns, the answer my friend is still no. Definaterly no. No guns."

"No. No. It ain't about that. It's delicate, like."

"Indeed. I am all ears, my man. All ears and all years." He sighed deeply. "More years than ears alas. Although my ears do seem to have grown somewhat. Small ears is a sign of youth. Did you know that? You have remarkably small earlets, young man..."

"Right... What do you think about Helen?"

"She is but yet fair and..." Norman paused, aware his finer conversation didn't always engage the coarser gears of Colin's mind. Or indeed, anyone else's now he thought about it.

"...she seems like a demure young lady."

"Yeh."

"Are you attracted to her, young Colin?"

"What? No. Yes. Well, I'd do her. Yeh I'd do her, but that's not what I meant. She's not my type, really."

"Eloquently put."

"No, no, no. That's not what I meant. She is... she's... uhm..."

"You find her attractive."

"Have you seen the news?"

"Frequently."

"No, I mean recently. A couple of weeks back. There's this girl who murdered this bloke."

Norman's face remained deadpan. "Many a man has died of a girl's broken heart."

"No, no, no, no. I mean, like, this girl, in Dorchester I think it was, this girl she murdered this guy, right? She got a meat hook and stuck it in his back then pulled him up off his feet."

"How gruesome."

"Yeh. It grew some, and then she chopped it off! Kerchunk!" Colin made a chopping motion with his hands. "And she forced it down his throat."

"What?"

"His todger. She chopped it off and stuck it in his mouth."

"How utterly vile."

"Yeh."

"This sounds like exaggeration to me. It isn't quite so easy to dismember as FaceTube would have you believe... eve." Norman hiccoughed.

"No, no. It's on the internet."

"Ah! YouBoob! That explains it then. It must be true."

"Yeh. That's what I thought."

"And you think she, this murdering witch, might be Helen?"

"You reckon?"

"Hmmm. I don't think so. The story sounds vile, if not impossible. Helen is such a quiet young lady. I don't believe her capa... apable of such a thing. She is but too frail, too comely, too feminin... anine for a start." The meal and the wine were now disagreeing, if not arguing, inside him.

"That don't prove nothing. Look at Caffee – matchstick legs and twigs for arms but she could deck a copper. No prob!"

"You've seen this?"

"Don't you believe me?"

Norman thought for a moment. If there was ever going to be an incongruous contest between a policeman and Caffee, his money would be on Caffee. Her clogs, when stamped down at a glancing angle against a man's shins, were weapons not to be underestimated. Then there was the quick flick of an ankle that sent the clog spinning up into the assailant's nose, or the bony dead leg in the thigh. And then there was the vicious kick into the testicular region and as the man doubled over, she would follow it with a flying drop kick to the victim's nose – and with the mass of those clogs it was guaranteed to rearrange the victim's facial furniture permanently.

Had she been twice as tall, fourteen times the girth, and male, she would have made a fantastic rugby player. Mind you, that was probably true of anyone.

Then there was the time she took her clogs in her hands, leapt onto the shoulders of a stunned mugger, pinned her pin-like legs around his neck and pummelled his head until he cried for his mum. Once started she could be ruthless. He had seen her in action at first hand and had never felt the paternal instinct to protect her. Her victim, maybe, but not that little spitfire.

He wondered what other moves she had, ones that he hadn't seen yet.

"I believe you. She is the mastress of her own misterial – ahhh... she is the mattress of her own marcupial..." He took a deep breath, suppressed another hiccough then, "She is the mistress of her own martial art."

"Caffee? Yeh, that's true. She twists her nails right into your ear 'oles. Does narf hurt."

There it was. Her fingernails. Another set of weapons in her arsenal. Then he remembered how she once broke one of her plastic bangles, held it in her fist and threatened a junkie with festering scars and instant blindness if he came any closer. Was she trying to be all girly-girly in that skimpy outfit? Or was it just an excuse to wear a wide range of weaponry in plain view?

"So, you are thinking that Helen is a murderer ...ress? One capable of coldly parting a man's member from his torso and then forcing it down his throat? It takes a special type of mental... mentality to be able to do that. I think not. Not even Caffee could go that far."

"Yeh. I suppose you're right. Putting it that way. She couldn't, could she."

"Indeed. Besnides, the police pointed out there had been at least two other... other murders where the victims were castranated beforehand. Their bodies were found in the city dump. She could not have... of. Now, I really *must* retire." He rose from the chair, wobbled a little, yawned and stretched while he waited for the room to steady itself.

"What? Give up your job?"

"Pardon? No, you fool. I must to bed. Retire for the night." Then a thought occurred to him. If Colin *was* attracted to Helen, maybe that would not be such a good thing. "Of course, some of the worst murderers *were* demure young ladies."

"Yeh?"

Norman took a breath and counted them off. "Well, there was Belle Gunness, she killed all her family – as did uhm... Mary Ann, what's her name... Cotton. Beverley Allitt; she liked to kill the little children in her care. Then there was... Katherine Knight. Yes, Katherine Knight, that was her name."

Norman grabbed the back of the chair for support. "Wonderful woman. She stabbed her lover then skinned him before roasting him as a meal for her children. She was quite eco... economaniacal what with the housekeeping as I recall."

"Bloody hell! What kinda people did you go knocking 'round with?"

"Helen could be one of those quiet, demure young ladies that, if you upset, upset in the *slightest* way, she could creep up on you when you're sleeping and carve you into several joints of meat. Or maybe she would drape your intestenines around the bedroom as a birthday surprise for when you awoke." Norman tried a little expressive dance, waving his arms to illustrate where the intestines would be draped.

Colin's face turned pale and his eyes opened wide. "Jesus! You reckon?"

"Oh, these sorts of psycho... pathenic killers usually don't kill other women. They prefer to kill men. Particularly attractive young men. Ones with small ears. Often spectaculan... larly. It is well known, my young man. Especially ones with earlets... like yours."

Colin's hand drifted to one of his ears. "Oh, fuck. Perhaps we'd better tell the police..."

"And they would believe you, would they?"

"Well, you said..."

"They would patiently listen to your story, then look up your extensive police record and arrest... who *would* they arrest, Colinin?"

"Fuck off! You're just trying to scare me. This is just bullshit!"

"Yes. Yes, of course it is. But best to play safe, my boy. If you leave her alone, I'm sure she'll leave your earlets and intestenines alone, too."

Colin left the room first, still fingering his ear.

"Goodnight. And sleep thee well." Norman grinned.

Meanwhile, the hunters were closing in on their quarry.

13
Picking Up the Scent

Terry had finally arrived in Gunnersbury by following the girls' route by train and underground.

The police were now hot on the trail of the girl too. Despite his attempts at sabotage, they'd figured something out and now the source in Doncaster had informed Jacket that they too were chasing her. At least it confirmed he might be on the right track, but most importantly, he was still ahead of them.

But only just. He needed to move.

Terry left the station and walked on, aware he was probably still on video, but at least not the one in the station. From a deep pocket he extracted a small stack of prints of the girls he'd taken from the supplied CCTV footage. There were pictures of the green anorak girl talking to another girl dressed in pastel blue and pink – if dressed was the right word. Pastel girl, the one known as Kathy, Cathy, Kathleen, Kate or even Jennifer Fiveash. She was the key. Picking up a stranger and taking her directly to another location meant she knew her way around therefore she was almost certainly local. People tended to bring new-found things home, and he figured the pastel girl did too.

The source in Doncaster had identified the new girl as being a drifter with a history. Each time she had been detained she'd given a different variation of her name. Several times she had been arrested; for theft, street trading without a licence, Grievous

Bodily Harm, threatening behaviour, attempting to bribe an officer of the Law, and twice for soliciting. But very few instances resulted in charges being brought. She seemed to be adept at getting away with it.

Her family background was sketchy and almost certainly inaccurate. It indicated that she came from a broken home in Essex (or maybe Tottenham or Enfield) and her age was put down as seventeen, nineteen, or twenty-two years. A sergeant had commented on one of the files that all this information was probably wrong anyway. Another comment, by a social worker, disagreed but the reasoning was unclear. She certainly looked young in some of the pictures, but older in others.

Her home address had also varied over the two years or so between the first encounter with the authorities and the last. She'd certainly lied in most cases and her records showed that she couldn't be trusted to tell the truth. She had been tested for drugs but there were no signs in her blood or urine. There were however, some small suspicious telltales on other parts of her body.

The results of a medical examination confirmed that she had probably been the recipient of physical abuse as a child.

On paper she seemed to be a handful, a troublemaker, but looking again at her picture that didn't quite seem to fit. GBH? She looked underfed and unable to hurt anyone. Her ridiculous footwear would be a problem too. He thought she dressed like a whore. Was that her income? Almost certainly.

But the good thing about all this was that she was readily identifiable. In a couple of places her records described her as a 'character'. The girl spoke with an exaggerated cockney accent as if she came from the nineteen fifties. There was conjecture she lived in her own fantasy world. That, as far as he was concerned, was a good thing. It made her vulnerable.

If he could find her then he'd find the target, or at least a clue as to where she went.

Now for the legwork. He selected the best pictures from his stack and approached some youths.

After nearly an hour asking questions and showing pictures of both green anorak and the pastel girl, someone recognised Caffee. She lived in squat just a few houses down a nearby road.

A few small WiFi cameras dotted along the street would get the exact house. He needed to hire a car. Something nondescript but which he could sleep in.

He looked across the High Street. He was so close. Maybe a quick look now wouldn't hurt? Wrapping his raincoat round him, Terry dodged the traffic and entered the street.

14
The Raid Starts

The next few days were spent discussing the plan in more detail. Caffee produced Adrian's master document. Everyone was amazed at the quality and lucidity of the work.

However, when they observed him making some last-minute changes to the plan, they couldn't help but notice how he set about it. He started by writing the middle of several sentences first, then filled out some of the endings before starting yet more sentences. After a short pause he filled in the beginnings of the first sentences before moving on to complete the remaining ones. It was like watching someone write as if they were painting a picture by numbers that was, at the same time, also a puzzle being assembled from random directions.

Jobs were a bit of a problem. Mam convinced her employer she needed to go abroad to visit her family, one of whom had 'lost their house'. It wasn't a total lie. She'd lost her house a while back and she liked to think of the others as her family. Her employer agreed and promised to hold her job open for her for when she returned. She didn't feel too guilty about stretching the truth as he was a Mormon and therefore, in her eyes, not a real Christian at all.

Caffee and Colin were self-employed so there was no problem there. Norman explained to his employer that he needed to take Barry away for a while, and surprisingly he agreed. Union members held a disproportionate amount of sway in management decisions. However, Norman had the strong suspicion that their jobs would not be waiting for them when they returned – the council were making cutbacks... or trying to. Helen was happy just to stop going to the bakery, confident that her job was secure. Especially after Caffee explained how she managed to blackmail the bakery shop manager in the first place.

There were still one or two items needed for the job, but these were easily obtained. Being employed by the council's waste disposal department, Barry and Norman had access to much useful stuff. Indeed, Adrian's reconstructed laptop and printer had originally been assembled from discarded machines.

All too soon it was 'The Saturday' and everyone was visibly nervous – except for Adrian who disappeared to his room to pack. Helen noticed that Caffee seemed a bit more tetchy than normal and - had also doubled her consumption of gum.

It was generally agreed that Adrian had done enough just to plan the caper and they all felt he was unable to take part. This decision was confirmed when they stood in the dining room drinking red wine while watching Adrian outside in the garden. He was dancing, what they guessed was an Indian rain dance, while at the same time trying to encourage a black-and-white cat to join in. During one of his crazier moves the cat wandered off – no doubt uncomfortable in the company of a demented human. It was replaced a moment later by a curious tabby. When Adrian finally stopped, he fell to his knees exhausted and, not realising his audience had been replaced, started apologising profusely (at least that's what Helen surmised) for inadvertently dancing a 'fur-changing' spell.

The clincher was when he offered to paint-spray the cat back to its original black and white, but then, after a moment's reflection, started apologising again because he didn't have any black-and-white-spotted fur-paint.

At that point each member of the audience started having serious reservations about the plan but apart from shared grimaces, no one had the courage to express them.

The truck with white tarpaulin sides had been acquired by Colin and Caffee on the Friday night without a hitch. They simply strolled up to the yard where several trucks were kept overnight, shot the cameras with the paintball gun while taking care not to get into view, then picked the lock on the gate. The guard dog, a large lonely old German Shepherd, seeing the gate now open and desperate to see what lay beyond, shot outside ignoring the two burglars who were now brandishing joints of steak. He bounded down the road, tongue lolling outside his mouth, skipping from side to side and almost dancing with excitement.

The two burglars paused, puzzled by the dog's behaviour. They were unaware, as was everyone in fact, that this particular guard dog had a poor sense of smell and absolutely no comprehension of his role at the truck yard. Years of being stuck in an oily garage with nothing to sniff at other than various chemicals, paints, and the dubious contents of some of the trucks, had taken a toll on his senses and even his instincts. More than once he had uncovered one of the driver's secret stashes and spent quite a time tripping out on some of the stuff he'd tasted. He would have made a wonderful pet for a hippy.

Colin asked Caffee what they should do with the meat. She shrugged and suggested that, to save money, they should return it to Mam's freezer. Colin didn't like to admit that he'd laced the meat with sleeping pills and quietly agreed, making a mental note to become vegetarian until he found a way of losing them.

"Just one question," asked Caffee. "Why have you got a paintbrush duct-taped to the barrel of your gun?"

"I used to play paintball with it."

"Yeh, I *know* that. What's the brush for?"

"It's a bayonet. When the enemy get too close you paint 'em with it. Especially their masks." Colin grinned. "Our team used to specialise in close combat. We had a few plastic bags of household paint too. We used them as grenades. Once my mate filled a fire extinguisher with paint, and we used it like a flame thrower. Then the bastards banned us. They said it wasn't fair on the kids."

"Kids? You took it seriously then, did yuh?"

Colin's grin was reply enough.

"We taught a lot of kids about the truth of war. Their parents were pretty pissed off, though."

"Fuckin' hell. Surprised, I ain't!"

Caffee selected a suitable truck and Colin drove it outside and waited while Caffee re-locked the gates. Several passersby noticed them and one even waved, but the two thieves acted so friendly and self-assured no one felt the need to wake the neighbourhood by summoning shouty policemen — what with their loud sirens and flashing lights. Besides, snitching is impolite. Moreover, the police had this nasty habit of asking so many questions.

Mam was up at the crack of dawn cleaning the inside of the cab. It was a typical delivery truck littered with fag ends, chocolate bar wrappers, cigarette boxes, half-eaten French fries, and a used pregnancy test kit. Mam examined the contents of the latter and was sorely disappointed the result was negative, unaware that her feelings were the direct opposite of the driver.

By nine o'clock the cab was spotless and smelling strongly of lemon with just a faint hint of bleach and diesel. It never occurred to her the confusion she could have caused on Monday morning when the driver would open the now super-clean truck. Fortunately, the driver was the sort of woman who blundered through life oblivious to such details. She still lived with her parents and had never thought to question how her bedroom always remained neat and tidy.

The rest of the morning they loaded up the truck and then set off for the garage for the rest of their kit.

Just before they left the house Adrian's babysitter arrived. She was a tall, gaunt, monochrome Goth of about twenty-four years who had often 'babysat' Adrian in the past. Her skin was a naturally unnatural pale white. The only makeup she felt she needed was black lipstick and copious black eyeshadow – which matched her long black hair. As is common for members of her subculture she had several ear and nose rings which were linked together by a chain. Barry always wondered how she managed to turn her head without the chains pulling at the rings, but no amount of explanation ever seemed to satisfy him. Mam disapproved of 'the witch' but no one else had ever come so cheap so it wasn't really a choice.

None of the gang had ever seen this vampire-like vision smile or even heard her speak. Her ears were permanently plugged into a black iPod and communication with her was always upstream against the sound of 'tshhhh d-tshhhh d-tshhhh d-tshhhh' from her earphones. Presumably she could lip read. They did learn from her flatmate that she was a student attending classes in Accounting and Business Studies. How *that* had happened no one was quite sure. They nicknamed her 'Morticia' and she never objected, if she ever even knew. She always turned up on time and Adrian always enjoyed talking to her at great length. Whether she understood, listened, or even realised he *was* talking to her was a mystery but while she was there Adrian never got into trouble and was always pleased to see her.

They drove to the garage where they all put on gloves and then loaded up the truck. Caffee checked everything against the lists on the clipboard. They replaced the tarpaulin sides with their dark blue substitutes and lay blue sheet plastic over the top and back of the truck which changed the apparent colour of the body, although the cab remained white. The number plates were covered with those 'acquired' on the Thursday night from a dark blue truck of similar size. The Blu-Tak wasn't strong enough to hold the false plates on and even the addition of Caffee's industrial-strength chewing gum didn't help. However, sticky tape wrapped round them worked a treat.

During the loading Caffee noticed Colin's lips moving silently as he calculated how much he could have earned from selling all this stuff himself. He never understood why she hit him, and she never explained.

They set off after lunch and arrived at Esher in the early afternoon, parking the truck in a quiet side street. Mam, of course, had to be helped down from the cab before they prepared for Phase One.

Barry, Helen, Mam, and Norman got dressed in their disguises in the back of the truck. Adrian had thoughtfully specified a stepladder for everyone to climb up behind the tarpaulin to get changed. Mam disguised herself as an African woman in a bright dress – which simply meant she wore a slightly more flamboyant dress than normal, but two sizes larger to fit over the dress she was already wearing. Apparently, it was the matching hat that made all the difference. Negotiating the stepladder back down to the pavement afterwards was a difficult operation assisted by Barry, Norman, Colin, and Caffee but then she asked...

"Do I look fatter in this, girl?"

"No, Mam." Caffee's standard reply was automatic.

"Oh, don't tell me that now, girl! I'm trying to look like a fat African woman!"

Caffee replied glibly, "Sorry, Mam. I thought you were someone else," to which Mam beamed.

Helen had acquired a sleek navy-blue velvet evening dress, high heels, a pair of vintage black cat glasses and a long, slightly chewed, woman's cigarette holder. It came complete with a cigarette super-glued into the end. She had also taped a sharp six-inch kitchen knife to her inner thigh, but no one knew this. She was very pleased with her choice of disguise.

Norman had managed a dapper tweed suit with flat cap, a pair of glasses, false sideburns and a matching pipe, probably acquired from a prop box somewhere. But Barry, sadly, could find nothing to change his appearance so had finally acquired a large milkman's outfit complete with peak cap.

"You're the fucking 'A' Team, yeh?" but Caffee's attempt at motivation fell flat on the nervous group.

As the four walked away from the truck Caffee watched them go. Mam and Barry holding hands and Helen staggering ungainly on her high heels and clutching at Norman for support.

Colin, for some reason, felt a twinge of jealousy.

"Fuuuck!" murmured Caffee. "I ain't so sure now..." The two swapped worried glances.

The A Team headed down the High Street and eventually entered the bank. Barry took out his cheque book and dropped it on the floor as they'd rehearsed, but a helpful old gent bent over and picked it up for him.

"I think you're in the wrong bank. This is a Barclays cheque book." The man smiled sweetly and handed it back to Barry, who froze in fear.

"Did you bring the wrong cheque book, Henry?" asked Mam. She winked knowingly at him.

Barry was now completely confused. "It's me. Barry, Mam," he replied, took the proffered cheque book and deliberately dropped it again.

"Your name is Henry, Henry." She made a point of winking again.

The old man frowned, and cautiously picked up the cheque book for the second time.

Barry screwed his face in confusion. "Who's Henry, Mam? Helen, you tell her."

"Mah nem izz Marta Harri," replied Helen, placing her hand on her hip and attempting to suck from her cigarette holder. She mimed blowing some imaginary smoke into Barry's face, coughed, then dramatically threw her head back. Her glasses went flying across the foyer. She squeaked and made a dash to grab them.

Mam took the cheque book from the bemused old man and gave it to Barry.

"He's not all there... ever since his mother died," she whispered to the old gent.

Barry threw the cheque book at the floor and stared at the old man – daring him to pick it up again.

The old man looked down at the fallen book, back at Barry, and across at Helen who, in her attempt to retrieve her glasses, had now tripped on the hem of her dress and lay sprawled across the floor. He looked up at the large sweaty black woman and said politely, "Well, I do hope it all works out for you. Good day." His attempt at a smile looked more like a grimace, and then he made sure he left them far behind.

Barry stooped down and picked up the cheque book.

By this time Norman had finished placing the smoke pot behind the radiator – completely unobserved by the other customers. He walked across the foyer and helped Helen up from the floor, brushed her down, re-balanced her glasses on her nose, and declared loudly, "God made woman beautiful and foolish. Beautiful, that man might love her, and foolish that she might stumble on her high heels."

Helen winced and replaced the cigarette holder in her mouth, unaware the cigarette had broken and that the tip was dangling precariously.

So far, so good. Sort of...

15
The Raid Phase 2

The A Team slowly returned to the truck. Helen was now limping and being supported by Norman. Caffee and Colin left the truck and walked toward them.

"So, how'd it go?" Caffee was concerned that things hadn't gone to plan.

"It went well." Mam beamed and dabbed a floral handkerchief at her forehead.

"But you did get my name wrong." Barry was visibly upset.

"Oh?" Caffee examined the state of Helen. "And what happened to you?"

Helen winced, handed Norman her broken cigarette holder and glasses, took off her high heels, and sighed with relief.

"Never again."

"Your hair's all a mess. What happened?"

"The fair maid hath stumbled and needed rescue."

"...and Mam forgot my name," whimpered Barry, clutching at Mam's hand.

Mam patted Barry's hand. "It was only pretend, Barry. We were pretending to be someone else. It was a game."

"I thought we were robbing a bank."

"Shush, now!"

"But the lady's minor mishap was but the merest

of trifles and yet it worked well in our favour," Norman replied to Caffee's question.

Colin was surprised. "She slipped on custard?"

"Custard? Pardon? No. No, I mean..."

"Did you slip over?" Caffee was concerned for her friend.

"I fell."

"On custard?" pressed Colin, wondering if he'd missed out on some sort of treat.

"Custard? Where?" Helen glanced down at her dress, concerned that her image of elegance had been compromised by a slimy streak of yellow.

"I like custard," whispered Barry.

"There was *no* custard," murmured Norman.

"Trifle, apparently," remarked Caffee.

"I did not see any trifle," declared Mam.

Norman sighed quietly. "Tis but a manner of speech."

Helen only caught some of that. "Butter of what?"

"What?"

"No. There was *no* trifle!" Norman's patience was wearing thin.

Helen looked up. "So, I did slip on butter, then?"

"Oh, dear Lord preserve my soul! Shallow understanding from good people be more frustrating than absolute misunderstanding from the cretin!"

Helen started checking her dress for butter smears.

"Anyway, it's all over now. Let's get on with Phase Two. But first – you all go get changed."

"I am indeed in need of refreshment. Then, let us

redress to the public bar."

"What?"

"What? I ain't dressing up in no fucking pub."

"Oh, Good Lord! I meant..." Norman sighed and drew a breath to calm down. "...once more unto the pub, my friends."

"In a mo'. Let's get you lot changed back first. Mam looks like she's going to melt."

Colin was still suspicious. "You lot had cakes, didn't you! And you left me out."

"No, Colin," said Mam. "They're too fattening." An excuse which only confirmed it to him.

Colin threw the steps back into place by the truck while muttering under his breath. The A Team entered the back of the lorry to change into their normal clothes.

After that the entire group wandered down the street to the nearest pub. They bought drinks from the bar but surreptitiously ate their packed sandwiches, and if the bar staff noticed anything they were too polite to mention it.

Later in the afternoon, as the sun set, the streetlights came on and the High Street submerged behind the shadows of the cold white and yellow. Save for the kebab take-away, the shop fronts also went dark as if to hide from the passersby. Colin and Norman returned to the truck. The two changed into overalls and carried the customised ladder back down the high street to stand outside the bank. Sure enough, high on the wall, the two alarm bells were clearly visible. One above the other.

Caffee located herself across the main road, still in her ludicrously short mini skirt, but now her hands were thrust into a white fake-fur hand muff that almost matched her white-edged fake-fur jacket. Her legs were now protected against the chill wind by a pair of maroon tights. She started walking up and down as the two men started their work, but then she changed her mind and leant against a shop front to watch for police or any nosy shoppers.

Colin took the step ladder and rested it against the top bell. A drill bit poked from one side and Colin casually pulled a lever and the drill, duct-taped to the top, started to whine. It bit into the casing of the bell but the sound of the traffic drowned out the screeching of the metal.

A small thump signified when the drill had done its work. The two then pulled gently on the ladder and it came away without a fuss. As planned, they then lifted it and moved it over so that the other side of the ladder leant against the bell inserting a nozzle into the hole. Colin pulled another lever connected to a duct-taped can of foam. A shushing sound emanated from the bell-housing as the foam was injected into it. This was soon followed by the sudden appearance of white foam around the edges of the unit.

Caffee was still scanning the street when the figure of a young female in a navy blue burqa appeared a few yards in front of her and stopped. Caffee frowned. Esher was not the sort of place she expected to find women dressed like pillar boxes and this particular pillar box was attracting glances from passersby.

Extracting the ladder again was straightforward

and also went according to plan. Norman shortened the ladder to the new height and Colin checked the drill and the foam nozzle. All was well so the fill-with-foam procedure was started on the second bell.

The flat top of the burqa slid slightly sideways at an angle and the woman, or girl, underneath must have started to spin as it turned round and round on the spot. It seemed to Caffee that the occupant of the burqa was spinning around quite fast and the garment was unsuccessfully trying to catch up.

She briefly wondered if burqas were worn by whirling dervishes' wives. Probably not. In any case, this one couldn't have been a expert Arab ballet dancer as she was starting to stagger.

Caffee was unsure whether this was a good thing or not. It was certainly taking the attention away from the men with ladders across the road. On the other hand, this one was attracting enough attention that a concerned nurse, or worse, a police officer, might start to get curious.

Across the road things had stopped going to plan. This time the drill had stuck in its hole. No matter how hard the two men pulled and pushed and twisted it would not break free of the bell housing. In the end Colin climbed the ladder and pulled the drill away from the top of the ladder and extracted it manually. Rather than waste time re-positioning the ladder to deliver the foam, he simply pulled the foam spray and filled the second bell by hand.

Caffee glanced around. No one was watching the two across the road. The woman in the rotating burqa must have stopped spinning and, like a puppy stuck in a duvet, was now struggling to find a way out.

But... the way the woman jerked, then stopped, then batted at the cloth, was vaguely reminiscent of...

"Oh, *shit!*"

Caffee moved quickly to the burqa ballerina and grabbed at the top. The occupant continued to punch and turn underneath.

"Is that you, Ade?"

The punching stopped abruptly.

"Coz if it *is*..." she hissed.

"Erm... if I positively agree in agreeable agreement..."

"What the *fuck* are you trying to *do*?" Caffee glanced awkwardly around at a few passersby. "Fancy dress," she called out. "Poor choice." She managed a sickly smile. Losing interest, the audience continued about their business. Caffee dragged the duvet-trapped puppy away from the road and dragged the costume off.

"What the *fuck* are you *finking*?" she scream-whispered.

"I couldn't see or view through the unfit eye slit bit and periscope-less I've never been and seen a mean and keen burglary of the non-cat kind of unkind cat..."

"*Shut it*! You were in a *burqa*, you wanker! If a muslin figured you out, he'd prob'ly wanna thrash you to a pulp. Christ! They chop off hands for this sort of thing, you know? You stupid wally! They take their thrashing seriously, you know? They have no fucking sense of humour. Wot a dick-'ed. What *are* you trying to do? Ruin the job? Start a jihad or

132

summink?"

Adrian went quiet and looked at the floor.

"How'd you get here, anyway?"

"A trained train training trailing carrying carriages," he murmured.

"You were on the train wearing a fuckin' burqa? Jeezus H. Bleedin' Christ! You're playing with fire, mate."

She glanced across the road. The two men had finished with the alarms, packed up, and were now walking away down the road towards the truck.

"...so how did you buy a ticket? Tell me you didn't go to the counter."

Adrian didn't answer.

"...and 'ow the *fuck* did you get hold of a burqa? I hope you didn't nick it from the neighbour's clothesline, coz' I'll brain you if you did!"

She looked around for anyone curious, but no one was paying them attention.

"Fuckin' hell! You didn't buy it, did you?" The thought horrified her. "Strolled into a muslin shop and bought a burqa for your girlfriend?" The idea didn't have legs.

"...and Morticia? Where's she? She was supposed to be watching you."

"She made us a bees and snake, buzz and hiss, dinner, yum, and then fell asleep, profoundly deep, not a peep, but not under but snores in a heap."

"Wot? I wish you'd learn fuckin' English. Bees and snake... is that peas and steak?"

"No chips, not of wood, but to eat because chips on the hips is bad and sad, skinny is good, bony is

133

better, she said..."

Caffee frowned. The only steak they had, had been used to knobble the guard dog when they had those sleeping pills...

"Oh, *Colin*. You wanker!"

"No, no, no. It's me, see? Ade, lemony, not lemony, Ade." He twirled and pointed at himself.

"*Fuck it!*" She threw the burqa to one side, grabbed Adrian by the collar and frogmarched him back towards the pub. It was tense enough with the crew she had. *Now* they had to include Adrian.

Well, what else could possibly go wrong?

16
The Raid - Insertion

The third phase went without a hitch. Later in the evening, well after the shops had closed and the High Street had emptied of shoppers, it started to fill with partygoers. Colin got into his overalls and wandered back towards the bank. He'd already located the street box which contained the telephone switching gear and opened it with a hand-crafted key and hammer. He then spent five minutes happily snipping away at the wires which a mate of his, Nigel (who worked at a telecoms company), had happily confided were the ones to attack.

The cost of that information had been just seven pints and a promise of an introduction to his 'nymphomaniac sister-in-law' – but only after her 'merchant navy officer husband' had 'put to sea' again. It was never actually discussed as a specific transaction. It's surprising how well the young male penile-driven mind can focus its 'intelligence' (if that's the right word) sufficiently to be able to work through a complex social interaction – particularly where there's a one-in-a-million chance of sex at the end of it.

The two started with a few friendly beers at the pub. Colin then described the young lady's attributes. Then, from Colin's casual inquiries, Nigel, now fully attentive, was happy to describe his role in British Telecom. As soon as Nigel started to feel uncomfortable with Colin's questioning Colin changed tack and discussed the girl's marriage to his 'merchant navy officer' brother explaining how he often left his young, nubile wife alone for long stretches. So much so, that he was frequently unable to satisfy his wife's 'strong feminine desires and needs' when he returned from a voyage. Nigel then found it much easier to disclose intricate details of how the street boxes worked – provided every now and then Colin regularly supplied more information on his lusty 'sister-in-law' and her licentious 'history'. Finally, Colin, now in 'awe' at Nigel's technical expertise, was able to promise an introduction to her. Apparently, Nigel was just her type and it only needed a bottle of vodka for her to 'party' too.

Naturally, Colin's sister-in-law was a figment of his imagination and also a star of many private fantasies. Soon, she would sadly disappear with a new lover ('sorry, Nigel') only then to reconcile with her 'husband' later ('good news, Nigel!') and then he'd be back at sea at just about the same time Colin needed a little more technical information.

Colin later mused that his 'sister-in-law' must have also appeared in many of Nigel's private fantasies too, but Norman assured him that there was no satisfactory way to claim copyright and collect royalties from that. And Norman was an expert on the matter because he'd been an actor at least once.

The insertion phase of the robbery started shortly after the telephone lines were cut. They didn't want the telephone repair engineers to appear and reconnect the remote lines between the bank and its head office too soon.

Satisfied with the technical quality of his

vandalism Colin stood back from the box and closed the door, sealed it with a tube of super glue, then looked across the road at Caffee and nodded. The others had already wandered down to the truck and after a quick call from Caffee they set off around a few backstreets to eventually cross the crossroads pulling up on the narrow pavement so that the side of the truck was almost touching the bank's windows.

Colin took out a little electronic box and, on Caffee's cue – but only after she'd checked the road again – he pressed a button. There was a little flash behind the blinds of the bank. Caffee swore, wondering if they'd set the premises on fire.

There followed a scream and wailing from the back of the truck. Caffee started to worry that something had gone seriously wrong until she noticed water pouring from out the side and onto the pavement. Then she remembered that poor Helen had just been doused with the anti-infrared-detector stealth-system – i.e. two buckets of cold water. Caffee looked at her clipboard and read the next item on her checklist. She called Norman and was informed that they were now busy trying to console Helen who had broken down into a vitriolic state of shivering rage. Caffee screamed down the phone that the entire plan depended on her being cold and wet. For the sake of his future potential to father children they'd better breach the window and get her into the bank, *now*! She was no good to anyone if she was warm.

Colin entered the back of the truck and Caffee watched with satisfaction as the side tarpaulin curled out to stick to the side of the bank. They made a short tunnel between the truck and the window. On her command the window was broken just as the traffic lights changed and the roar of Saturday night traffic covered the sound.

Inside the truck Helen was given a pair of safety glasses, a paintball gun and coaxed through the short tunnel and into the sprinkler's downpour inside the bank's dark foyer. She wailed again as the downpour from the ceiling soaked her before she started shooting at the motion detectors and cameras, finishing just as the sprinkler system ran dry.

Colin, Norman, and Barry jumped down from the window ledge into the pool of water covering the floor. They erected a ramp from the floor to the bottom of the window. Adrian passed a black holdall to Colin then followed them.

Helen, already standing in the water-covered room, dripping from head to toe and still shaking from both cold and fury, put her hand to her hair. She paused then raised the paintball gun and took aim between Adrian's eyes.

The four men froze.

She snarled "My h-h-hair w-w-w-will t-t-t-take w-w-w-weeks b-b-b-before I-I-I-I c-c-c-can b-b-b-b-b-brush it a-a-again. YOU B-B-BASTARDS!"

Mam appeared at the window with a flask of hot soup. "Now, now, Helen my girl. There's no need for..."

Helen opened fire. Fortunately, for the other three, she only had enough ammunition to take her vengeance out on the one man who'd dreamt up the idea. Adrian squealed as balls burst all over him. Most of the paint missed, Helen's shivering translating itself into an equal covering of paint (and bruises) over Adrian's torso. The wall behind left an Adrian-shaped shadow.

When the gun had emptied, and still pulling at the unresponsive trigger, the other three gave her a wide berth and continued with the job at hand.

For a moment Mam stood there shocked. Then she took one look at Helen's expression and decided to act as if nothing had happened. "Here's your soup, girl. You drink that while I take Adrian back into the truck and clean him up." Helen snarled but the look on Adrian's pathetic green, yellow, and blue face and with his eyes now firmly closed, must have triggered something. She reluctantly handed the gun to Mam and accepted the soup.

Mam ushered Adrian back into the truck just as Caffee climbed into the back from the cab.

"What the fuck happened to him?"

"Helen was a little upset." Mam, wary of getting brightly coloured paint over her dress, despite the fact that the two colour schemes looked surprisingly similar. She started to pick away at Adrian's clothes but his eyes remained shut allowing Mam to do as she wanted. Every now and then he let out a whimper.

"Why?"

"I don't think she realised how cold it would be."

At that point Helen, clutching the half-drunk soup, re-entered the truck up the wooden ramp.

"Watchya do that to Adrian for?" Caffee was furious.

But even in the dim red light of the back of the truck, Caffee could see Helen still shuddering from the cold and her dark expression. The black-clad demon shivering before her looked nothing like the demure Helen she knew. This was something else. Caffee's sense of self-preservation snapped into place and her anger morphed into cautious diplomacy.

Mam felt the tension between the girls but wisely concentrated on undressing Adrian.

"I don't fink he meant you any 'arm. He just

needed someone to disable the..." Caffee's eyes darted all round Helen looking for weapons. "How about we get you out of those wet cloves..."

Helen gently put the flask of soup onto a box and, without taking her eyes off Caffee, started to unzip her very wet wetsuit.

Caffee realised that Mam was stripping Adrian out of his greasy-stained clothes while Helen was stripping herself too. Slowly, not wishing to cause alarm, Caffee reached for two towels, passed one to Mam and the larger to Helen.

With none of her usual modesty Helen stripped until she was naked, her eyes never once leaving Caffee's. Mam had stripped Adrian down to his 'Spiderman' underpants, his skinny body covered with reddening welts.

Helen dried herself with the blanket, but glanced every now and then at Adrian who, still in shock, held his eyes tightly closed – which was just as well.

Helen's hair, once brunette, long and reasonably straight, was now curly, tangled and in the poor light appeared jet black. Caffee was certain she was looking at a Jekyll and Hyde transformation and wondered if she'd lost her friend permanently. Helen finished drying then started dressing herself again from the clothes box.

When she'd finished, and clearly getting warmer in her dry clothes, she looked again at Adrian, the murderous expression fading. Mam was still sorting through Adrian's things trying to find him something to wear.

Caffee decided that now was a good time to see what the lads were up to in the bank. She edged past

Helen and walked down the ramp into the pool of water in the foyer. The lads had broken their way through the protective barriers in front of the cashier stations using a car jack and some blocks of wood to smash open the door. Colin had remembered to cover the radio phone and they were now standing around the safe. Caffee was pleased to note that all were wearing gloves. She pulled her own pink ones on, the ones with the fake fur edging and the sellotaped fingers.

She noticed a handwritten sign stuck to the wall. "The management request that all staff dismount their pogo sticks before assisting customers," and wondered what the story was behind that.

The safe was the expected tall grey iron box standing over six feet high with large metal handles and a dial in the front.

"Aha. Tis our mistress of this night, this night of dastardly deeds. Do we but fall behind our illicit schedule?"

"Wot? No, we're okay. Have you got your magic powder, Colin?"

"Yup." Colin placed a baked bean tin on top of the safe at the very front. "This'll burn down to the door."

"I shall fetch the vacuum cleaner," declared Norman, and disappeared into the darkness.

Caffee checked her notebook. "And bring the fan, the extinguisher, the grabber, and the safety glasses." She looked up at Colin. "There are no fingerprints on that, I take it?"

"There won't be." Colin grinned and proceeded to insert some paraffin-soaked string into the top.

Norman returned with the vacuum cleaner and

the fan and handed out the safety glasses. Colin waited until Barry had opened the back window. They plugged in the fan then Norman stood there with the fire extinguisher. Colin lit the string.

The flame snaked up the fuse, spitting every now and then as if angry. It crept over the lip of the can and then all hell broke loose as the custom thermite mixture inside caught fire. Smoke and sparks sprayed everywhere and the intense light lit up the inside of the bank like a volcanic eruption in a petrol-filled hell. The noise was pretty loud too, something they hadn't reckoned on.

Barry was visibly shaken and stepped back while the others watched the firework show covering their faces against the acrid smell and smoke. Colin had the foresight to bring some dark glass to keep watch on the fire's progress as it melted through the top few inches of the safe.

"I hope the ploppers don't turn up!" Caffee yelled over the racket.

"What?"

"Ploppers – fuzz – pigs. I hope they don't turn up."

"Turnips?" Colin was concentrating on the fire. "No! I don't wear turnups."

17
The Raid - Extraction

After a short while the inferno died down to a spitting fizzle and Norman shot it with the fire extinguisher, blowing dust, ash and smoke away to the far side of the safe. Standing on a plank of wood between two chairs Colin and Norman peered down into the hole.

"Yes!" Colin punched the air.

Next came the small tins of beans on the centre of the safe. Before lighting each one Norman filled the safe with CO_2, then Colin lit a piece of string and stood back. As there was a smaller amount in each bean tin it took three attempts to burn through the top.

Caffee and Barry left the two men and retired back to the truck. The smell and dust were overpowering. Even dipping handkerchiefs in the water and covering their faces didn't help much.

Within two minutes Colin and Norman returned to the truck, their faces black and eyes smarting. They had made a third hole and then made the second hole larger to facilitate extraction. Apparently, some bank notes and papers had caught fire but Norman's prompt flooding of the safe with more fire extinguisher gas prevented it from spreading.

Barry, Mam and Caffee now went to the safe. Mam dropped one of her large handbags, handles tied with string, through the hole in the top. Barry held a flashlight through one hole and Caffee used the grabber to knock and/or place bundles of notes into the handbag. The handbag was lifted and emptied by hand into a thick plastic bin bag before being lowered and refilled again.

Caffee had methodically emptied the uppermost shelves first, then one by one lifted them off their runners and dropped them down by the door before emptying the next level.

There were a lot of papers, several metal boxes and bags of loose change which were too heavy for the grabbers so Caffee just dumped them on the floor too. The lower shelves proved too difficult to reach even using two grabbers, one to support the other. She did manage to extract a couple of boxes of unknown content, some tubes of one-pound and two-pound coins, but mainly it was the notes that Caffee concentrated on.

At the end of the half hour, they sat back. "Time to go." Caffee smiled. "We got quite a bit, didn't we?"

Barry peered in through a hole. "I still see some money," he mumbled.

Mam also peered in through the top. "There's still some money there, girl. And there's some boxes we might be able to lift out too."

"Yeh. But time is pressing an' we got enuff so let's not waste time and get greedy, hey?" Caffee lifted the bin bag. "It's heavy enough. Let's go."

Barry and Mam looked at each other. "There's more money just for the taking, girl. We can do it, now."

"Mam, you *ain't* a proper feef. Okay? Take it from me, if you try too hard then, when you look up, there'll be a whole bunch of ploppers watchin' you incriminate yourself. Trust me. Let's go while we're ahead." And she splashed out toward the ramp. It was true, Mam thought, the skinny girl probably had far more experience than her.

Wrapping up the operation took another five minutes. Caffee went through her checklist making sure that all the equipment was stowed back on the truck. She wiped down most surfaces just in case something was left. Mam passed out a bag of dust from the van she'd collected from their street, the local café, and the local pet shop. Caffee liberally spread it around all the dry surfaces before brushing it onto the pool of water.

Satisfied that all was in order Caffee returned to the safe, extracted a plastic bag from a small holdall and, using tongs, extracted a black leather glove and dropped it into the top of the safe. "Take that! You bastard," she whispered. Then she extracted a hammer and a greasy pair of pliers and dropped them onto the floor.

On impulse she grabbed a still dry post-it note and wrote 'The Pogo Stick Freedom Fighters strike again!!!' on it and dropped it in the safe. Finally, she extracted an envelope addressed to the bank and dropped that onto the top of the safe before leaving the building.

The letter inside the envelope was pristine and untouched by human hand. She'd made sure of that. It read: -

Sirs,

According to my records you have several

times allowed unauthorised payments to pass through my bank account against my explicit wishes. Furthermore, these payments caused my account to go overdrawn and then you had the audacity to send me a letter and charge me for the same privilege while you knew I was unable to afford it.

After spending much time explaining my financial situation to you, I received no apologies or assurances that the same series of mistakes would not occur again. I was however, still charged for the letters and for your time.

It is not my policy to pay for your incompetence.

Consequently, I have taken steps to redress the balance by making a personal withdrawal from this branch. The discrepancy between your bank charges and the amount taken will pay for my time and act as compensation for my spouse and family who, like me, find our relationship with your money

grabbing bank very stressful.

Ever Your Servant

The letter was a complete fabrication of course, but Adrian had known that the police had only so many resources they could dedicate to the investigation. The details in the letter could well have been written by hundreds, if not thousands, of disgruntled customers; none of which applied to The Gunnersbury Gang. It would tie up personnel and time investigating the many false leads, and with any luck, maybe even get into the newspapers.

The dropped tools, the hammer and greasy pliers, had been removed from a shed in a private hospital several stops on the underground from Gunnersbury. Yet more fingerprints and clues for forensics to follow.

As for the glove, well... that was *covered* in DNA. None of it Caffee's.

She ran through her checklist again. She extracted the smoke pot from behind the radiator and splashed around in the filthy water while wiping surfaces with a dirty rag until she was satisfied that all was... well, 'clean' is hardly the right word.

Once Caffee had finished, she left. Having recovered from the smoke and fumes, Colin and Norman pulled up the ramp and replaced the window frame. A sheet of plastic over the front was held in place by small tacks. Another quick wipe down and the short bridge was pulled back. The canvas side of the truck was straightened up and clipped together.

Caffee hopped out the truck with the paintball gun, now reloaded, and casually walked down the road away from the traffic lights to the traffic camera. She took aim and shot it, watching with satisfaction as the paint splattered over the lens.

"What are you doing, young lady?"

Caffee froze.

"Well?"

She turned to see a little old lady in a raincoat squinting at her over the top of rimless glasses.

"Owls," said Caffee saying the first thing that came into her head. "They're watchin' me."

"Bowels?"

"Owls. Mmm." Caffee nodded.

"It is illegal to have firearms, you know. You are not allowed to own guns without a licence. You might shoot someone." She tapped the paintball gun with her walking stick.

"Oh no, it's alright, mum. This is like a water pistol, yeh? It doesn't fire bullets, just pellets of... owl deterrent."

The old lady frowned and looked down at Caffee's enormous wet boots.

"'ere look." Caffee opened the top of the gun and took out a paintball and squeezed it between her fingers. It burst, spraying yellow paint over her gloves, up her arm and in her face. "Fuck! 'scuse me... it's filled with a chemical to scare away owls, see? It stops 'em looking through my bedroom window." She nodded to one of the cottages.

"I haven't seen you here before." The old lady's eyes narrowed.

"Hello." Caffee smiled and extended her hand. "Pleased to meet you. I've just moved in... with my new husband."

The woman stood back from the proffered sticky yellow glove.

"Mam said you should come back to the truck now."

The two turned to look at Barry silhouetted in the street light. "Before we get caught, she said."

"This is 'im." Caffee sidled up to Barry and took his arm.

"Who?" Barry frowned.

The elderly lady squinted harder and eyed him up and down. "My, my. He's a big lad, isn't he?"

"Yeh. My hunk. Aintchya, darlin'!" Caffee looked lovingly up into Barry's wide eyes.

"...and you... such a slight, little thing," observed the old biddy.

"Yeh. That's me. Slight."

"Tell me, does it hurt?"

"'scuse me?"

"I'm a widow now. I was married very young, you see. My husband, well, he was such a little man. I didn't know at the time, of course. Nothing to compare him with, you see? I didn't go in for that sort of thing when I was young. All smutty it was, in those days. So, we were told... Silly girl, I was. He was such a little man. In so many, many ways." She sighed wistfully. "But I've always wondered, if he were bigger, would it have hurt?"

Barry was struggling to get to grips with the conversation, his lips moving as he silently repeated the words to himself. Caffee on the other hand knew *exactly* what the old lady meant. "Only the first time, but then you get used to it and from then on... oh, it's *heaven!*" Caffee grinned cheekily. "But we've got to go now, his Mam is calling for us."

"He was always at it though. Never stopped. I was just telling Margaret – she's my friend you see – he was like a frustrated rabbit with Parkinson's, he was. We used to keep the neighbours awake."

"Uhm. Too much information, luv. We've got to go now..." Caffee's cheeky grin faded.

The elderly lady's eyes turned misty. "The neighbours thought I had a noisy sewing machine."

"Uh... yeh. *Too* much, missus. We've *really* got to go now."

"I never could sew. I bought a sewing machine once. Does *he* go like a rabbit?"

"Uhm... wot? Him? No. No, he's very quiet. He's very gentle, but..."

"Oh, that's nice. You won't have to worry about the neighbours every morning, will you. Besides, Margaret is quite deaf. She won't mind. But if you ever feel the need for a little more, you know, pizzazz, try giving him a good dose of speed with his dinner. It did well for Jonathan. Made up for his... you know... *size*. Well, until he passed away, of course. But his brother likes it too. Ooooh, a much bigger man and he's not afraid to use those blue tablets, either. That reminds me, I must get back soon or Lancelot will wonder where I am. Well, nice speaking to you. I must get home now. He's poorly, you know. It's his heart. Poor thing. I need to catch my bus. I live in Surbiton, you see. Too far to walk.

151

Especially with my back. Good luck with your bowels, young lady. Goodnight."

She waved her walking stick and the pair watched the elderly lady waddle off down the road.

"Goodnight."

After a short pause Barry asked, "What was that about a rabbit?"

"It kept the neighbours awake."

"Why?"

"It liked sewing."

"Ah..." Barry nodded, understanding. "I like rabbits."

"One last job though." Caffee extracted a plain envelope and clumped off to the nearby post box.

18
The Raid – Withdrawal

Caffee and Barry returned to the truck. There was an air of impatience from everyone but Caffee made sure that nothing was rushed. She ran through her checklist again making sure that everything was accounted for and questioning everyone about their use of gloves. Only then did she allow Norman to drive off down the road, round the corner, and off to a quiet country lane.

As soon as they reached a secluded stretch Norman pulled over. They all got out and replaced the tarpaulin sides with the original white ones before peeling off the dark plastic strips over the body and removing the false number plates. Despite their apprehension, they let Adrian out for a dance in the woods – he was overjoyed at the success of the operation but, as yet, no one else was quite ready to celebrate.

For Helen, Mam, and Norman the guilt was starting to set in. Colin was continually looking up and down the road for police cars, and listening to the police frequencies on a radio scanner. Caffee was running through her checklist for the twentieth time. Barry simply put all his faith in Mam.

When the outside of the truck was made righteous, Adrian was grabbed and everyone got inside. They set off for the gypsy rubbish dump further up Portsmouth Road. There, they unloaded all the used materials into a skip and, once Caffee had checked with the checklist yet *again*, poured a can of petrol over it and set it on fire.

They all boarded the truck this time with Colin driving and Norman and Caffee sitting beside him.

As they drove away the sky lit up orange behind them.

"What the fuck was that?" Caffee craned her neck to look in the mirror at the receding glow in the trees. "How much fucking powder dew make, Colin?"

"I put all of it in the skip – like we agreed."

"Yeh. But the skip's just bloody vapourised... you *wanker*! The fire engines will be here any minute."

"So?"

"This was supposed to be a stealthy getaway – not Her Majesty's Fucking Fiendish Fireworks Festival!"

There was an uncomfortable pause.

"Jesus H. Christ. It's like bloody Chernobyl back there! How much effin' powder woz there?"

Colin thought for a moment. "And how are they going to connect the bank job to the skip? It's vapourised, remember?"

But what was done, was done. There was no use in upsetting anyone at this point of the job. "At least we can be sure there ain't nuffink left for the forensics."

"Except the ash," whispered Norman.

"What?"

"Forensics will link the two by the unburnt powder particles, but I think we're still in the clear. Unless we've left tyre tracks by the skip."

For a few minutes there was another silence in the cab as the truck sped on up the A3.

"We need to change the tyres."

"Fuck that! Pull over and let the tyres down. Not all the way, just 'nuf to wear 'em down quick like, yeh?"

Colin pulled the truck over and leapt out. After a few minutes he returned and they started off again.

"Nice idea. They should wear away around the edges now. By the time the police check 'em they'll have a different wear pattern." Colin grinned.

"But we won't get a puncture, will we?"

"I fuckin' hope not."

"Danger knows full well that Caffee is more dangerous than he. We are lions littered in one day, and I the elder, but she the more terrible," misquoted Norman.

Caffee frowned. "Is he calling me terrible?"

Colin shrugged. "I dunno. I got lost after the lions being rubbish bit."

Norman sighed... as usual.

Barry's voice piped up from the back. "Who's Bloody Chin O'Ball?"

They were off now, back to Gunnersbury to transfer everything to the van then wipe down and return the truck.

By two o'clock in the morning the gang were in the Volkswagen van heading up country on the A40. Colin drove for the first two hours before Norman took over. Only Adrian and Barry slept at first but after Barry took over the wheel the rest were asleep

155

or dozing.

By nine o'clock the next morning, after three short fuel and 'comfort' stops and further changes of driver, they were near the cottage in Dumfries where they planned to hide out until the dust settled. Colin extracted a map and guided them around the country lanes.

Then they arrived.

"Cor! Posh innit!" Caffee – it was her turn at the wheel – was impressed with the new dwelling and its large tinted windows as they pulled into the gravel driveway. "I 'ope we don't spoil it," unaware that the van had developed an oil leak and was already spoiling it.

"I like this place. Are we staying here, Mam?" Barry's eyes were drooping after the long drive.

Mam turned to Colin. "Is this really where we are going to stay for the next week, sonny?"

"Yep. Unless they come home early. I reckon we're set up alright for a few days at least."

"Who comes home early?"

"My friend's girlfriend's brother's girlfriend's parents."

"Are you sure now?"

He worked through the relationships on his fingers. "Yep. Positive."

Norman got out the van first, stretched and yawned. His breath steamed in the cold morning air, waking him up but he didn't mind. "Houses are built to live in, and not just to look upon. Therefore, let use be preferred before the uniforms come."

Barry grinned. "Oh good. I like unicorns." He

shivered and yawned.

Helen got out, ran across the drive and started peering in through the windows.

"It should be empty," called out Colin.

"Why can't we live in houses like these all the time now?"

"Because they're holiday cottages and they're not available all the time. Besides, this one cost me a bag of ganja." But the loss wasn't *that* great. It was stale.

Mam nodded and joined Norman who was now busying himself unloading clothes. These were carefully packed in their cardboard dressers now doubling up as packing boxes. Adrian fell out the door, stood up, brushed himself down and pointed over the road at a black heifer that was idly watching them from a field. "Moo!" he declared triumphantly.

Caffee smiled to herself. No one had mentioned the robbery since the last comfort stop, and no one had looked at the haul since the event. At one point during the long drive, she did get paranoid and rummaged around in the back to make sure they still had it. They did, and yet no one seemed concerned.

More than once the thought had crossed her mind that one of them might double cross them and steal it. She knew Mam and Barry wouldn't. Norman, well she was sure he wouldn't. He was as straight as they come and had never cheated, stole, or done anything improper while she had known him. Colin might. In fact, if he was given the chance, he might just take all the money and run – but he'd run back to London. In fact, he'd run back home to Gunnersbury and she knew that he knew that she'd find him and exact her revenge. He was still afraid of Caffee after that groping affair.

That had been when he had sneaked into her room one night. He'd said that it had been simply to ask her if he could borrow some money, but at one o'clock in the morning when everyone else had been asleep? No. Fortunately, his groping hand on her, albeit small ('pert' was her preferred word), breast sparked a reflex reaction. Within two point three seconds she had his head in a scissor lock and a pair of tweezers held firmly two inches up his left nostril.

Caffee let him go after she had explained, in eye-watering detail, what she'd do to his genitalia if he ever tried anything similar again.

Norman arrived on the scene shortly after, no doubt disturbed by the scuffle. Although both assured him everything was fine Caffee noticed that during the explanation, when Colin had tried to leave, Norman had subtly placed a firm hand on Colin's chest and pinned him against the wall. Colin's watering eyes and a trickle of blood down his left nostril probably revealed the real truth in any case.

Caffee took a lot of comfort from that. She also felt more secure when Helen had moved into her room. Caffee believed in security of numbers. Nevertheless, every now and then something in Helen's eyes made her feel that if Colin tried something with *her*, well, he wouldn't remain alive to make up any feeble excuses later.

She pondered a little more and then admitted to herself that she was more afraid of Helen than Colin. She had seen it in the van after she'd been doused under the sprinklers. And then there was also something about the way she handled kitchen knives. She idly wondered what would have happened had Helen been near a kitchen knife then.

The key to the cottage was left under a flowerpot. The first thing on the agenda was carrying everything from the van into the hall. The second thing was for Mam, Barry, and Norman to find the kitchen and make a pot of tea while Colin, Helen, and Caffee ran upstairs and allocated the bedrooms. Once Adrian's bedroom was assigned then his old mattress could be placed on the ground outside, beneath the window.

Meanwhile Adrian was talking to a bunch of flowers. His talk was quite profound, all about his friends and how he felt he had the right people around him. He told them of the bank job in terms of the colours he felt and the dampness he heard. Of course, anyone listening would not have understood any of that, let alone the marigolds.

Inside, Colin and Norman decided to have a drink. Norman found a small wine rack and chose a suitable Merlot. Colin visited the fridge and swore.

"Have you, perchance, struck lucky?" enquired Norman. "Is there any beer?"

"Fuckin' homo-pathetic beer only."

"I beg your pardon?"

"They only got bottled water. Fuckin' toffs don't drink beer."

"But if at church they would give some ale; and a pleasant fire our souls to regale. We'd sing and we'd pray all the livelong day; nor ever once from the church to stray."

So, they relaxed on the two large sofas, Colin slumming it with a glass of the Merlot. Soon the others came and joined them.

"He that is robbed, not knowing what is stolen, let him not know it and he's not robbed at all."

"Yeh, whatever. We got to count our loot." Colin glanced over his shoulder to the hall where the remaining bin bags held the contents of the safe. "No rush, mind. I guess it's all going into the kitty."

Caffee got up and disappeared for a minute then re-appeared with a handful of old newspapers. She spread them on the floor. Then Colin and Caffee carried the bags into the living room and started emptying them.

Most of the bundles were ten- and twenty-pound notes and were put on one side. Colin found six large bundles of fifties. "That's fifteen hundred there," he declared, grinning.

Helen leaned forward. "That's more than that. There's one hundred notes in each bundle. That makes it... a hundred and fifty thousand pounds!"

Norman shook his head. "Batches of fifty notes. Six times fifty times fifty pound notes is... fifteen thousand pounds."

They stopped while they did their calculations, mostly on fingers.

"Yeh. He's right."

In the end they reckoned the grand total amounted to around one hundred and sixty-four thousand pounds plus change plus a small box of legal papers, two bundles of letters and two wooden boxes.

"It's not enough." Colin sat back crestfallen.

"It's one hundred and sixty-four-fousan' pounds more than we had yesterday!"

"We can't buy the house for that."

"But we can pay the rent for a very long time," Norman suggested.

"That's about ten or so years of rent. Not bad really. If we ain't been caught already."

Colin did another quick calculation. "That's about twenty-three and a half thousand each, if we include Ade."

"We include Ade." Caffee said sternly "...and the money is for the kitty."

Norman sat forward. "But have the notes been registered? Will we have to launder it? We can't simply deposit it into another bank account now, can we?"

"He's got a point. If the bank has a list of the numbers on the notes then we need to swap them with others. That's going to cost us."

"Do they do that?"

"Dunno. I never worked in a bank. Might do though."

"We could bet on the gee-gees," suggested Colin.

Mam shook her head. "I do not like betting. Betting is wrong."

"Oh, right. But robbing banks *is* okay?" Colin raised an eyebrow.

"The Good Lord punishes sinners with his wrath. I have taken a lesson set by example from our Good Lord and helped punish those that have punished us for being poor."

161

Colin was about to answer back when he felt a sharp jab in his ribs. Caffee stood up. "The notes are all used, so I reckon that's good news. It won't be checked until it gets into the banks – *if* it's checked at all. So, we can spend it if we need to. We got loads of dosh 'ere and we need a couple of weeks' supplies. I suggest that this afternoon we drive out for about an hour an' buy stuff in a supermarket. If they detect the notes next week they still won't know where we are."

"...and we're moving on in a few days anyway." Colin sat back. "Sounds like a plan."

"Do you think we have got away with it, girl?"

"Yes, Mam. Provided no one gets stupid and we don't spread it all around, I reckon we're alright."

Helen suddenly blurted out "...but what about Morticia?"

There was silence for a moment.

"Oh, *fuck*!" Caffee's face turned white. "We forgot about 'er."

"She's alright," said Colin, more concerned about the meat with pills being discovered.

"We paid her, right?"

"Yeh. She was paid up front."

"Fank Christ for that!"

Mam got a little indignant. "There's no need to take the Lord's name in vain, girl."

"You're right. Sorry, Mam. Fank God, yeh?"

In a white Georgian mansion set in its own grounds, deep in leafy Surrey, a muscular man in a tailored black suit knocked on a door.

"Enter!"

He opened the door cautiously. "I got an alert, boss. From Esher. It's on the move."

A dark-skinned man, probably in his mid-thirties, looked up from his desk. "The box?"

"Yeh, I guess so. It's being moved."

The dark-skinned man sighed. "Curse them! They took the box. We shall have to retrieve it. They shall pay for this! Round up the others then inform Imani and tell her I have to go away for a while – but I will call her as soon as we are on the road."

19
Hiding Out

Tiredness from the night's drive and worrying about the consequences of the job seemed to put a damper on the general mood. It was cold but sunny outside – what the Scots might describe as a 'Fresh' day – so Norman and Barry put on coats and gloves and joined Adrian while Caffee and Helen went upstairs to unpack and clean up. Mam rooted through the kitchen cupboards before working up a list of things she needed for the next few days. They had brought some food with them, but not anything that needed a refrigerator.

Colin was the first to find the TV control. He flipped it on and went through the news channels. He found nothing but it wasn't the top of the hour. He flipped through to the adult channels but it was too early in the day to discover if the owners of the house had a subscription. Most of the sports channels were not subscribed to and neither were the movie or the documentary channels.

There was a muffled squeal from upstairs.

He did find a free sports channel with football and put his feet up. Mam's domestic radar must have pinged because she immediately re-entered the living room and forcibly flicked his trainers back to the floor.

"You go and change!" she demanded. "Look what you did to the sofa, boy. Shame on you! Shame on you!" She flicked him with a tea towel and watched him retire to his designated bedroom.

Within a few minutes he had returned and glanced at the clock. It was now on the hour which was pretty much news time so he switched on the TV and, sure enough, the robbery was being reported.

"...unusual raid. The robbers, allegedly allied to the 'Pogoshlick Freedom Fighters', a new terrorist group reported to be based in Azerbaijan, had broken into the premises during the night by removing a window and climbing through before vandalising the premises. The police have sealed off the centre of the town and are now undertaking an extensive forensics examination of the scene. It is unclear at this time if any money was taken, but we were informed that they did leave some surreal art on one wall. The bank was quick to assure its customers that all their accounts were safe."

From upstairs came another muffled squeal followed by swearing.

The next news item was about a car bomb in the Middle East which had claimed four lives. Colin shook his head sadly. So far, so good. Terrorists indeed! And since when did stealing money from a bank trump the pointless murder of four people? That was the 'News' for you.

A muffled shout, another squeal and more swearing, but Colin was oblivious to it. The TV still had his attention.

Flicking between the football and news channels he noted that nothing new was coming from the news. The police must still be deciphering the evidence and deciding what story to peddle. He observed that in the background were several different news vehicles, so this was going to be a big story very soon.

When Caffee came down Colin stood up and grinned. "We're on the news!"

"Yeh? What do they say?"

"Nothing much. But it'll be on again soon."

Colin called out the window and Norman and Barry rushed inside to see. Adrian followed too – in a roundabout fashion.

Mam came in and sat down with the others when the half-hour news started running through its cycle. Only Helen was absent.

The first item featured a member of parliament explaining – in the usual web of waffled vagaries – how politicians were motivated by their 'sense of duty to the public' and were therefore, by their very nature, fully prepared to 'sacrifice some of the major benefits of their lifestyle' for the public interest. He did this while simultaneously insisting that they should be paid several times over and above the UK's average salary. On asking why their pay should not be linked to average pay the politician adeptly provided a long and exhausting reply which, as far as anyone could tell, did not answer the question.

Norman scored the bastard as a nine-point-five. "Political language is designed to make lies sound truthful, murder respectable, and to give an appearance of solidity to their pure wind. I am fond of pigs. Dogs look up to us. Cats look down upon us, but pigs treat politicians as equals."

Barry agreed. "I like pigs. Especially baby pigs. They have cute little tails."

There was a murmur of assent, or it would have

been assent had they known what Norman was talking about – but they all knew that they didn't understand the MP. They concluded therefore that he was lying. It is, after all, what *all* dodgy salesmen did by default – something that politicians the world over never seemed to grasp.

The next news article was about the daring bank robbery. The family sat back wide-eyed as they watched the footage of the outside of the bank. It showed the police removing the plastic window where they'd broken in. Strewn around the outside were lots of numbered plastic tags against items of litter, and even two against some dog turds. On the alarm bells there were plastic bags protecting the evidence from the weather.

The newsreader gave them the summary. "Daring Bank Raid" – "Done in full view of everyone on the street" – "Dark-coloured lorry used to cover their entrance," before turning over to the reporter on the spot who took great delight in repeating the exact same summary but with slightly different words and more references to the previously unheard-of terrorist group. He then turned to interview a police spokesperson who described "The Daring Bank Raid" – "Executed in the street in full view of passers-by" – "A large dark commercial vehicle was used to cover their break in." Yet a fourth account was stated in words that were only slightly different from the previous versions but at least this one managed a reference to the surreal art on one wall. "Police are working on the assumption that it was done by a serious artist with some previous experience. At least one member of the gang is probably an Azerbaijani immigrant studying art at a

British university."

The newsman then asked for the help of the public. If anyone was there during the time of the robbery, or if anyone had spotted any suspicious characters over the past few days, they should contact the local police.

But this was Esher, so the local police station was flooded with reports of suspicious characters.

"Fat chance!" laughed Colin. "Last time I tried helping the police they arrested *me*."

"Was that the time you told them about the mugging in Chiswick Road?"

"Yeh. I told them who I thought did it and the bastards listened to every word I said then locked *me* up. Fucking ungrateful bastards!"

"They nicked you coz they watched you while you parked your stolen car in their car park. Dipshit!"

"So? I was still trying to help, wasn't I? They didn't have to fucking charge me for it. It wasn't my fault. I was trying to help. I ain't going to help them no more."

"Very wise," nodded Caffee. "God forbid they should let naughty crims get away when there are honest car thieves out there spreading malicious gossip."

Colin glared at Caffee but decided not to respond.

Caffee sighed. "Colin? Seriously? Are you a psycho?"

Colin felt a little indignant at that. "No!"

"Right. Well, let's see... if you were on a footbridge over a railway line with a fat man standing beside you, and underneath was a train was running out of control towards five workmen and it was going to kill them – would you toss the fat man off the bridge, in front of the train, to save the five workmen?"

"No."

"Oh," she frowned. "That's good. You ain't a psychopaff, then."

"I couldn't lift a fat man. He might fight back. Besides, I ain't ever seen a train kill people before. Have I got a phone with a camera?"

Caffee's mouth dropped open. "You wouldn't…"

"Can I jump on top of the train? You'd get a fantastic view from just above the cab."

"Fuckin' hell, Colin!"

He grinned back at her with his best Hannibal Lecter grin.

The room went silent when Helen entered. She stood silhouetted against the bright light in the hall. Her hair was now formed into a large loose ball of frizz. Inside that frizz two hair brushes hung, trapped like helpless flies in a tangled, matted, web of barbed wire. Her eyes were dark with seething anger.

"Oh God!" Norman muttered. "Oh God. How wiry, stale, matt, and pointless seem to me to be all the hairstyles of this world!"

Mam went to stand up to help, but then thought the better of it. Her hair remedies didn't extend to calamities on this scale.

Caffee's silently whispered 'Fuck!' was followed by a strong urge to start giggling – but Helen's evil eyes iced that idea on the spot. She strained valiantly but kept her face straight, biting her lip instead.

169

It was Barry who rose to the occasion by first stating the obvious. "I think that your hair might need brushing."

Helen slowly turned to face him – hands firmly balled into fists. "Y'think?" she growled.

"Yes." Barry nodded, oblivious to Helen's subdued rage. "You have got brushes stuck inside your hair."

It was only Barry's open expression and simple honesty which prevented Helen from removing limbs from torsos.

"My sister's friend had hair like that," he continued. "Let me comb it down for you." He got up and walked to the door taking hold of Helen's hand as he passed.

She didn't budge for a few seconds. She stood rigid, her eyes narrowed accusingly at Adrian, then she snatched her hand from Barry's and shook a finger. "Never again! Never... ever... *ever* again!" she snarled before letting Barry lead her upstairs to the bathroom.

Caffee waited until Helen was out of earshot. She had the most peculiar feeling of not knowing whether to burst out laughing or prepare herself for having her throat cut during the night.

"I forgot to put hair conditioner on the checklist. Sorry, everyone."

But it was understandable. Who would have thought hair conditioner to be part of a burglar's toolkit?

20
Neighbour

The next morning, they were spread about the house. Norman was in the dining room reading a tatty old book he'd found on a bookshelf. Barry and Colin were in the lounge watching Greek football. Colin had described to Barry how he could make a sheep run really, really fast with just the use of a long broom handle and a jar of English mustard. Fortunately for Barry's sensibilities, he couldn't get his head around the idea, so now they watched the TV in silence – save for the sudden interjection from Colin regarding the quality of the tackles.

While watching the sport, Colin's subconscious was trying to firm up the broom handle concept into another one of his business ideas. 'Formula One Sheep Racing'. He wondered how fast a sheep could really run and if it would improve the flavour of the mutton.

Perhaps the idea would be better for livening up greyhound racing? He could see it in his mind. 'The National Hot-Arse Turbo-Bitch Event of the Year'.

But would English mustard count as a sport-enhancing drug?

This *must* be a marketing coup, he thought. Think of the branding: 'English Mustard – Hot enough to win this year's Greyhound Turbo-Dog Finals.' Although advertising a mustard that one puts on one's sausages because it works so well when stuck up a dog's arse, was probably going to be a bit of a difficult sell.

Perhaps something heavier, more dramatic. Maybe. 'The Eye-Watering Spectacle of Super, Hot-Arsed Bulls in Havoc-Making Tournaments to the Death!' And the losers could be sold as fresh burgers to the public. This sounded a far better idea than what those cowardly Spanish bullfighters did.

But what if the bulls should turn on the men that were handling the 'Bovine Anal Poking Devices'? On the other hand, think of the TV ratings...

And so, he thought on...

Mam was vacuuming the upstairs hallway.

Caffee and Helen were with Adrian in his room above the kitchen. Most of the chatter was between the girls while Adrian sat facing the wall doodling on a sketchpad, sometimes his left arm, and sometimes the wall. When he spoke Helen translated what she thought he was saying but most of it was just too surreal.

"Baby cat but not a baby cat, hungry, but not hungry, still, but not stationary. Remaining in fact, but not remaining. We fell without falling, falling short without being shorter or falling anywhere. Financial energy in paper from the metal-covered reservoir isn't enough. Oh, woe, woe, woe but we dent the rent that is good, good, good. Some goodly good is good."

"Wot?" Caffee raised her eyebrows at Helen.

Helen screwed up her face in concentration. "I don't know. A baby cat? A kitten? Falling? I don't know what he means."

"Tell him to write it down on the laptop. We can afford to get him a proper one now." Caffee got up, irritated by Adrian's indecipherable chatter and went downstairs. He was trying to tell them something but it just didn't make any sense.

As she reached the hallway there was a knock on the front door. She froze. No one was supposed to visit them here. This was their hideaway. Looking at the front door window she could see the outline of the person outside. The profile didn't look very policeman-like.

She decided to take a chance and clumped over to the door.

"Who's it?"

"Helloo," replied a high-pitched Scottish accent. "Ah've come to say helloo to you."

"'allo then."

There was an awkward silence until Caffee realised that more discourse was expected.

"Hold on to your muffin', gel. I'll open the door." Caffee cracked the door open and peered around the edge. It was a large lady, probably in her mid to late fifties wearing a large, green National Trust anorak, brown woolly skirt, large, green National Trust wellington boots and carrying a leather bag.

The broad-beamed lady beamed broadly. "Helloo. Ah'm your neighbour. Ah thought I'd come over and say helloo."

"Congrats. You managed it."

The woman smiled awkwardly at Caffee's blank expression. The silence lasted a few seconds before Caffee realised that, yet again, terseness was not the appropriate response. It could be construed as suspicious behaviour so it was probably safer to let the nosey biddy in. No need to let her spread gossip about the horrible Sassenachs from the South.

"Come on in and 'ava cuppa. Nice to meetchya!" She opened the door. "My name is Caffee. Wot's yours?" She extended a hand but the woman ignored it.

"Oh, that's so kind. Thank you. Mah name is Margaret but you can call me Maggie, everyone does. Everyone except the postie, that is. I canna stay long, mind you. I've got mah own dinner in the oven. Oooh, this is a nice place you have here, isn't it? Have you just moved in? Ah live just down the road, Bramble Cottage, the one with the white roses around the door, and I saw the van when I walked by. Ah often pass by, you understand. Ah like to walk. What brought you to this quiet part of Scotland? It's not often we get people moving up into this part of the country. Are you here to stay? There was a young couple from Cardiff who came here a while back. They were very quiet, they didna like people visitin' them, at least I think they didn't. Ah like to think they were on their honeymoon, y'know? Ah told ol' Jesse that. She's the receptionist at the doctor's and a personal friend of mine. We've known each other since we were wee lassies. But I coulda been wrong, they didna seem too close – you know what I mean? In the end they didna' stay long. Moved away, I heard. Here, I've brought you a little housewarming gift." She extracted a large cling-film wrapped fruitcake from the bag.

"Fanks. Cor – Fuck! – It's heavy!" Caffee grimaced as she took the cake and nearly dropped it. "Lucky you was just passin' then, innit. Otherwise, you'd have to drag this one 'ome again," she puffed.

Mam appeared at the kitchen door. "Hello. Are you going to introduce me, girl? Would you like a cup of tea?"

Caffee, still struggling under the weight of the cake, tried to answer but Maggie beat her to it.

"Helloo. Ah was just telling your... well, Ah'm guessing she's not your daughter... anyway... I was telling the gel here that mah name is Margaret but you can call me Maggie. Everyone does. Except the postie. Ah was just passing by. Ah do that a lot, and I thought I'd leave a little housewarming gift for you. Do you mind? Ah hope you like cake. Ah made it mesel'."

"That is very kind of you. Come on in, come on in. You are very welcome, now. Excuse Caffee here, she's not used to people. I'm very pleased to meet you. You can call me Mam, everyone does. Oh, that's a lovely cake. What is it? A fruitcake? Caffee, would you bring it into the kitchen, there's a dear."

Mam beckoned Margaret to join her in the kitchen.

"It's mah own recipe Dundee. Fewer nuts and a little more fruit. Not so much cherry, I'm afraid. Ah used them all up, but a little more fruit and a little zest will make it better. Ah do like to make my own cake. So much nicer than shop-bought, don't you think? Oh, that's a nice kitchen you have here."

Caffee, still struggling under the weight of cake, cursed under her breath. "Fuckin' Dundee, my arse. Fuckin' rock cake. Fuckin' granite cake. Fuckin' lead ore..."

Mam made them a pot of tea and they drank it standing in the kitchen. It was surprising how much the Scot could talk. Within ten minutes the names and histories of all the locals had been passed on and, had Caffee been taking notes, they would have known enough to blackmail most of them.

In the living room the visitor's voice was strong enough to distract Norman from the local newspaper he'd found. He'd turned to page four in the hope of finding something intellectual to read. Sadly, the only articles were titled 'Red Tape Holds Up New Council Offices', 'School Coach Crashes: "Something Went Wrong" says Expert', and 'Glasgow Girl Wins Dog Show'. He figured that someone in the newspaper office had more fun writing the headlines than the articles themselves.

He decided to satisfy his curiosity with the new voice and get a cup of tea at the same time. He put down the paper and went to the kitchen.

"...so Ah said to Belinda, 'Since his wife passed, he's been a very considerate shepherd, has he not? He must love his flock. Whenever I see him in the fields, he's always trying to help a sheep get o'er the hedge.' and you know what? She just said 'Oh, no. I dinna think he's helping the poor lamb!' And she laughed and laughed. She's a funny woman, that Belinda..."

Norman caught her eye.

"...ooh helloo. You're a hunk, aren't you? Mah name is Margaret, but you can call me Maggie. Everyone does."

"'cept the postie," Caffee sighed.

"Oh, aye. Except the postie. And what's your name?"

"My name, madam, is Norman Winchester Haine

176

Le Burgulian. At your service." He bowed with a flourish like a seventeenth century dandy, then took Margaret's hand and kissed the back of it.

She flushed. "Oh my, my. Ah've never had my hand kissed like that 'afore." Grinning she tried a curtsy but stumbled and Caffee and Mam had to rescue her. She quickly regained her composure. "He's quite the charmer, is he not?"

"To mine own self I be true, and it follows as night follows day, I canst not then be false to Mam." He winked. "May I impose for a hot beverage from the pot?"

"Would you like a cup of tea instead, Norman?"

"Indeed," he sighed.

Mam fetched a cup and saucer from the cupboard and poured.

"You seem very... are you an *actor*, by any chance?"

Norman grinned broadly. "'tis in the blood."

She looked at Mam. "Aye. I can see that. And are you married at all?"

The bluntness of the question caught Mam off guard and a quick glance at Norman's expression would have seen the surprise in his eyes too.

Maggie picked up on the awkwardness.

"Oh, Ah'm terrible sorry. Ah didna mean to intrude. It's just that up here where there's so few to chat to, one gets a little direct. Yah ken? Are you married, Norman? Or are you of the... other persuasion? I know these days so many *actors* are." She paused expectantly.

"If men could be contented to be what they are,

177

they would fear in marriage," misquoted Norman.

"Ah see. But is there a Mrs Burger-Ian?"

Norman frowned. His previous life had always been a closed book and even the family had not pressed him on such matters. It was an unwritten rule and everyone seemed happy with it, probably because everyone was hiding something. Provided each personal history was respected, the family respected each other – but now this battle tank of a woman was barrelling through it with the sensitivity of a German blitzkrieg.

"There was indeed, madam. A lady most fair whom I loved so very deeply. But alas, she liked to talk, to chatter, to gossip, to pry and she never stopped. So, I left and the silence of the lack of inquisition has, until now, been such bliss."

"Oh, Ah'm so sorry to hear that. Ah know that sometimes women canna stop the gossip, they canna help themselves, y'know? It's in our nature. Do you have any children? Will you be staying long? Are you appearing in a production?"

Norman accepted the cup of tea proffered by Mam, quietly smiled a thank you and left.

"Oh, did Ah upset you?" she called out. But Norman ignored her and started up the stairway. "Did Ah upset him? Ah hope not. He's a sensitive fellow, is he not? A bit of a dark horse, perhaps. Ah hope I didna upset him." She seemed genuinely concerned.

"Oh, don't worry 'bout Norm," said Caffee. "He's a bit like that." And with that she took her leave too, ostensibly to comfort Norman but actually she went to see what Adrian and Helen were up to. Anywhere to escape from Margaret.

"Ah there any others staying in the hoos?" Margaret started on Mam again.

"There are seven of us. Norman and Caffee you've met. Then there's Helen and the boys, Barry, Adrian, and Colin."

A dark shadow flashed by the kitchen window followed by a thud, a short scream from upstairs and a groan from outside.

"That will be Adrian. Sometimes he forgets when he's upstairs." Mam opened the kitchen door and called out. "Are you hurt, Adrian?"

The young man looked up from the mattress and smiled weakly at the kitchen ceiling. "I forgot... windows... prefer stairs... to stars." His voice trailed off weakly. The sound of rolling thunder coming down the staircase alerted Mam. She stood back from the door and gently moved Margaret to one side as the two girls stormed past.

"Adrian! Adrian! Are you alright?"

"The one with the dark hair is Helen," whispered Mam to Margaret.

"Wot the fuck did I tell you 'bout climbin' through windows?" Caffee sounded angry but, like Helen, was really quite concerned. The two girls ushered him back through the kitchen and upstairs.

"Bouncy, bouncy mattress surprising. Bruise count rising."

As they dragged him back upstairs Helen started brushing his hair with her hands and Caffee brushed at his cardigan.

Margaret's eyes were wide, unsure if the girls were

trying to tidy him up or beat him for falling out the window.

"Is he alright? Is he all there?"

Mam nodded. "He sometimes forgets to use the door. That's why we leave a mattress outside his window."

"Oh, my gosh." Margaret, frowning in concern, peered through the kitchen door and into the hall following the progress of the retreating group upstairs. "There's quite a party here, then. Are you all on holiday? The countryside is nice but I wouldn't say much for the night life. You're nae here for the night life, I'm thinking."

"Yes... no. We are all taking a break. It is so nice and quiet here."

"Ah see. Ah couldna help noticing the bags you had in the living room. Are you still unpacking?" Margaret glanced at Mam who had a sudden need to hold on to the cupboard for support. "Are you alright? You've gone very queasy. Is it something I said? Here, let me help you..."

21
The Bug

"...but she didn't suspect anything. She just saw the bin bags. We already put the dosh back in the bags. It's alright, gel." Caffee was trying to be gentle but Mam was still visibly upset and her hands were shaking.

Margaret had finally left and now Colin, Norman, Barry, and Caffee were all trying console Mam in the living room.

"I do not know. I hope not. Oh, I hope she doesn't go to the police. Oh, I'm so worried. What if they discover what we did, now?"

Colin tried next.

"She's a fuckin' nosy biddy and it ain't your fault, Mam. She shouldn't have been let in. Anyway, she won't know it's full of cash. For all she knows it could be bits of a dismembered body."

"Yay, Colin! That's really fuckin' helpful, that is! Be sure to make Mam feel better, wontchya?"

Caffee was certain they were still safe. Only Mam's profound guilt could give them away.

"You know what we could do, Mam? When we leave here, we could write a postcard to Maggie and write on it, 'Having a lovely time in Corfu, wish you were here. By the way, have you told the police about your thieving gay postman raping all those little boys, yet? Love Doris.' – that'll distract her."

Norman was more thoughtful. "Like as the waves

make towards the pebbled shore, so do our minutes hasten to their end. We thieves are possessed with fear and the stuff sweats to death. The loot must be hidden."

"What? Waves? Oh, right! Good thinkin'. But where?"

"Oh, I hope she does not go to the police."

"*Stop* worrying, Mam. She didn't see nothing. This is just a wake-up call, right? God's telling us to be more circumcised, is all. We got to hide the dosh somewhere. We can't leave it in plain bloody sight in the living room."

"I could bury it in the woods. No one would know where to find it."

"Yeh, right Colin, 'cept you of course. You just drive off with all the cash and we wait here for your return. Is that the plan?"

"Yeh. Sounds good to me."

"I love all, but trust few," smiled Norman. "The loot stays where we can *all* see it."

"Yeh. That's a Conan-drum tho', ain't it? We keep the dosh here and along comes Mister Plopper, discovers the dosh, and we say what? 'My goodness. How did those plastic bin bags full of pub vouchers happen to follow us from a place we ain't ever visited, let alone robbed?'"

"Like I said, I could bury..."

"No thanks, Colin. The money stays here where we can see it. We put it up in the loft and hope Mister Plopper ain't got a warrant if he visits, okay?"

"Besides," said Norman, "our DNA is on the notes already."

"Yeh. Our DNA is on the... *what*?!? Oh, fuck!"

"She would not go to the police, would she?"

"No, Mam. And what would she say? I saw some strangers with a couple of bin bags in their living room? I don't think so."

Barry perked up. "There might be mice in the loft."

"Yeh, thanks Barry. Make it easy, why don't you?"

"I like mice."

"Yeh, thanks Barry."

"They make nests..."

"Yeh. *Thank you*, Barry!"

Barry fell silent and held Mam's hand. She gripped his in return. Colin realised that they hadn't examined all the loot.

"What's in the boxes? We ain't looked proper yet. Might be diamonds. We might be millionaires and not know it."

"Yeh, might be. We could have a million pounds of diamonds or a few pence worth of glass beads and we wouldn't know the fuckin' difference, would we? So, we take the jewels to a jeweller who says to us, 'Oh dear me, take a look at these. These are those famous stolen Crown Jewels. Please hold on a moment while I make a quick phone call to the local law enforcement.' You *wanker*!"

"Well, I know someone who..."

"Yeh? And he lives in London, is really honest, and you happen to trust him with all our money, and subskently your life. Right?"

"...uh. Yeh. Maybe... Well..."

"Look, Mister Cheese-For-Brains, it don't matter what's in the boxes. If it ain't cash we can't cash it coz we don't know its worth. Besides, it could be traced back to us."

Norman sat forward. Curious. "But we could at least behold the beauty of such wealth, even if we dare not partake of it?"

"What? Oh, you mean open the boxes? Take a sneaky? Yeh, well... I suppose so. Let's do that. Let's take a gander."

Colin and Caffee seated themselves in the middle of the living room cross-legged and dragged the bin bag with the boxes towards them. Colin reached in and took the largest box out. It was made of rosewood with delicate inlays. It looked like a small jewellery box but only a few centimetres deep on each side. It had a brass six-digit combination and a key lock. The key lock was easily picked but it took a few minutes to get the six digits of the combination. Fortunately, they were so worn as to be no real challenge to the amateurs. Despite this, Colin suggested smashing it open but Caffee pointed out that the box itself might be worth some money. It looked old. Colin made a sarcastic comment about not knowing its worth just before a pink fingernail suddenly appeared dangerously close to an iris. They continued in silence.

Before Colin opened the lid Barry whispered, "Be careful. It might be a bomb."

Colin paused and thought for a moment. Norman dove behind the settee and, seeing him move so quickly, Caffee scrabbled across the carpet to join him. Colin gently raised the box to his ear then shook it and listened. It rattled.

Upon detecting not even the slightest of explosions, he opened it.

"What the fuck?"

"Wot?" demanded Caffee, popping her head above the back of the settee.

"It's got electrical stuff in it. Look, most of it is batteries, then there's wires, a broken mobile phone and another smaller gizmo." He frowned. "Could it be a secret design for something?"

"Let me look." Caffee crawled over Norman who was still prostrate on the floor. She took the box from Colin and looked at the phone. "Fuck! it's switched on. It's a bloody bug! They've been listening to us." Her mouth dropped open.

"They know where we are…"

"INDEED, WE DO."

Five heads snapped round to see four men in expensive black suits and dark glasses standing by the living room door. The man who answered Colin, a dark-skinned man, probably in his mid-thirties, was clearly the leader of the group. His suit was light tan while the others were all dressed exactly the same – black with white shirts and black ties. Their cold stares were enough to transfix the gang in the room, save for Colin whose eyes flashed from the door to the windows. But it was already too late. He was still sitting down and one of the henchmen was on the way to blocking one window while another was moving around the outside of the room towards the other. They looked and acted like professionals, seemed well-rehearsed and were probably ex-military. Moreover, each one was well endowed in the muscle department.

The leader removed his glasses and smiled while glancing at each of the gang in turn. "I also have a man on the stairs in case your two friends would like to join us." He walked to one of the easy chairs. "May I?" and not waiting for an answer, he sat down, carefully extracting an ornate glasses case from a jacket pocket, putting his glasses into it and re-pocketing them.

"You ain't a plopper," Caffee stated. "Who are you and what do you want?"

The man reached across to the dining table where Norman had left a glass of red wine. He took the glass, sniffed it, and then wrinkled his nose, tutted, and shook his head disapprovingly before replacing it.

"Those boxes. Hand them to me please." He held out his hand. His voice had the air of one used to giving orders.

Colin went to rise but the man held up a hand. "Just reach across. I wouldn't like any of my colleagues to get the wrong impression."

Colin glanced at the impassive faces of the dark-suited gorillas then reached over and passed the man the two boxes.

"Thank you." He seemed more interested in the smaller box. "I am pleased you did not break it. It is a nice piece. Not that rare, but it has some sentimental value."

"What's in it?"

He held up the larger box. "You were right, young lady. In this box is a bug. If it detects movement it is programmed to call me and then it tells me its location. I can also listen in on your conversations. I

186

must say, it has been most entertaining listening to you talking on the way up here." There was a short pause before he continued. "I did like Colin's – uhm, you must be Colin, correct? – I did like your idea of singeing the ends of men's beards just enough to – how did you describe it? – 'to frizzle the end bits so that the whiskers would act like Velcro'. However, I don't think sticking things on them would catch on. Do you?"

Colin slowly shook his head.

"...and your subsequent idea – you *must* be Cathy? – of frizzling ladies'... how did you describe them? – 'short and curly gardens'? – in order to keep those Velcroed men in *just* the right position. That had us all very amused. I thank you for that. It made a dull car chase so much more entertaining."

No one laughed.

"And you must be the quiet but erudite thespian. Your name is...?"

"Norman," replied Norman. Deadpan.

Barry whispered to Mam, "What's an Araldite Lesbian?"

Mam shushed him.

"And of course, Mam and Barry. I have been able to compile a surprisingly comprehensive dossier on most of you in this short time."

"You ain't police though, are you? Hey? What are you? Men in Black? The Black and White Menstruals? The Society of Monochrome Male Morons? Lost your funeral, 'av yuh?"

"No. No, you are correct. We are not the police, Cathy. They are still scratching their heads down in

Surrey. But I must say, the Esher job was a masterpiece. No one got hurt, and you all got clean away. Well... almost."

Caffee wanted to rip the smug smartarse's face off. "So, wotchya want? You come to nick your dosh back?"

"Relax. Relax, young lady. No. In fact, I'm inclined to let you keep it. All of it... perhaps." He smiled again then noticed where Caffee had fixed her gaze and crossed his legs. He continued, "At first, I thought you'd be the usual type of bank robber. Hard men. Sad men with a history of violence and treachery. A gang. Maybe even a group of desperate junkies – but all certainly prone to violence. Definitely undesirables. But listening to your chatter, well that was most... intriguing. I discovered this was your first, and perhaps only, intended robbery. And yet the plan was so well executed. So precise. So well thought out. I thought you would be a motley gang of experienced professionals – not destitute amateurs."

"So? Give us a medal."

"So, I got to thinking. Maybe there's something we could do for each other."

"Are you saying you ain't gonna nick our dosh back?"

"That depends. I have a proposal."

There was a thump outside the back door and a squeal from upstairs. A shout in a foreign language followed by a scuffle. The black suit by the door dashed out to the kitchen and through the back door. The two remaining gorillas reached inside their jackets, but they didn't withdraw the expected weapons. Not yet.

A moment later Helen and Adrian, hair all mussed up, appeared by the door, each firmly held by a black-suited man.

"Attempting to escape is futile," the dark-skinned man declared.

"He wasn't escaping. He just doesn't understand doors."

The man obviously didn't believe her.

"...or windows, for that matter."

He beckoned to the captives. "Please come and join us." The two were released and they staggered into the room. Helen, wide-eyed and confused, went to sit on the floor beside Norman. Norman took her hand reassuringly.

Colin frowned.

Adrian pirouetted, staring at the pattern on the carpet before falling in an untidy heap close to Caffee.

The two suits by the windows removed their hands from their jackets. The fourth left the room, presumably to check upstairs and secure the floor.

"Now that we are all together, perhaps I might be able to continue." The dark-skinned man's mouth smiled warmly but his eyes remained cold.

"Who are you?" Norman asked quietly.

"Hmm. My name is unimportant. I'm sure if you tried hard enough you could discover my identity. However, my proposal, I'm sure, would be of significant interest to you. Do you wish to hear it?"

Colin and Norman nodded. Caffee's eyes narrowed in suspicion while she calculated the time and distance for a hand-thrown clog to his kneecap, or would bashing his balls be more productive?

"I am employed by a... Middle Eastern person of great wealth and influence. Sadly, he is not a direct member of the Royal Family, but his family is very noble and well respected."

"You mean they were like the Mafia a few thousand years ago. All protection rackets and threats, but *now* they get to be called noble coz they got everyone's money. Right?"

The dark-skinned man paused and raised an eyebrow. "A student of history, Cathy? I would not use such terms in front of them, if I were you. You must understand that old Mafia habits die hard." He paused. "Respect, no matter how undeserved, is still a requirement. May I continue?"

Caffee's face remained dark, and the man couldn't help noticing that she was now recalculating the distance between her feet and his shins. He cleared his throat and re-crossed his legs, slightly unnerved.

"A lowly and undesirable member of the Royal Family has taken a romantic interest in my employer's eldest daughter. The young lady is reluctant, but alas, if a member of the Royal Family takes such an interest, then there is little that can be done. They are to be wed in ten weeks' time."

"Congrats. Does she wanna get spliced?"

"I beg your pardon?"

"Does she wanna get 'itched? Married?"

"No. No, she does not. She is quite appalled at the idea, but she is a dutiful daughter."

"Why her?"

"This... the royal prince wishes to have a trophy bride. The young woman is very eye-catching and very elegant."

"Why doesn't her dad just say no?"

"There is a reason why my employer stays in favour with the Royal Family. He is very loyal."

"What a bastard! She can't be forced to marry though, can she?"

"We are very devout. It is also a tradition. Women in our society do not have much say in this matter."

"So don't be devout, fuck it! She doesn't have to marry him if she don't want to."

"Ah yes, but she does. If her father says, then she is so obliged. To disobey would be worse... for everyone. Do you understand?"

"So, the Royal Family is still the fuckin' Mafia, even under all that nobility crap. Yeh? Fuckin' hell. You guys are still living in the med-evil ages, aintchya? Sounds just like my old school playground."

"Hmm. Quite. However, I suggest you not be too judgemental towards our people."

"So, Dad's quite happy to pimp out his daughter, and little Miss Elegant ain't got the balls to leg it, I suppose. And you got a soft spot for her yourself, yeh?"

There was a short pause while the two stared at each other before Colin asked, "Soooo, what has this got to do with us?"

"Ah... Yes... My proposal. The wedding preparations are well under way. We have invested much in the ceremony, and it is my employer's wish that the ceremonial jewellery will be much admired for centuries to come. We are having a good portion of our family heirlooms reformed into new, matching sets.

"Consequently, we have obtained the exclusive services of a company based in London. They are at this moment creating the tiaras, bracelets, necklaces, etcetera, etcetera. They are to create three complete sets. One for the wedding ceremony, one for the public appearances, and one for the private party thereafter. There will also be matching jewellery for the groom and the immediate family. All three sets will have much symbolism. They will consist of different combinations of alloys for each event. There are nearly one hundred matching pieces in gold, platinum, and silver."

"And you want us to nick it all?"

The dark-skinned man smiled. "Thankfully no. That would be impossible. Besides, different pieces are being formed at different locations."

Colin's eyes lit up. "Then you want us to kidnap the princess?"

A momentary look of horror flashed over the man's face before his smile returned. "No. No. Certainly not!"

"Then what?"

22
Run Away

The next day was miserable, and not just the weather. The clouds were low and grey and a light rain pattered gently on the windows. The tick-tick sound had that sharp tang that meant ice, the sound that told you it would sting if it hit your skin. This is what the Scots would no longer refer to as 'Fresh' but would now refer to as 'Brisk' – but what Londoners refer to as 'Effing Cold'!

Colin spent most of the morning on his mobile phone. The rest of the family were quiet, subdued. When Colin announced he had another cottage for them they immediately sprang to action and started packing, cleaning and re-loading the van.

Caffee pointed out that the Arab guy had already heard of their plans to run, but the general consensus was that it was better to try than be forced to do another robbery – one for which they had no plan. Besides, he knew where they were and his gorillas looked mean. They could turn up again at any time – maybe even in the middle of the night. They didn't want to have to barricade the doors and windows. They felt like rabbits in a glass burrow in a zoo for hungry crocodiles.

Worried about their fingerprints and DNA, Mam bustled to the kitchen and started scrubbing everything in sight. Caffee, Helen, and Barry tried to console her but she would have none of it so, rather than waste time they all started to help clean the place.

Within a half hour they were startled by the sound of a strident voice from the hallway.

"Helloo! Is anyone there? It's only mee, Maggie. May I come in?" She stood inside the front door dripping, beaming, a visitor most unwelcome on the welcome mat. The Scottish battle cruiser stamped her green wellingtons and shook the rain off her coat.

Helen came out to her from the dining room, holding a spray can of polish in one hand, one of Adrian's worn socks in the other, and wearing her anorak and a red bobble hat.

"Helloo. Mah name is Margaret, but you can call me Maggie. You must be Helen, am I right?"

Helen nodded, her red bobble nodding much more enthusiastically.

"Ah see you're going oot somewhere. I hope I'm not inconveniencing anyone. Did you try mah cake? Gosh, it's a wee damp, brisk day outside, but at least it's nice and cozy inside, aye?" She laughed. "Is your Mam aboot?"

A flash of horror followed by a moment's confusion crossed Helen's face before she realised she was referring to Mam.

"You mean, Mam?"

"Aye. That's what I said. Your Mam." Margaret squinted. "Or would that be Cathy's Mam – Ah'm sorry, child, I'm not sure of whose is whose and what is what's yet. It's all buns an' baps, you ken? You'll have to forgive me."

"MAM!" Helen called out.

Caffee stuck her nose around the kitchen door.

"Oh, fu... Hello." She grinned weakly. "Wait a mo' while I peel Mam off the floor."

"Oh dear. Is she alright?" Margaret became an instant picture of concern and steamed towards the kitchen.

"Yeh, yeh. She's fine. She's just removing our fingerprints from under the bloody oven!"

Helen frantically shook her head and hands, trying to stop Caffee from giving the game away, but Caffee ignored her. "Mam's got it in 'er head we've got to be cleaner than clean. Maybe you can stop her."

Margaret got to the kitchen just as Barry helped Mam to her feet. "Helloo. It's me, Maggie. Are you alright, dear? You look flushed."

Mam just nodded.

"You dinna have to clean so much, mah pet. The house is spotless. Here, let me take thaht." She took the floor-cloths from Mam's hands and placed them on the kitchen top. "You dinna need to worry so much."

Mam shook her head.

"There now. Ah come to see how you're getting on. Did you like mah cake? Was it all right?"

Mam nodded.

Barry said, "I nearly had a piece. It is a big cake." He smiled.

"Aye. Did you no try it?"

Caffee felt she'd better interject. "No. We saved it."

Margaret looked at the waif. "You need filling out,

195

mah girl. My, my, you're all skin and not much bone. You'll be blowing away in the wind."

"Not if I ate your cake, I'm guessing. Anyway, we're going out."

Mam nodded again.

"Going visiting, are you? Oh, how nice. You have friends near here?"

"No. No, we saved your cake for the picnic. We're going on a picnic."

"Picnic? In this weather? You're nae going on a picnic in this weather."

Mam shook her head.

Caffee tried to recover. "We heard that the wevver was gonna improve," she tried.

"Improve? Nae, you silly gehrl. The storm hasna come yet. The man on the TV said it'll be here this afternoon."

"Oh, silly me."

"The weather will not improve until late the morrow, or the day after, and even then – I wouldna recommend a *picnic*. The grass will be all wet and besides, your nae dressed, are you? You'll freeze to death. You'd better unpack everything and settle in. Mam, talk some sense to your gehrl, you shouldna go out in this weather."

Mam shook her head again.

"And I hope you don't take this the wrong way – but I really think you should put some clothes on, mah dear. You're just walking around in your underwear, and with men in the hoos too – well, between us gehrls, better be safe than sorry, I say. Yah ken?"

"Gels? Anyway, I *am* dressed."

Margaret looked askance. She didn't want to push it and by now Mam had realised that she should be acting less like a muppet and more like a host. She fell into default hostess mode. "Would you like a cup of tea, Maggie?"

"Oh, no. It's alright, Mam. I just popped around to see how you were all settling in. Ah couldna help but notice you had visitors yesterday. Friends, were they?"

"You saw them?" Caffee was aghast. "How? You can't see us from your place."

"Oh, aye. The two black cars and all those handsome men. Friends of yours, were they? Cousins, mebbe?"

The pause caused a little discomfort, but not for Margaret who waited patiently for the reply.

"They are business associates," explained Caffee. "Came up to see us and wish us well."

"Oh, I thought as much. They looked like office people, what with the suits an' all. Very smart. You must work in a very smart office. Anyway, I must be going. The weather's soon to turn and I have to see to the door of mah shed. It opens when the wind is strong, ya ken? And then it slams open and closed all night. It frightens the sheep."

Barry perked up. "I like sheep."

"Oh, that's nice, dear. You'll like it here, then. The farmer sometimes puts the flock into the field behind your garden – but Ah'm sorry I must go. Ah canna stay. The weather is closing in and I have a cottage pie in the Aga. Put any thoughts of a picnic from your mind, but do try mah cake and let me know if it's to your taste. Ahm thinking of making another, maybe I'll make it with real cherries this time – what d'yuh think? Ah do like to use real ingredients whenever I can."

"So, your cottage pie is made with *real* cottage?"

Margaret paused. "You dinna use cottage cheese in pies, mah gehrl. Did you not know thaht? Tusk. Mam, you should teach her to cook n'all and she does need feeding up, do you not? You're all skin and not much of the bone. Oh, what they teach gehls these days – that and the price of fish, well I dinnae ken." Margaret left the kitchen but her gravity seemed to drag Mam, Caffee, Barry and Helen along in her wake.

She reached the front door. "Ah'll drop in and see you again tomorrow. Do try mah cake, I'd like to know what you think. Well, I'll be off now. Cheerio." And with that she set course out into the rain with her scarf flapping in the wind like a tartan battle ensign. They waved and watched her sail across the gravel driveway, down to the country road and disappear into the gathering mist.

"Right! Let's all bugger off quick, like," yelled Caffee. "Barry, 'elen, get Mam into the van sharpish before she decides to clean the underside of the barftub. Colin!"

"The van's open!"

"Where's the dosh?"

"It's all in the van."

"What else do we need to pack away? Where's Norman?"

"Norman is standing here in waiting for the ladies. And I am packed." He patted his old suitcase patched with duct tape and tied with string.

"Put your stuff in the van and check the 'ouse again. We gotta make sure it's pristine before we go. The owners must not know we've bin."

"...and you think the Scottish dragon would not mention our presence?"

"Who cares. Git!" Caffee stabbed a finger toward the door. "Colin?"

"Yes, Sergeant!"

She ignored the sarcasm. "Did you nick anything?"

"No."

"Nothing?"

Indignantly, "No."

"Nothing *at all*?"

"What do you take me for?"

"A liar, a habitual thief, and sometimes a bit of a wally. Put what you nicked back else they'll believe the fat Scotty woman and set the ploppers on us. Yeh?"

"It don't matter. The owners can't stand the woman!"

"If they know they been robbed, or that we stayed 'ere, they'll believe any and everyone."

Without a verbal answer Colin sighed and disappeared. Caffee figured that he'd return at least some of the stuff.

Norman and Caffee did the rounds of the house making sure nothing obvious remained. Helen stayed in the van to try to console Mam. She also needed to console Barry who had just realised they were moving away and he hadn't seen the sheep yet. Adrian was piled in the back with, and amongst, the bags of clothes.

When they finally departed, they took care not to drive past Maggie's cottage.

As the van's engine whined, complaining with the weight, and the wheels bumped their way out the drive and onto the country lane, Caffee sat deep in thought. She stared, without seeing, through the window at the grey clouds. What else could go wrong? She felt uneasy. Something was telling her this wasn't over. The tan-suit man would not have left them alone without ensuring he still had control over them.

This was too easy.

23
The Second Hideout

They arrived at the second hideout just over two hours later. This time they were less enthusiastic about exploring the building let alone the surroundings. It was a large whitewashed house with four bedrooms, much older than the new property they'd come from. The building was simply a brick box painted white with a grey slate roof and situated on the side of a hill amongst a lot of trees.

Mam was still worried about the DNA they'd left behind but Caffee was happy that the house was clean enough. If there were any signs that the house had been occupied then it would be a while before the penny dropped.

The only fly in the ointment was Maggie. The woman could identify the van and the occupants. To solve that one, they parked the van behind the house, out of sight of the road, and then the following morning, after a rain shower, they set about spraying it black. Lots of old newspaper had been sellotaped over the windows, lights, and chromed bits. They were very, very careful – even covering the concrete patio with newspaper.

Luckily the weather held for a few hours. It remained cold despite intermittent sunshine, and the van soon became matte black – as did one side of someone's tabby. Curiosity sometimes has a price.

During the next few days, it rained again and the boredom and the tension started to get to them.

Mam spent a lot of time cleaning the house and removing their DNA, Barry tried to help but fell to watching children's TV in the dining room and avoiding Mam. Her anxiety was increasing and it was showing. Colin and Norman watched Serbian Football and Arabian camel racing for want of anything better. They did manage to find an Indian test cricket match, to which Caffee's passing comment was: -

"They're *still* testing it? You'd have thought they'd have fixed the fuckin' thing by now."

She was ignored.

The girls kept to themselves either in Adrian's room with Adrian or they spent a while in their own rooms. Norman and Helen found a bookshelf and spent a few hours reading some old novels.

It was the morning of the third day when the sound of a motorbike was shortly followed by a knock on the door. Norman answered.

"May ah help you?" he said, in his best Scottish brogue.

"Sign here," said the obviously-from-London leather-clad motorbike courier. He held up a package, delivery form and pen.

"Ahm thinking you have the wrong address..." Norman's face fell as he looked at the writing on the label. "Oh dear." He signed the form on top and was slightly taken aback when the courier used his phone to take a picture of him, before taking the form and pen back.

"Cheers!" The bike rider waved a cheery goodbye, mounted the bike, kick-started it once, and drove off with a roar.

The envelope was from the tan-suit man. Norman closed the front door, opened it, and peered inside. It contained sheets of names, places, dates, times, and even photographs. A memory stick had recorded telephone conversations and there was a transcript and translation of the Hebrew and Arabic conversations.

When Norman called out to everyone to join him in the living room, they came quickly. At first, they came because it was something to break the boredom. Barry was already in the living room and Norman asked him to mute the TV.

"A missive from Malik," stated Norman.

Colin saw the envelope in Norman's hands. The address simply read, 'The Gunnersbury Gang'.

"Oh Jeezus H. Fucking Christ! Fuck me a hairy midg..."

"Colin!" Mam appeared, furious at the outburst.

"Sorry, Mam. But it's from the bloody Mafia! How the fuck did they know we were here?" He flopped into an armchair and stared at the ceiling.

Caffee clumped into the living room next. "Wot's that then? Oh, *shit!*"

Adrian ran out of his bedroom into Caffee's, closely pursued by Helen. He grabbed one of Caffee's plastic ponies before Helen managed to steer him away from the bedroom window, out to the landing, past the top banister rail and point him to the top of the stairs where he then successfully ran down of his own accord. They both entered the living room, saw the darkening mood and sat cross-legged on the bean bags.

Caffee took the envelope and some of the

extracted sheets from Norman. She flicked through them.

"Fuckin' 'ell! This is comprehensive, innit?" Caffee was impressed, passing the sheets over to Colin as she extracted them.

"How did he get all this stuff?" Colin was flicking through the private folders of the employees, but was disappointed to note that the three women were happily married and, in his eyes, too old for him. There was nothing sinister or erotic about them; but he was nosy, nonetheless.

He passed the sheets on to Norman.

"It appears he had intended a robbery in any case." Norman stared intently at several lists and schedules. "This material is professionally gathered. It would have taken time. I wonder why he wants us to do the job?"

"Coz we're expendable. It's bleedin' obvious."

"Or maybe his original plan was discovered. Oh, how joyful be they that find deceitful means anew."

Mam, Barry and Helen took separate sheets in turn and examined them. Adrian started blowing on his fingernails and reciting something incomprehensible.

Save for the odd remark, the group were quiet while they read, or scanned, the information. Some of it was personal, all of it was private but nothing in there deserved further comment. An employee and a security guard had some gay experiences, some of the staff had some affairs, but not with each other. So what? Some of them had financial problems and one was spending too much gambling online, but nothing in all this information gave them inspiration. None of it was serious enough.

Somehow, they had to rely on Adrian.

After a while Adrian started to take some interest in the data and scanned the photographs and maps. He began taking the sheets of information from the others and placed them in piles on the table, then went through each pile spreading the sheets amongst the remaining piles. He repeated this several times, sometimes stopping to sniff a page or lick it. Sometimes he tried reading them upside down or sideways. Three times he held a short one-sided conversation with a photograph and once argued with a file before throwing it to one side. A couple of times he tried scratching at the words to look underneath, but after a while he turned to Helen.

"Where ever it is it must be will be was, for I need it, not a lap or the top of a lap but the laptop for the table top, for tippety-tappety tip-tap on the unmusical keys with no set key that are never bored. Please, please, please?"

Helen got up. "I'll get you the laptop," she said, pausing to watch his expression, not quite certain if *that* was what he had really asked for.

"He's got a fuckin' plan. Ain't you, Ade?"

Adrian grinned sideways at the ceiling and words gushed out, "Give me seven kisses for the seven simple sinister sisters, but the simplest sinister sister is really the most complex, the simple complexity revealed in its complex simplicity and called elegance, so it is the most elegant sister I need to espy like a spy spying on the seven sisters, a voyeur of an undressed scheme, and she must be chosen on the criteria for not crying tears, for a crying elegant sinister sister isn't. Got to get, or be, closely close without being seen. You see?"

Caffee sighed. "If you got a plan just fuckin' nod yer head!"

Adrian held up Caffee's plastic horse and nodded it seven times.

Mam said, "I think we all need a cup of tea. Give me a hand, Barry." Barry helped her out of her armchair and they both went to the kitchen.

"But how the fuck did the bastard know we were here?"

Norman thought a while. "While he was talking to us, were all his 'neanderthals' in the house with us? Who was watching the van?"

Colin wrinkled his nose. "What?"

Caffee's eyes widened. "Oh, *shit!*" She stood and went through to the dining room where she stood and looked out at the black van. "That fucker is as slimy as a slick snail sliding on silver snot! Colin, tomorrow morning, when you can, work through the van looking for another one of them bloody bugs. The git must've bugged it!"

"What? You mean he put a tracker in it?" Colin joined her at the window.

Norman nodded. "He may well have done. They had plenty of time to think and plan ahead, did they not?"

"Fuck, yeh." Colin went outside to start looking anyway.

"I suspect the men of evil are practised in their trade and find such precautions but second nature."

Caffee came back. "Good thinking, Norm. Fucking slimy git prob'ly has us buggered all over."

"And the fool doth think he is wise, but the wise man knows himself to be a fool."

"What? Watchya mean?"

"Let's check all for bugs. Clothes, and loot, and van. For he is a master of his trade, and we must know ourselves to be but mere fools in comparison."

"Cheek! I ain't no fool."

"No, indeed not, my fair spitfire. For 'fool' read 'amateur'. But we must be careful. We have been trapped by this man, the man who calls himself Malik. He is clever, while we are yet still learning."

"Check everything, then? Mam will go crazy!"

"Let us not burden her with the search."

Caffee thought for a moment then... "Oh yeh, right. Let's not tell 'er. Good thinking."

Caffee clumped out the room and called back to Helen, "'Ere 'elen – you check your stuff, Ade's and Barry's. I'll check mine, Colin's and Mam's."

Colin yelled out from the van. "No. I'll check mine! Leave my stuff alone!"

Helen rose. "What do I look for? I don't know what to look for."

"Neiver do I, gel. Jus' look for anything that might be spy stuff or that might have spy stuff in it. Look for electronicy bits, or bits that shouldn't be there. Norman, you check your stuff and check the loot. He might have placed more little buggers in it."

"Buggers indeed." Norman rose.

Caffee knew she had been right to feel insecure earlier, and now they knew Malik still had a grip on them. She also knew that even if they discovered the new bug, Malik would have thought of something else too. He wasn't going to let them escape so easily. They needed a way to escape his clutches.

They also needed a way to make more money. The loot they had simply wasn't enough. Quietly, she wished they were back at the house and the only problem she had was how to blackmail, or reward, the baker into giving Helen a job.

24
Esher Fades

The next morning found Mam in the kitchen making tea and toast. Despite knowing what was happening, she didn't really understand it or what it all meant, but she knew that if she kept working all would eventually sort itself out. She wondered if the Good Lord was punishing her. But then why would he have put her on this path in the first place? He *had* given her a sign after all.

That mouse had cheekily stolen the bacon rind and had gotten away with it, just like she could steal from those wicked bankers and she too would get away with it. Then she dropped the toast – but the Good Lord had made it land butter side up. He was there for her. The preacher was right, the Good Lord did move in the most mysterious of ways.

The woman sighed. If only the Good Lord would talk to her rather than just give her these obscure signs – signs that she couldn't always interpret. She wondered how many she'd missed. Perhaps her heart just wasn't open enough?

Mam reminded herself that God, or Jesus, or both (she wasn't terribly sure which version of these she *actually* believed in) always liked to test the faithful through trials and tribulations. Maybe all this uncertainty was just another trial to be endured. How many times had He put his faithful through, what she considered to be, completely unnecessary trials and tribulations in the Bible?

She admonished herself for thinking these things and then hoped that God would forgive her.

But of course He would. He would understand. He was a kind and thoughtful God and she was just another one of His flock. She prayed quietly for strength and guidance in the sure belief that He would eventually see her right. Time would tell. Mam had faith. Her fate was in the hands of Jesus... or God... or both. One of them at least.

Barry was already in the lounge watching cartoons with the sound very low. He liked sheep, and rabbits, and pigs. All animals, in fact. He wondered if there were any close enough to see from the cottage. He would have to ask Mam if he could go out for a walk later.

Adrian was fast asleep huddled in a corner of the room clutching a cushion from one of the chairs.

Caffee's clumping down the staircase woke Helen. Eyes still closed, she stretched and yawned. Before she went to sleep, she'd been seriously thinking as to how she could escape from the group. The plan to steal the jewels from the Docklands jewellers looked impossible to her. The entire idea was silly. Thinking back, she was surprised she'd allowed herself to be talked into doing the bank robbery, let alone a jewel heist. She needed to find where the loot was hidden, grab a suitable amount, and then find a way of leaving and getting as far away as she could.

Helen did not intend taking all the loot though. That would be theft. She would take just her share, a few thousand to tide her over until she had a flat of her own and a job. Then she could plan a future, a real future, but that's where it got vague.

Could she take Colin with her? He made her laugh. He seemed nicer than her previous boyfriends. Maybe. He was *so* distant, though. Maybe he was shy or insecure. Who could tell with boys? The others had just wanted her for sex, but they had paid the price and she had 'dumped' them in her own, special, way. They would never disrespect women again.

But ever since the other 'incident'... Then her mind went blank and she couldn't think further ahead. Wait and see. Wait and see. Sitting up on the edge of the bed, her heel nudged the kitchen knife underneath and she was reassured.

Colin was awake too. He lay in his bed thinking, worrying, planning. Everything about him was starting to fall apart. Time to move on. The bank job had been cool and that made him smile. Finally, he had some street cred. It might put him in jail, but at least now he had a reputation – a 'rep' – and it opened so many doors of potential. Pride – a rare feeling for Colin. Sadly, he'd had to leave the old house, his private hideaway with all its secret nooks and crannies. It had taken quite a while to relocate some of his stashes. He'd miss that old house. It was a strategic loss.

He'd thought about splitting from the gang and reckoned he'd only take about one hundred and forty thousand pounds, maybe a *bit* less. Maybe. He'd leave the rest for the others – that seemed fair. He was still young. He had all his life in front of him. Would Caffee join him? That was a definite 'No'. That bitch was too disrespectful. And too unpredictable. Anyway, she was all bones and no tits to speak of.

Helen? The Doncaster murderess? No fear! She did have a body though. Anyway, he'd have to share at least some of the loot with her. Fuck it! A prossie would be cheaper. And safer. Maybe one of them classy ones, one of them university birds desperate to pay for their university fees and maybe wanting a bit 'o rough too. He was a gangster after all and ever since those politicians had introduced fees to learn there were a lot of desperate girls out there – or so he'd been reliably informed. Way to go, government! He vaguely wondered if the politicians had done it deliberately. Dirty old sods! Almost certainly. How else could ugly old rich men get a continuous supply of needy young ladies? They weren't daft – and they had the power.

An image of Helen came to him again. Maybe not. Something about the quiet one made him think again. What did she see in Norman? He was old. But... then again... why not Helen?

Then he remembered Clair, an old flame. In his view she had been *hot*. Grinning and grimacing in equal measure, he recalled the time he finally managed to lure her back to his place.

They had been partying and she was even more drunk than he and so, as far he was concerned, well up for it. Even in the dark he managed to get her to the bed without bumping into too many things. He remembered the heavy breathing, the quick groping of body parts that, in his mind, counted as foreplay. Then came the shedding of clothes – all managed in the blackness of a damp concrete council flat without electricity. Then came the frantic scrabble for the condom in his top drawer (she had insisted), the frenzied tearing at the packet and then the incongruous explosion of German mustard over the belly of his half naked conquest-to-be.

Her cries of disgust grew louder and higher in pitch as, at first, she assumed that his manly essence was not only premature, but cold and slimy. The girl was already dressed and halfway out of his flat before Colin remembered the boxes of condiment packets. He'd lifted them two days previously and put a sample in his top draw until a buyer could be found.

As she left his flat, the harsh hall light revealed the true nature, and colour, of the mustard. It was now smeared over her favourite t-shirt, low cut lace-bra, and cock-baiting micro-skirt. While getting dressed she must have brushed at it to try to get it off. It was also on her hands, legs and face. She could feel the cool clammy substance across her stomach too.

At this point it hadn't reached her belly piercing.

Her monosyllabic screaming, staggering gait, and flicking of the wrists caught the attention of the neighbours who opened their doors, more in curiosity than to assist. What she actually thought the substance was no one could really tell, but it didn't take much imagination to guess, it being of a slimy brown consistency. By then she had got some in her eyes and up her nose resulting in a third wave of even more distressing screams.

She hated mustard.

Colin, now standing half-naked in the flat's doorway, mouth wide open in shock, was too stunned to move. The bruiser from the flat across the hall had opened his door first as soon as he had heard the screams. He muttered an expletive in Colin's direction and our valiant hero retreated and locked his door. Nevertheless, even as he pulled on his clothes, one part of his brain made the mental note that the Germans didn't know what they had there; the mustard seemed to be an excellent instant cure for teenage drunkenness. This seemed to be another business opportunity he would explore at a later date.

By the time the well-meaning lynch mob had broken down Colin's door, Colin was streets away. He did regret losing the consignment of packet condiments because sometimes stock had to be written off. All proper businesses had to do that from time to time.

Also, his condoms. He'd spent good time hacking at a machine for those. They too were casualties of this misfortune.

And Clair, of course. Colin felt sad at that. His luck with women was patchy at best. It always had been. Like the time he nicked a packet of chipolatas for a girl he fancied. He knew she liked cooking so he thought a present of food would put him in a good light. That night they had gone out to the cinema with friends so, in the dark, while the adverts were still playing before the start of the feature, he tried surreptitiously passing one of them to her.

She had reacted in a similar way to Clair. Screaming, hysterics, the slapping in the face. He *tried* to explain that she'd misunderstood. Nevertheless, she and her friends left in a hurry and despite his wish to remain and quietly watch the film, the cinema staff had thrown him out too. It was a wasted ticket but at least the sausages were nice –

that is, all of them except the one the girl had fondled before dropping it.

Perhaps there was something about girls and food that just didn't mix.

After the 'Clair Event' he moved to Gunnersbury, unable to face his peers and, no doubt, their ill-informed girlfriends.

He had burnt many bridges in the past. Now a part of him didn't want to hurt his family here, but...

Yeh. One hundred and forty thousand pounds, or thereabouts, that would be enough to see him right. He'd return to London, maybe not Gunnersbury but somewhere nearby. Chiswick sounded cool, if a bit expensive. Maybe the pickings were more expensive there too? He'd have to find out. His remaining mates, or rather his contacts, would be able to advise him where to settle. He could get himself a decent car too, once he had a couple of driving licences made up. His mate Jamie could help with that one. That was another argument against asking Helen: if he had a car, he could find a girlfriend – easy. There were benefits to being a gangster.

But he didn't *want* to burn Helen.

Or the others, come to think of it. Caffee...? Maybe. But Mam? Barry?

...and Helen *had* smiled at him. More than once. And she had nice legs. Ones that seemed to reach all the way up to heaven. This decision was going to be harder than he thought.

Norman lay in the bed on the other side of the room. Believing Colin was still asleep, he cried to himself quietly. His thoughts and fears incoherent, just the knowledge that his nightmare wasn't over yet. But then again, maybe he deserved it. He had a debt to Adrian and he was damned well going to pay it.

Caffee could sense the tensions rising within the group. Colin was the most likely to do damage and disappear – possibly taking all the loot with him. Would he leave them high and dry? Possibly. He was stupid enough. But Caffee also knew Adrian. She had confidence in him. He'd come up with a plan and then it was simply a matter of making everyone accept it rather than choose their own fate.

Adrian dreamt while he slept. In his dream the colour pink was arguing with a pigeon on whether it had enough smiles to buy a wobble on roller skates. Anyway, who owned Thursdays? Certainly not the Indians. A two-foot spider with a syringe, a bald patch, and wearing a green face mask with a picture of a squirrel on it, was sneaking up on him. He stamped on it over and over and over again, but the spider was made of rubber. He was only hurting the squirrel.

"Oh look. He's chasing rabbits! Has he been here all night?" Caffee demanded of Barry.

"He was asleep when I got here."

"I hope he was working on a plan."

Barry shrugged and continued to watch cartoons.

Caffee slumped into an armchair and stared at Adrian, not wanting to disturb him, yet anxious to know if he'd solved the problem. After a short while the laptop on the table caught her eye so she rose, sat at the table and opened it up.

Yes! There were several documents but the one she was interested in was clearly marked as the 'Jewellery Job'. She started to read it when Helen came in.

"Is that Adrian's plan?"

"Mmm."

"Is it a good one?"

"Mmm. So far..."

"Fancy a cup of tea?"

"Mmm. Yeh..."

Helen left her to it.

When she'd finished, Caffee got up. She was beaming. Adrian had done it again! A bit ambitious, she thought, but what the fuck! So was Esher. And who would have guessed they would have ever pulled that one off?

It had been several days since the bank raid and the police still had no idea who'd broken into it. They were overloaded with clues and had many possible lines of enquiry. Nevertheless, other events had pulled their attention into a different, and a far more newsworthy direction. The investigation was quickly being 're-prioritised'.

They had successfully identified one old crook from his DNA. This suspect was now retired and living at an old people's home in North Gunnersbury. However, it was clear that he hadn't equipped his zimmer frame with a jetpack or equipped his colostomy bag with a blagger's toolkit. Besides, the old codger couldn't even remember who he was, let alone follow a plan.

During the first visit to the old people's home a couple of young policemen were placed in a moral dilemma after being sexually assaulted by an eager Mrs Tappenden. Afterwards, they were reluctant to revisit the premises and, more because of the attendant ridicule than her age, they were also reluctant to press charges. They withdrew their accusations of 'definite cupping', much to the amusement of their colleagues.

Despite this, they did discover that the old lady had been married some three times before, and that there was no record of divorces or deaths of any of her partners. Some idiotic bureaucrat sent two WPCs to question the lady further on this issue. On returning to the station, they were adamant that the lady had Alzheimer's and it was therefore not fruitful for the police to follow up those enquiries.

It also transpired that Mrs Tappenden wasn't too fussy about the gender of her next 'conquest' either.

It was because of those events that the police checked the staff records only at the most cursory level. Of the three missing part-time staff members, Mam did not fit the profile of a bank robber.

How their DNA, and those from various other people in London, got there was unclear. Thus, over the next few weeks that evidence was logged, filed, and forgotten.

However, the letter they found proved to be of *much* more interest. Two teams of investigators looked into the bank's records and found many letters from disgruntled customers. They found scores, but this was typical of all the high street banks. Some could easily be discounted but many others could not. It would take a lot of manpower to work through all those lines of investigation and, knowing that they'd already been fed a batch of false leads, they felt that, in the end, this line of investigation may well prove fruitless too. Besides, they were conscious of the limits on their budget.

They had also found the glove. That had been exciting for the forensics people for it had DNA evidence: the fingerprints and the envelope had traces of yellow paint that matched the paint used in the bank job. The fingerprints turned up trumps, being those of a District Judge, a Malcolm Laufeld.

This particular character had no friends amongst the police community, whom he often accused of incompetence. His reputation was such that both criminals and police would sneer at the name. His ego had ballooned in line with his rise to judicial power to the point where even his wife found him insufferable and often dreamt of finding a way to leave him.

One day her dreams would come true.

The Wednesday after the robbery the Daily Telegraph received a photo of a glove under a bed. The photo was in a brown envelope with a small sticky yellow patch on it. The picture was sealed inside a small plastic bag. Written on the back was the name of a girl, two dates and two addresses. The first date was that of the robbery, and the first address was that of the robbed bank in Esher. The postmark confirmed its origin.

The editor of the Telegraph sent the package directly to the Metropolitan police, after having it photographed in detail at his own office beforehand.

The Metropolitan police took great care in the forensic examination of the package and its contents.

Within forty-eight hours the police raided the second address. This was a private address in Knightsbridge, only to discover that it was a 'gentlemen's club' of some notoriety. Amongst its distinguished members was a certain District Judge Malcolm Laufeld, a man who also indulged in some of the less reputable pastimes that, for a small consideration, a 'gentleman' of his status could satisfy himself with complete discretion.

The story quickly came out. Over time the club had acquired certain links with an Eastern European entrepreneur who supplied young ladies for domestic purposes such as cleaning and cooking at a very reasonable hourly cost. Once he'd been given the business the entrepreneur gently encouraged the club into offering services that became less and less legal. Together with the income from such operations, the enthusiasm of its more 'adventurous' members, together with the club's otherwise spotless reputation, it became impossible for the club to change direction business-wise.

The name of the young lady on the photo had been an underage prostitute taken from her Romanian family at the age of fourteen and had been peddled for the fun of the older men in the club. She was advertised as a 'youthful' seventeen-year-old whore. The young lady had attempted to take her own life by slitting her wrists after 'pleasuring' the judge. The entrepreneur, realising that her future as marketable commodity was now in question, finished the job for her but only after reassuring everyone else she had willingly returned home to her family.

The girl's body had been discovered some weeks before the robbery but at the time the police had insufficient evidence to identify who she was or from where she originated.

The investigation into this sordid affair soon took all the Met's spare resources. The Surrey Police and the Met set up a liaison group but apart from this one link, they had nothing else in common. The Met's investigation made the national headlines with several high-profile prosecutions related to the girl's plight and the bank robbery became a mere footnote. With no discernible progress the Surrey Police soon moved on as well. The liaison group was unable to resolve the connection between the two crimes.

And so, when a little old lady, a person who may have been able to identify at first-hand two of the *actual* bank robbers, gave her account of how she met a strange little girl with a yellow gun trying to shoot her bowels off a lamp post – and her big well-endowed giant of a husband with sparkling white eyes and flashing white teeth – well, she was wasn't taken seriously at all. Perhaps it was the memories of a predatory Mrs Tappenden that coloured that line of the investigation.

The Esher Bank Raid disappeared quickly, and quietly, into history. A situation that the bank was also keen to encourage.

25
The Jewellery Job

It was eight o'clock in the morning. The sun would have been shining brightly if it hadn't been for the dull mattress-like grey clouds in the way. Considering the thickness of the clouds it was amazing there was enough light to illuminate the Scottish countryside underneath, but there was not enough for shadows to form clear edges. A cold drizzle pattered on the windows.

Mam was the only person up and about at that time. She had been in automatic breakfast-making mode since just after seven but as it was a sort of holiday, or hideaway, she was taking her time and seeing to herself first. As soon as the others appeared she'd start breakfast properly; although she wouldn't wait for Colin. Sometimes, back at the house, he wouldn't rise until the afternoon and often he'd skip breakfast altogether and go straight out.

There was a knock on the front door. Without thinking, she put down her cup of tea, walked through the hallway, and opened it. She could only watch as Malik, the tan-suited man, smiling all the while, gently pushed the door aside and entered.

"Good morning. Not a pleasant day, but pleasant enough for a visit. I do hope I am not interrupting anything. I suspect everyone is still in bed?"

He stopped at the door of the lounge and spoke quietly to two of his black-suited associates who had followed close behind. Two more entered. One stood by the front door and closed it for Mam with a nod, and what was probably a genuine smile. The other strode through to the back door in the kitchen and waved a hand signalling something to a hidden colleague outside. Entry, and domination, had been achieved again.

The first two goons ran upstairs, heavy shoes on thin carpet, without any consideration for the dozy occupants. Taking the stairs three at a time in just a few strides they were soon at the top. the first turned left to the first door while the second stopped on the landing, eyes flicking back and forth as each door was opened in turn and the man announced loudly, "D'broe uhtro!"

Within minutes all seven inhabitants had been herded into the lounge where Malik had already made himself comfortable.

Adrian, being guided by Helen, was the last to arrive.

"Hello, again." Malik glanced at each in turn, his smile fixed in place. "This is a *pleasant* cottage, is it not?"

"How'd you find us?" Caffee's eyes burned with the indignation of a wildcat that had just been released from a Hotpoint's rinse cycle.

He laughed gently. "We have been watching you. My colleagues are all ex-military and some of them relish living outside in the fields and in the woods. You may have wished to escape from me, but I assure you that is not possible. If any of you should try and run, I will *always* find you."

Caffee would normally have scorned such a claim. Bragging about such things by the London gangs or the local psycho was the norm in her social circles. In this case though, she suspected it was either the truth or as close to the truth that made little difference.

There was an awkward silence during which Malik's smile never wavered. His eyes however, remained clear and impassive.

He looked directly at Adrian. "How did you find the information I sent you?"

Adrian made a dramatic huffing sound, blew out his cheeks, then, "Inside beside both sides the whiffy stiffy down brown paper shaper envelope with the edged edge that could and would cut and hurt, but tore... hmmm. Never mind, my mind never minds mind you, you don't mind minding though, do you? Not much ripping, ripping Christmas used to be better for such a letter."

Adrian looked up at the ceiling then down at his trainers, one blue and white, the other red and white. "Colin sold me his this these but not a train but training trainers for fifteen pounds of sweet honey money but I didn't need training to train the train - Wooh! Wooh! Chuff! Chuff! Chuff! Chuff! The plan is my trained train, one uncarried, but pulled carriage after the other quickest logic, see? Not holistic. My thoughts but not enough so much for the after diversion needed no time, no time, train leaving station too soon. Wooh! Wooh! Shame. Shame, but some risky risk trades off well, I hope. The line is wet but good enough, the underwater train needs training you see under the wet water? But is your promise still good?"

The man looked at Caffee. "What did he say?"

"He said we have a plan. Is your promise still good?"

"Oh. Really? May I see it?"

"No. Is your promise still good?"

"I *would* rather like to see it." The man held out his hand.

All eyes were on Caffee.

"Fuck off, dimbo! You got military muscle protecting your arse all over the bleedin' place. If you could pull this job off yourself, you wouldn't need us little bunch of bunnies, now wouldya!" Her eyes narrowed. "I reckon you got someone close to you who's fuckin' you about. You daren't make a move on your own. If we told you what we got then maybe that person would find out and then we would both be up shit-creek. Yeh?"

The man sat still, a little taken aback.

Caffee continued. "As I see it, we're both safer with you not knowing the details. Anyway, you got all the uvver cards – we need *summink* for us, if only for our pride. Yeh?"

The gang's eyes, growing wider with fear, snapped to the tan suit.

The man thought for a moment. "How can I be sure that... Adrian... has come up with a workable plan?"

The gang's eyes snapped back to her.

"Don't call me so stupid as not knowin' you ain't too stupid to have not already thought that through."

She stopped, surprised at the sentence and going over it again in her mind before nodding. She continued, "I don't, for a minute, think that you ain't got a continence plan in case we fuck up. Jus' let us do our bit and if we deliver... well, is your promise good? Or are you going to fuck us over? Jury says the latter."

The gang's eyes snapped to him.

"You must understand, I do have concerns..."

Eyes to her.

"After you play your psycho card with you dominating our house, gettin' all of us out of bed with your monochrome musclebound morons and making us all feel helpless? *You* got concerns, mister? Seriously? You think we're all so stupid as not to notice your intimating us with these thee-attricks? We may be daft – but we ain't idiots!"

Eyes to him.

His expression remained fixed as his mind whirled, weighing up options.

Finally, "I apologise for intruding on you the way I did. I shall endeavour to be more polite the next time I visit. I need to return to London this morning and I needed reassurance that the plan would work before I left. You can understand my position. I can only hope that my future visits will not require me to be so... theatrical... as you put it."

"'*I can only hope*' – there you go again with your fucking veiled frets! You're like a three-legged tabby with a sparrow at a disco. What is it with you, you can't treat us with just a *little* respect? Hey?"

In the short silence that followed the tan suit's opinion of Caffee rose immensely. He also knew that, unless he immediately resorted to violence, he'd just lost a battle; but resorting to violence would also lose him the jewels. He wanted to save face but at the same time, he conceded to himself, she had a point. Nevertheless, his pride was more important to him than the opinion of this jumped-up little bitch. His eyes narrowed and he glanced at his gorilla by the door.

"I like cats," offered Barry.

The incongruous sentence snapped him out of his mindset. He looked at Barry's open face then at each member of the gang's saucer eyes in turn. There was no challenge from them. What did it matter if he lost a little face, considering the rewards? Only this mini-skirted vixen counted in this group. The rest were, in his view, harmless.

He didn't know how very, very wrong he was.

He reconsidered his position. If he did intend to use their services in the future it would be best if they did so in an atmosphere more conducive to cooperation. Abject fear was not always a successful motivator, despite what his father had taught him. It certainly wouldn't work on the bitch in front him.

Perhaps he could teach them proper respect *after* they'd delivered the jewels? Or, as would be most likely, if they didn't deliver – well then, he'd deliver this bunch of lowlifes to his men as playthings.

He laughed dismissively and rose from the chair.

"Well?"

"Trust shall be earnt over time. I do intend to keep my promise. If you deliver, so shall I." He walked to the lounge door. "It was such a pleasure to see you all. I shall be in touch."

"Yeh, but next time, can you come in all polite like? Like a normal person?"

The man looked at the black suit by the lounge door. "My colleagues are there to ensure my protection. They like to be sure that what they encounter is not... unfriendly."

"Yeh. I can imagine you got a lot of unfriends, aintchya?"

"If I can be assured your plan is workable and you've started upon it..."

"You can. We'll do our bit. You do yours."

He nodded. "But I will *not* take failure well. Remember that. Good day." And he left followed by his men.

The gang waited until they heard the sound of the two Range Rovers depart and all was quiet again, save for the patter of rain on the windows.

Norman sighed, "The native hue of resolution is sicklied o'er with the pale cast of thought; and enterprises of great pitch and moment, with this regard their currents turn awry and lose the name of action."

Colin ventured a thought. "You did come across a bit strong, Caff. I think you upset him."

"Fuck him! He's a bleedin' pest."

Colin nodded. "But those apes got shooters, though. I ain't fucking with them. We do this job but then how do we know we ain't going to get fucked over after?"

Especially now you upset him, you stupid cow! He screamed silently.

"Time shall unfold what plighted cunning hides. Who cover faults, at last shame them derides."

"What the fuck, Norm? Have you gone and caught

228

what Adrian has? What the fuck does all that mean?" Caffee held up her hand and turned to Colin. "Norm's read the plan. It's just you now. Are you in?"

Colin sat back in a huff. "I ain't read it yet."

"It's lots of bits of cool stuff nicked from Hollywood. We get to go swimmin' like James Bond but it's a doddle. It's just gonna be cold is all. Do it Colin, and you'll be famous."

He didn't say anything but sat there pouting with his arms crossed for a while. Famous but dead, he reckoned. The alternate link between being 'famous' and being 'in jail' didn't occur to him. Neither did he think deeper on what 'famous' would mean in any case.

Norman spoke up. "I do believe the suited devil when he says that he can find you. Wherever you are."

Colin slowly nodded. He believed him too. "But he's gonna fuck us over, isn't he?"

Caffee stood up. "Maybe. Maybe not. I don't know. But that's part of the plan..." She grinned wickedly. "He's a fucking pro and 'e could easily fuck us over. That's why we need that warehouse." She winked and clumped out the room calling out behind her, "Come on, Mam! Let's make breakfast! Barry, you make the tea."

Colin sat deeper in the chair and folded his arms. Helen saw him, walked across and sat on the arm.

"It is a good plan." Colin looked up at her and noticed her, soft, dark brown eyes. She reached down and took his hand in her own. It felt warm and comforting. "How do you feel after Esher?"

Colin was taken aback. This was the first time
229

Helen had shown him any real interest.

"Cool," he muttered.

"I could tell. It *was* exciting, wasn't it?"

"Yeh. Yeh, I suppose." He felt his heart beating faster than it should.

"This one's even better," she smiled. "Read it." She leant forward and gave him a peck on the forehead.

Colin's brain seized up. Another part of his anatomy did its utmost to embarrass him. Fortunately, she returned to her bedroom and no one else noticed.

Mam's voice could be heard from the kitchen.

"Barry? Have you been cleaning the non-stick frying pans, boy? I could have sworn there were black non-stick ones here."

Malik sat quietly in the back of his Range Rover as it sped down the road. His mood had darkened and he was debating whether to keep to his word or not. The women in Europe had a nasty habit of stepping out of line. All too often they showed him disrespect. It was as if they saw themselves as his equal. To *their* men, maybe, but he was not used to such defiance. This one had the temerity to go even one step further; she had verbally challenged him – even from a position of being dominated.

Yet somehow... he felt some confusion... somehow, he liked it. She had spirit, this one. There was no way she should hope to threaten him at all, and yet...

To earn her respect would mean a lot. A lot more

than from the women he usually mixed with. His mood changed again and he grinned. Let us see what the tiger cub will do next time. He rather looked forward to their next meeting – whichever way it went.

26
A New Base

The fact that it was still winter hadn't escaped the gang. However, they were now heading back to 'The Smoke', as Caffee called it. Only Norman knew why London was referred to as 'The Smoke' and wondered why Caffee used such old slang when it was no longer appropriate. Then again, a lot of her language wasn't contemporary. He wondered if she'd been brought up by her great grandparents.

Colin seemed to think it meant the place where the most people smoked weed, and, as a part-time distributor, the thought of a ready market made him feel happier.

It was still cold but several degrees warmer now and the wind seemed a lot less harsh. Caffee made the observation that English breeze was 'The same effin' wind but with less of the fuckin' Scots' attitude.'

On the return journey they'd taken their time and even stayed overnight in a motel. Now that they had a little money, they'd taken a diversion into Sheffield to buy some warmer clothes. This was mainly prompted by Mam's desire to look after Barry who seemed to feel the cold more than the others. It was also because the van's heater had packed up. A cold draught whipped through the van until Norman covered the dashboard with a folded blanket and duct tape.

On their return they had made a point to drive into London and passed the old house in

Gunnersbury. They were all pleased to see that decorators were in there repairing and repainting the old place. At least the sign outside implied that was the case but they couldn't see any action through the windows. The building definitely needed some TLC and the family had never had enough to spend on it themselves. Norman had tried a bit of do-it-yourself once or twice, but most of the work was beyond his abilities and a couple of wonky shelves proved that. He claimed that welding was his strength, simple carpentry being quite beyond him.

But their hearts dropped when they saw the 'For Sale' notice. They'd hoped for the better 'To Let', which might have given them the chance of buying a short lease on the property. It brought home to them how little the Esher job had in fact achieved. Thoughts of a cold, and possibly a homeless, Christmas lurked in everyone's mind. Colin suggested he might be able to find another abandoned property — but they weren't too hopeful. This old house, and the timely passing of the resident old biddy, had been a lucky fluke, or a miracle, according to who you asked.

As time progressed, they got more and more resigned to doing the jewellery job. It seemed to be the only course open to them. The pressure from the dark-skinned tan-suit man and his gorillas was undeniable. The reward, if real, was also tempting. Adrian's plan was ambitious and daring but the more they talked about it the more it seemed workable and quite doable. In fact, the scariest part — the underwater stuff — Norman assured them was to be the easiest. It transpired that Norman, for some inexplicable reason, knew a lot about swimming and scuba gear.

Barry, Colin, and Caffee pressed Norman on the subject. Didn't divers get bendy if they go too deep? Wouldn't they sink if they drank too much water? If they sucked in too much air, would they fill out like balloons and float away? What if the air pressure was so much that they expanded like balloons and then farted so strongly that they zipped through the water like rockets making a 'bpbpbpbpbpbpbpb...' sort of noise. Would they have to breathe in that helium gas and then talk all squeaky? What does SCUBA actually mean? And is it anything to do with Scooby-Do? Would there be sharks?

And finally, how come Norman knew so much about all that stuff, anyway?

When his answers to the last question were very vague it was Mam who stepped in and stopped the interrogation. Nevertheless, even she wondered how the old thespian knew so much, and furthermore, how come he was so confident about the diving being easy? Getting wet in anything but a secluded bathtub was not her opinion of a good idea.

Caffee made sure that every other reservation they had, and there were many, were addressed one by one. It was a long list. From boats, air tanks, to woolly hats, scarves, a little flashing black box, wigs and makeup, and even water-resistant brown spray paint for a mannequin.

Adrian had been diligent in his planning. He always was. It seemed to come naturally to him. Furthermore, behind his butterfly mind was a prodigious library of knowledge. For instance, he knew how to calculate the times of tides of the river Thames and how murky the water in the old London docks was. It seemed he also knew why Norman was such an expert, why he would support Adrian's plan, and why he knew that Norman had confidence in him.

In fact, the entire strategy plan revolved around it.

Now they were spending the Esher loot on petrol and a rented house in a town to the North of London, called Harlow. The house had to have a garage for they had purchased lots of equipment. Colin put the Volkswagen in for a full service and he and Caffee acquired another two white vans for cash.

They tried several places for the vehicles. They looked for the dodgiest and least honest dealers to buy from. Furthermore, they were looking for a seller who preferred cash and wasn't too bothered about paperwork. They were really looking for vans that had probably been clocked, weren't too old, were somewhat cheaper than they should have been, and preferably stolen. The last requirement was something they couldn't explicitly request, so they had to rely on their judgement and the dealer's lack of character.

The men joined the local swimming pool. This was as far as they dare go in public, but it was necessary. Barry was, at first, the least confident but he trusted Norman implicitly and simply did as he was told. Although he'd earned the 'Swam the Width (Without Walking on the Bottom *Too* Much) Certificate' at school, it was Norman's slow, steady, and patient tuition that taught him how to work along the edge to the deep end, breathe in, and push himself under. Then, later, he managed to breathe out and wait a little longer before pushing off to swim to the surface. This demanded a great deal of confidence for a near beginner but, with the support, Barry turned out to be a natural. Someone like Norman being at his side, and giving him confidence, had never been the case for Barry before. Furthermore, Norman found himself a new talent, that of being a teacher.

Colin looked on and slyly copied the lessons from afar. He'd been quite a good swimmer at school and it was a skill he hadn't forgotten.

Barry was overjoyed at his accomplishments and couldn't wait to tell Mam whenever they returned from the pool, declaring, "I like swimming," more than a few times.

At one point in the changing rooms, after a particularly successful lesson, Colin sidled over to Norman.

"You've done all this stuff before. Yeh?" He eyed Norman suspiciously.

Norman continued dressing and didn't answer.

"You seem to know all about this swimming stuff. I can tell. Adrian knows about you too, doesn't he? That's why he planned it this way. What's your secret? How come you know all this stuff?"

Norman stopped and sighed. "There are no secrets that time does not reveal," he muttered.

"Seriously. How come you know so much?"

"I used to be a diver." He continued dressing. "A long, long time ago. In another life."

"Oh? That's cool! How come you never said?"

"It's not something about which one should brag."

Colin took a second to unravel the sentence, then, "I bloody well would! That's real sick, that is. Being a diver, underwater and all that stuff. Where'd you work? The Bahamas? Coral reefs and sharks and stuff?"

Norman nodded. "Here and there. It certainly was a compendium of experiences."

Colin punched him on the shoulder. "Who would've thought, hey? You're a dark horse, mate. A bloody dark horse. You'll have to tell us all about it." And walked back to his changing cubicle, feeling a little less embarrassed at ever having been threatened by the older man. A diver? Sick! Respect, even.

Norman finished putting his wet trunks and towel into the duffel bag and watched as Colin did the same. He had an unwelcome flashback to his youth: an underwater exercise, squatting, hunched side by side with his teammates, all anonymous in their black air tanks and scuba gear, seated in a rubber-covered metal frame embedded into the back of an old 'O' class submarine but open to the ocean around them. It was cold and murky. Streams of bubbles of spent air from each of the men floated up to the brighter surface only to be lost in the ocean even before reaching the crinkled, cresting waves above.

The only sounds he could hear was the regular hiss of air as he breathed in, the sounds of escaping bubbles as he breathed out, and the thumping of his heart as if it was trying to hack its way out of his chest.

This was a joint anti-terrorist exercise run by the Royal Navy and Army. The submarine was underwater and drifting south in the icy currents of the North Sea. Speckled green-grey light filtered down from the choppy surface just metres above them. Their equipment sat uncomfortably between their legs and against the rubber-covered hull and his silenced MP5, sealed in a plastic bag, was strapped to webbing on his chest. The cold green light, the sound of his heart, and the hardness of the submarine were all surreal, and frightening, even for the experienced men in the team.

Then, in the near blackness and without making any sound, loomed a huge ominous shadow over them — the enormous metal leg of an oil rig drifted into view. It rose from the black depths right up and above the ever moving, ever rolling and rippling surface above them. The mass of the structure was blotting out most of what little light they had. Then he felt, rather than heard, the ocean rushing past his head, pushing against his face mask, as the submarine engaged its propellor to give it the needed headway to avoid a collision. It was time to disconnect his lifeline and swim away from the safety of the boat. He and his colleagues would swim over the black abyss toward that metal leg. Each man had to grab hold of one of the metal ladders attached to that leg and then ascend it, fighting the currents and the chopping waves. He knew that if he missed that ladder, if he slipped, if he failed in any way, he'd be swept away into the cold vastness of the North Sea with little hope of struggling back...

Norman doubled up in painless agony. His face screwed up so hard he started to cry. He sat on the wooden bench, face in his hands, frozen for several seconds.

There are no secrets that time doesn't reveal.

Eventually.

A few seconds later Colin and Barry were ready to leave and returned to find Norman.

"You ready?"

Norman looked up.

"What's the matter with your eyes?"

"Chloride," he muttered, and stood. "It gets to me sometimes. Let's move." And they strode out of the changing rooms.

27
Contact Again

It had been several days, and Lieutenant Commander Evans was sitting in the coffee shop staring at his espresso and musing on the mission so far. This was his fourth operation involving the tracking of missing persons, but his first in his beloved Motherland, the United Kingdom. This should have been the easiest of missions but was far from it. This one was proving to be a dud. Any moment he expected to be recalled and re-assigned. He was not looking forward to that.

Even worse, he would have a failed mission on his record. That would be recorded as a simple 'tag-and-bag' he managed to flunk. It wouldn't look good. Something must have spooked the gang. They had all disappeared – lock, stock and barrel. The entire household. Vanished. He felt, rather than knew, it wasn't him. It must have been something else, but what?

He looked up and decided to make the most of it. It had been a while since he'd been in the UK and some weeks since he had an affair. He examined the talent sitting nearby. There were two young Japanese girls at the bar by the window, chatting. Another two wearing hijabs at a table – one reading her Kindle, the other texting someone – probably a friend.

It was a brunette in her early thirties, clearly an office worker, that caught and held his attention. She was sitting alone, wearing a lemon blouse, dark red jacket and matching skirt. Her earrings and the way she'd made herself up interested him. Either she was going to meet someone, or she usually took the time to make herself attractive. She sat cross-legged a little way back from her table reading a novel.

A half-finished latte and lightly nibbled cream cake remained in front of her, so he assumed she was treating herself. He watched intently for a few seconds then, as she turned a page, he saw the engagement ring – but no wedding ring. He took out his silver-handled comb and quickly brushed it through his hair while deciding on his approach strategy. In his experience women that were engaged required more finesse.

His mobile rang.

His heart sank faster than his sigh. Dreading the coming conversation, he re-pocketed the comb and extracted the mobile from his pocket.

"Evans."

"We have them again. Leicester emptied the account from a post office in Harlow."

"Harlow? Where's that?"

"It's a town, north of London off the M11. Get up there, can you? I'll get a copy of the CCTV and confirm it is Leicester. I'll ring you with more details later. Stay in touch."

Evans glanced again at those enticing crossed legs and sighed again. Did he have time? No. Not if he was to have a chance of turning this mission around.

"Alright. I'm on my way." He decided to look on the positive side. The mission was still active, and he was still in the UK. Besides, he might find someone in Harlow.

He gathered his coat, left the coffee shop and walked to the car park, searching for his rental BMW. He'd grown attached to that, and wondered if he could afford to buy a new one of his own. He hoped this posting would last a while longer.

28
Harlow

Caffee insisted they spend a few nights before the jewellery job at the River Lee practising in the cold murky water with the wetsuits. It was getting used to the shock of cold water that seemed to be the most important thing, along with not panicking when the lights went out – which came a very close second. Working in murky water was problematic enough, but powerful torches strapped to their face masks and shoulders helped. The main problem was the half-buried branches of trees in the soft mud. None of these was an issue they expected to face on the day.

Despite this, Norman insisted they practise with few, and even once or twice, with no, lights. Just in case they lost vision. Besides, it built confidence and after watching and listening to Norman both Colin and Barry discovered that acting calmly in times of stress always helped them to resolved the problem.

In the end, all the rehearsals paid dividends. It gave everyone the assurance and the faith that were needed for the job. In fact, it gave them all a spurt of confidence and pride in their new-found abilities – none more so than Barry who, eventually, and after a lot of personal tuition from Norman, took to the project like a proverbial duck to water – albeit one that sometimes had to struggle to stay under the surface, often ended up facing the wrong way, had to learn to cope with sneezing into the face mask, and then discover – and come to terms with – what divers did when they needed to pee.

Norman also took visible pleasure from how his personal attention to Barry paid such dividends. Even Colin showed him a little more respect and paid more attention to the lessons. As time went on, Norman could be seen smiling a little more and walking a little taller.

Mam, Caffee, and Helen managed to hire a dirigible despite it being off season. They practised driving it around the boating lake and found it to be quite fun. At first, it was assumed that Mam would not be interested in any of the diving activities, although that might have been a mistake. The major issue that everyone quietly understood, but was left very much unsaid, was trying to find a wetsuit of suitable dimensions and the support she needed in the necessary places. Furthermore, safely overcoming her abundant buoyancy might have been a challenge.

Caffee specifically said no. Incongruously, she felt naked without her clogs, bangles, and micro mini-skirt.

No one dared to ask Helen.

Apart from the public pool and access to the river, one of the reasons for choosing Harlow as their temporary base was the Templefields Estate. It was there they managed to hire a small warehouse with its own wire-fenced perimeter. When they weren't swimming, boating, or testing equipment they were cutting up metal and rehearsing the handover of the loot. After all, they didn't want to squash the hand that might feed them.

One evening, when they were exhausted and recovering from the day's exertions and they had just finished watching a game show on TV, Colin asked, "How are we going to look after Ade? You know, while we're on the job? We need another Morticia."

Caffee was reading a girl's magazine. "Hospital," was her reply, not looking up.

"What?"

Helen looked up and frowned.

"Hospital. We take him into Harlow Hospital and tell 'em we found him wandering the streets. Then we bugger off. We do that early in the morning. Knowing the NHS they'll sit him in A'n'E for about six bloody hours during which time they'll figure out he's a drug-addled homeless guy, and then they'll put him under a trainee nurse for observation. By the time they figure out he really is a sandwich-free picnic we'll have done the job and be on our way back. The only problem then, is how to break him out of the nutters ward. I reckon we can leave him there for thirty-six hours, no prob."

Helen perked up. "What if they medicate him?"

Caffee looked at her and smiled. "For a flake that doesn't understand that stepping through open windows results in a slight case of plummeting... I fink that's prob'ly a *good* thing. What do you think, Ade?"

Adrian had acquired a small Lego toy. He was repeatedly connecting and disconnecting two of the bricks.

He looked up to the ceiling and squinted his eyes. "Adrian can paddle if dropped and plopped, but then

245

which way to go, Westward Ho, Ho, Ho? All three dimensions have ends which terminate the water but it's the breathing he be needing meanwhile, and it must be fare air and soon, and he doesn't want to return to the dropping place if unfriendly. Decisions, decisions. Love to watch the choo, choo go by but London so issy, busy missy. Not Esher, not at all. I can pay and boredom in hospital okay, for a day, may I say. Let's play that way."

"Mmm... Wot the fuck did he say, Helen?"

She shook her head slowly and shrugged. "I think he said it's okay."

"Done then. Hospital it is. You gotta thank our national health system. It's always there when you need it."

Norman frowned. "Even for jewellery heists?"

"Yep!" she grinned. "Especially for jewlerry heists. It's what them waiting rooms are really for. Why else would they keep all them ill people sitting together, knee to knee, bored mindless, and coughing and infecting each other for hours on end? Apart from the vending machine profits of course – which is needed to pay for it all."

She stood and stretched. It was cold outside and not too warm inside. She contemplated putting on a pair of striped blue and maroon tights. "You know, I could eat half of a sausage sandwich. A pork'n'beef butty wiv mustard, or brown sauce. How about you, Helen? Barry? Colin? You up for it? Make us one. Yeh?"

Colin's brain jumped a gear. Girls? Up for it? Then came the association with his nightmare, sausages... mustard... sauce...

A cold shiver ran down his spine. "No. Not for me!" he whispered and he stormed off to his room.

"Fuckin' hell! What's the matter with him?"

Helen, Mam and Barry swapped glances. Helen shrugged.

"Bleedin' lazy sod. Try asking that wanker to do you one little favour an' he jumps up and legs it. Come on Helen, you wanna share a sozzy sarni?"

Helen nodded.

"Who else? What about you, Foghorn Norm?"

"I am a great eater of the pork'n'beef butty and I believe that does harm to my wit. But let me help you, anyway." He rose from the chair.

Barry's answer was simply, "I like sausages." Mam declined. Adrian was offered one but, they assumed, he also declined.

"I'll just check on Colin first," offered Helen. "He seemed upset."

She ran up to his room and knocked on the door and peered in. He was laying on his bed, so she sat beside him.

"Don't you want a sausage sandwich?"

Colin shrugged.

"Not even with us? What's wrong?" She took his hand, looked into his eyes and could sense his feeble defences crumbling. She felt warm inside.

After a short spell of stuttering and throat clearing, Colin explained about the cinema and chipolata incident.

Helen smirked. Colin smiled. Then she sniggered and he sniggered too. She laughed, and then he laughed out loud. Helen, he realised, seemed to understand. She even promised not to tell anyone. Somehow, her response to his misfortune had turned the traumatic incident into an anecdote. And a good one at that. Something to joke about. Maybe later, even with the others. Her gentle laughter had quietly dissolved that demon in an instant. Something that had haunted him for years was now gone – in just seconds. Holding his hand, she pulled him up and led him downstairs to join the gang.

He didn't know it then, but in that moment, he'd fallen for her and in a way that he'd never felt about anyone before.

What he did know though, was that he should dispose of his stash of those bastard mustard packets before they got him into trouble again.

Moreover, the consequences of *English* mustard would be a lot worse than German.

29
The Lure

Evans was pleased. This time Leicester had slipped up. This time the address on the pensions form was correct. Probably because it was validated and he couldn't get away with a fake one. That made his job a lot easier. He parked at the end of the road and watched the comings and goings of those living at the house, and the neighbours. For this he had retrieved a small pair of handheld binoculars from his suitcase. They were good quality Russian ones, discreet and surprisingly cheap too. Also, a voice recorder from which he could write up his notes later.

There seemed to be a lot of movement during the day. Vans were arriving and departing, boxes were being delivered and sometimes, of all things, scuba gear was being unloaded and then reloaded into one of the vans. Presumably, this equipment was going to be used somewhere. The market in Harlow for such gear couldn't be that large. Fifty years ago, this town was a new town for young couples but the population had since grown old and now it was inhabited mainly by geriatrics – not a demographic renowned for scuba diving. He was tempted to follow them but couldn't. He needed a win. If Adrian was in the house he needed to know and the best way to find out was to stay put and hope for a direct view of his target.

The BMW had comfortable seats, but no car seat yet devised was comfortable enough to sit in for hours on end. He seriously wondered about waiting until they'd all left then breaking in and simply snatching the man if he was there. That would be his Plan B. But for the moment, time was on his side and he'd play cautious. Better to go in with good intelligence, than make a balls-up because of one silly oversight.

He didn't see anyone who could have been taken for this mysterious Adrian Channel. He saw the others many times. He counted them. The tall man was Leicester, the others were a heavily built black chap, another young man, a rotund black woman, and two young ladies in their early twenties. Six altogether. Quite a group really, all living in a single house.

The skinny girl always wore a short mini-micro skirt and, for some unaccountable reason, huge clogs. She was both trouble and asking for trouble, he thought. Her laugh was coarse and loud too, like some sort of demented baying hyena that even reached the end of the road. A stereotypical Essex girl? A clown in any case.

But the other one kept his attention. This one was quiet, had a demure walk and there was something more mature, more elegant about her. He liked to see her smile and sometimes she made that feminine coy look which he found quite attractive. He wondered if she'd find him too old. In any case, she was his means to find out if Adrian lived there.

Evans took out his silver-handled comb and, while running it through his hair, thought about how to introduce himself. Not knowing much about the target, he decided on the sketchbook ruse. That would impress her and account for him being older too. It had worked on impressionable young girls before when he had just a few days of shore leave. He was sure it would work again. He didn't like the false pretences that went with it, but it was fast and convincing. Well, convincing enough, anyway.

The next morning Evans was back in his BMW parked at the end of the street. He was wondering where he'd fix up the cameras he'd requested earlier. He needed them to keep an eye on the property. It was inconvenient, but not fully secure to have to be so close to the premises to observe them.

After an hour the two girls came out. The clown had her usual mini-micro skirt, a small fake-fur jacket and some ridiculous striped tights, confirming his nickname for her. She would be impossible to lose in a crowd. The other girl was wearing much more sensible jeans and white shirt under a worn green anorak. They got into the van, the clown into the driver's side, his princess into the passenger side, and they drove off. This time he decided to follow.

They didn't go far. After ten minutes they parked in the big car park in the town centre. Evans couldn't tell how long they'd paid for, so he opted for six hours. He reckoned, rightly, this was to be a shopping spree.

The two meandered through the shopping centre, working their way through no end of women's clothes shops. Every third shop seemed to be selling women's fashion of some kind or other. Thank God for big windows where he could watch them from a distance in the reflections.

Surprisingly, for the time spent in each shop, they

purchased little. He reckoned they were mostly trying things on rather than actually buying and he was right. With only a couple of bags each they returned to the van and deposited them in the back before going to a Chinese buffet-style restaurant and having some lunch. His feet ached and he felt bored and miserable. Didn't they ever tire of this?

While he watched them pick away at a shared dish from the outside, the clown received a call on her mobile. It was brief. She hung up, had a few words with her partner and then left. He followed her part way back to the car park. It was most likely she had been called to pick someone up, leaving his target alone in the town centre. He turned back. Finally! This was the opportunity he'd hoped for.

He returned to the Chinese but the girl wasn't at the table. She'd already left? Damn! He ran for the door and glanced around. Had he lost her? Then she came out behind him. She must have been in the toilet.

He let her pass, then followed. To his surprise the first few shops she visited were the same ones she had visited earlier. He couldn't figure out why.

As she stood outside a shop looking at the window display, he decided to make his move and strode over.

"There you are!" He put his hand on her shoulder and laughed. She turned, startled.

He stood back and feigned surprise. "Oh, dear. I'm terribly sorry. I thought you were the model."

She looked at him blankly.

"Sorry. Ah, from behind, you look exactly like her. I'm so sorry... I didn't mean..." He paused. "I'm

small sketch pad fell out and landed on the pavement.

"Oopsy! Excuse me." He grabbed it and picked it up, then handed the card over to the girl. It simply read 'E. Stephenson – Media Artist' and gave a mobile and fax number. Had Helen been observant she would have seen that the sketch on the sketchpad was a scene from the film Avatar.

"Erm... this is awkward. I'm a professional artist. I work on storyboarding. For the media. Do you know what storyboarding is?"

She shook her head.

"Okay. I read scripts. Plays, films, TV series that sort of thing. I sketch them out on paper so the director can get an idea of what camera shots to use. Here... here's some of my work." He handed the sketch pad over to Helen, then snatched it away and turned to a series of sketches showing a cops-and-robbers car chase and people shooting at other people. The style was like a hand-drawn cartoon, but in places quite detailed.

She turned a few pages then found some scenes from the Lord of the Rings, then some more from Avatar. Some of the pages seemed to have comments in them and one two contained names like 'Sigourney loves this. Can you keep her left profile in shot? James C.'

"These are good," she said and handed it back.

He nodded. He hoped the name dropping would impress. He was mistaken, though, Helen simply liked the pictures.

"Great. Look, I've been let down and I really need some help. Can we chat? Can I take you to a coffee

254

bar somewhere? Just over there? It's all on the up and up." He paused for a second and before she could say no, he continued, "Splendid." He pointed to a Starbucks nearby. "Let me treat you, then you can decide."

They walked a few steps then he asked, "Tell me about yourself. Do you model at all? I think you should. What's your name? Where are you from?"

"Doncaster," she replied.

"That is an unusual name. I've not met many people called Don Caster. Nope, no girls I know called Don. And where are you from?"

She smiled. "No. My *name's* Helen. I'm *from* Doncaster."

"Ah!" He laughed. "Of course. Stupid me. That makes sense. I wondered where the accent came from. What made you come down here? Down to the ugly South?"

She shrugged.

They entered the shop and he ordered lattes for them both. He chose a table toward the back.

"Tell me a little about yourself. What sort of things do you do? What sort of things do you like?"

Helen thought for a moment. Her hand wandered up to her hair as she unconsciously flicked it back, looked at him sideways and smiled coyly.

Bingo! The old charm still works.

"I don't know. A lot of things really."

"Are you working at the moment?"

She shook her head.

"Great. No, sorry, not great you're not working it's just... Well, the chances of that. This could be my lucky day. Look, I need to get some sketches done. I have a script to run through from the BBC. It's a new TV series. I can get most of the scenes done, car chases, the yacht, the interrogations, that sort of thing. But a lot of them involve the heroine and I need a model. It's only for sketching, you understand. There's nothing dodgy about it. It's mostly head shots. You know, shock, horror, laughter, love, that sort of thing. There's no dressing or undressing or cameras involved." He paused, "In fact, you can bring a friend with you if you like. Just to be sure, how does that sound? And, of course, you get paid. This will be for the BBC after all. Are you up for that?"

Helen thought for a moment, then nodded once.

"I tell you what, this is all a bit sudden, isn't it? You tell me more about yourself first. Where are you living at the moment?"

Helen shrugged. "I don't know. We've only just moved in. Somewhere in Harlow."

"How many in your family?"

"Seven. There's seven of us."

He had six on his list, now he knew there was a seventh. "Mother, father...?" he ventured.

"No." She laughed and shook her head. "I'm living with friends."

"Friends? They can't *all* be your boyfriends, surely?" He laughed and she laughed too.

"No. No, I don't have a boyfriend at the moment."

Bingo! He could press her further. There may even be an opportunity to bed her – for King and Country, of course.

"Who else is there?"

"There's Norman, Barry, Caffee, Mam, Colin and Adrian."

Bingo again! He was on a roll now. The chances were piling up in his favour. "That's quite a few. Must be a houseful. I bet you're pleased to get out of the house? Hey?"

She nodded. "Sometimes."

"I bet they all do, don't they? They all like to get out?"

She nodded. At that point her mobile rang. "Excuse me." She stood and answered the phone. After a moment she returned. "Thanks for the coffee. I must be going. My friend's coming to pick me up."

"I see. No problem. Thank you for agreeing to model for me. Look, can I have your mobile number? I'll call you and let you know when and where. Then you and your friend can come over while I sketch. Is that alright? Is tomorrow okay?"

"We're busy tomorrow. Maybe the day after?" Then she read out her number. He tapped it into his phone, idly wondering what she would be up to.

He placed a hand on her arm. "Thank you. We agree then. I shall pick you up at two o'clock under the town clock. Now don't forget, you can bring a friend, okay? In fact, bring two if you want."

She nodded and took her bag.

"Nice to meet you, Helen. Don't forget then, two o'clock – day after tomorrow. Goodbye."

"Goodbye."

He waved as she left. Would she look back? Was she intrigued by the stranger?

Yes! She glanced back at him before disappearing around a corner. Victory! He stood and left the coffee shop, unconsciously taking his silver-handled comb from his inside pocket and running it across his hair.

Helen arrived back at the house in a dream, running straight upstairs and humming to herself. Caffee followed behind her carrying the shopping and closed the front door by leaning against it. Norman was standing in the hall and reached out to help.

"But, oh, how sweet a thing it is to look into happiness through a young girl's eyes," he declared.

"Been at the wine again, have yuh?"

"Abstinence engenders maladies."

"What?"

"Yes. I have had another glass... or two. But not too many. I see our fair maid skipping up the stairs and singing. Did she find a rare bargain in the sales?"

"Helen? Nah! She's got herself a hot date."

"Oh?"

Caffee dropped the bags and entered the living room before flopping into a chair. "She met this old geezer in the town centre. She says he's an artist who wants to draw her face. I say he's an old letch that just wants to get into her knickers."

"What does this gentleman look like?"

"Dunno. Never saw him. Helen reckons he's the dog's bollocks, though. 'Mature, immaculate, and fit,' she said."

"A well-dressed artist?"

"Apparently."

"I see. When are they meeting?"

"Day after tomorrow, under the clock. Any chance of a cuppa?"

Norman nodded. "Yes. Yes, let me make us all a cup of tea." He rose, deep in thought.

30
The Big Day

Then came the big day.

It was very early in the morning when the men dropped Adrian off at Harlow's Princess Alexandra Hospital Accident and Emergency Department, before driving down to London. After they left, he sat in the waiting room playing with his Lego toy for an hour before a passing nurse asked if he was alright. She assumed that his smile, rather than his actual answer, indicated everything was okay so it wasn't until well into late afternoon that the receptionist realised something was amiss and mentioned it to a senior nurse. After that, it became an awkward situation because he clearly wasn't an accident, an emergency, or an abandoned baby. Well... not exactly. On the other hand, something had to be done.

All attempts at questioning him resulted in indecipherable mumbles. So, a physical examination, blood tests, and observation it was. It was a start. The NHS had him in its comfort zone... for a few hours anyway.

When the men arrived in London Docklands they first had to steal and reposition a JCB digger and then dismantle a section of the chain link fence on the quayside. This gave the big yellow digger a clear run at open water. Adrian had previously identified the building works taking place close by the jewellers and somehow verified the presence of the digger, a key part of the plan. Relocating it simply meant hot-wiring and moving it together with other building paraphernalia a hundred yards or so closer to the quayside to make it all look legitimate. They did this dressed in hard hats, gloves and yellow high-visibility vests moving quietly and casually so as not to attract attention.

Then they prepared their two boats according to Caffee's detailed checklist.

During this time only two CCTVs could have recorded them. A Vaseline-covered paintbrush on a broom handle did that job. The paintball gun would have been a little *too* conspicuous at that time of day.

The women had dressed themselves, packed away all the gear and travelled down in the other van.

It wasn't raining, it was overcast and not too windy which was helpful. It had rained earlier which was even better. Caffee was standing on Connaught Road looking up towards Helen on Connaught Bridge. They were relying on the Tan Suit's timings of when the aircraft would be unloaded at London City Airport, and it wasn't accurate. Fortunately, from her position Helen could see onto the apron in the distance and identified the three unmarked courier vans. Two were to be diversions and only one would have the safe and the jewels.

She used the camera on her new smartphone and managed to get a shot of the number plates of the vans as they were parked by the hangar. Only one had its back door open.

She watched the private jet pull up and men in suits milling around aircraft. The jet blocked the view but she saw the bottom of a forklift truck under the fuselage, so she knew something heavy was being unloaded.

Mam remained in the second of the gang's vans. Unable to park nearby she was waiting a few streets away. She dare not drive around in case cameras photographed her. Nevertheless, Caffee and Helen had applied some serious makeup and she looked like a convincing Rastafarian complete with a multi-coloured woolly scarf and Helen's matching bobble hat. Annoyingly, the bobble in the hat had come loose and it kept tapping Mam on her nose or ears but she valiantly ignored it, determined that the 'Satan's Tassel' was not going to interfere with today's plans.

Helen had applied makeup and dressed herself in a trouser suit to look older than she was. The girl hoped she'd be disguised as a 'senior office lady' and even had a slim briefcase to look the part. This time she made sure she wore sensible shoes. Caffee briefly wondered why Helen had included a sharp kitchen knife strapped to her leg, but thought nothing more of the matter.

Caffee had been more radical and obtained a punk outfit. A bright pink wig, short black skirt, laddered stockings, boots, black gloves, and leather jacket with studs made her look the part. She drew the line at piercings though. Colin thought she looked really cool and preferred the black leather look to her normal pastel. However, Norman thought she looked more, as he delicately put it, 'like a lady of the night addicted to coca of the cracked variety', which was the point of Caffee's disguise and pleased her no end – until Colin responded...

"Nah, she don't. She looks like a crack-whore," which landed him a bruised rib – not because he was wrong, but because he was Colin.

One of the objectives of the face painting was to use eye shadow and mascara to 'move' and 'resize' the eyes in order to make recognition less likely. In Helen's case it was also to make her look somewhat older. It was quite difficult to find commercial makeup to *add* wrinkles, but the internet helped. Helen also added a beauty spot on her left cheek on the understanding it made her *less* beautiful.

All that disguising was a hoot for the girls and took some of the edge off the pre-job nerves.

When the courier vans started their engines, Helen walked away from the fencing and approached the side of the road. To avoid suspicion, she signalled Caffee by dropping her briefcase and then picking it up again before walking as fast as she could down to Connaught Road.

Caffee rang Mam on her new smartphone. Being nervous Mam promptly stalled the van. Luckily, she didn't flood the carburettor and was on her way within seconds.

Colin also got a text message from Caffee and commenced his walk south towards Marsh Wall. Although the weather was chilly, he was hot. Underneath the jeans and jacket, which he'd borrowed from Barry, he was wearing a wetsuit. Without a mirror to confirm it, he felt as if he had acquired the body of Arnold Schwarzenegger and strutted accordingly. Luckily, no one that passed him offered to correct this delusion.

The three courier vans pulled out of the service

road in convoy, but Caffee was already in position at the side of the T-junction. She identified the van with the jewels as the last of the three and as it passed her, she reached into her bag pushing her hand past her personal box cutter and petrol-filled drink can (kept for those 'unsocial' occasions when pepper spray simply wasn't enough). Whipping out a spray can she sprayed paint stripper on the side. The driver and guard inside didn't notice being too intent watching Mam flashing her headlights and batting at her wayward bobble.

Caffee re-bagged the spray then ran toward the junction, crossing in front of the vans and waving her hands in 'delight' at her 'Rastafarian' friend.

It was clear to the guards that the punk rocker wasn't any threat and all three vans sped away. The van with the 'Rastafarian' bobble-batting driver did not follow.

At this stage the last van was still white, the paint bubbling away unnoticed as the chemicals got to work.

The vans now had to get to the Docklands. They sped along Silvertown Way and turned left over the Lower Lea Crossing. During this drive, as pre-arranged, a black Range Rover joined the small convoy at the rear. The first van, van one, broke off from the convoy and took the direct route to the Docklands turning left into Aspen Way then left again into Preston Road.

At the roundabout van two circled back around behind the Range Rover so that now the van with the safe, van three, was first in the convoy followed by the Range Rover then van two – which had now become the 'back door' in case of a problem.

The small convoy continued along Aspen Way before turning left down Westferry Road and catching the start of Marsh Wall. This unlikely route along such busy roads was thought to be safer. The bridge at Preston Road being a natural choke-point.

Meanwhile Mam had picked up Helen and was driving the more direct path. She drove down Preston Road and into Coldharbour where she and Caffee got out.

So far, so good.

So far, nothing had gone wrong.

31
Splash!

The small convoy reached the end of its short journey and turned left off Marsh Wall and drove slowly into a courtyard. The Range Rover moved off to one side and parked, letting the final vehicle move up behind the van with the safe. They passed the relocated 'Men at Work' signs and the construction works and turned left again onto the quayside, moving along the edge towards a waiting reception committee of four black-suited men.

Colin, now hiding under the dashboard of the digger, reached up and started the engine. He peeked over the dashboard as the first of the vans drove towards him. This had the safe and a large discoloured yellow patch of bubbled paint on the side. Some of it had peeled off revealing undercoat and bare metal underneath. His target was clear. As it drew level, he revved the engine and let out the clutch.

The digger, with the bucket low, lurched forward two metres and struck the left side of the van halfway up. Colin yanked a lever and the bucket lifted that side of the van a few inches pulling the wheels clear of the ground. The front wheel spun wildly having lost traction as the driver tried to accelerate away. Colin revved the digger's engine again, harder this time, and shoved the van sideways up to the edge of the quayside then remorselessly continued pushing it over and into the river.

It fell onto its right side onto the grey-green of the Thames with a dramatic splash and started to sink quickly. The guard had released his seat belt and opened the passenger door just before it fell, just before the weight of the door and the impact with the water slammed it shut again pushing him back inside. He landed on top of the driver. The driver's window had been open so he was stuck inside the van trying to reach for the seat belt release, but the van was sinking too fast. With the shock of the fall, the sudden weight of the passenger, and the cold water pouring in beside his head he started to panic.

They both went under, trapped inside.

As soon as the van hit the water Colin, already stripped to his black wetsuit and with his clothes in a couple of plastic shopping bags, leapt from the digger's driver seat and ran along the short bonnet. He jumped as high and as far as he could out into the dock. Overdosing on adrenaline, he remembered dive bombing girls at his school swimming pool so he rolled into a ball and yelled, "Geronimo!"

The young man was completely unaware of the four guards running towards him. Two of them drew handguns and one managed to get off two shots. Had Colin known about that his mood would have been very, very different. As it was, he was jubilant – there were no teachers around to send him to detention this time.

He hit the water beside some floating planks of wood and his weighted belt immediately dragged him under. In rehearsals he'd practised waiting for as long as fifty seconds before striking out for the surface, but the freezing cold of the river struck him like a hammer and the shock was so great it took all his willpower to prevent himself from breathing in. Instead, he screamed and immediately started struggling with the belt buckle.

But Norman was beside him within seconds. Waiting under the planks of wood he reached across and grabbed Colin as they both started to sink, and as they'd practised in the river Lea, he placed a face mask over Colin's face even before he'd stopped screaming.

Colin breathed the air and forced himself to calm down. A finger and thumb forming a circle from Norman meant all was okay and restored the young man's confidence. He wasn't about to chicken out in front of the old coot now. The river water was still unbelievably cold but he regained his composure in seconds. He had rehearsed this and he knew what to expect. An image of James Bond on a sunny Caribbean beach flashed into his mind. Interestingly, he was accompanied by an image of a tanned Helen, long hair billowing in the wind, clutching at Colin's arm. She was wearing a skimpy white bikini with a large kitchen knife strapped at one side.

Unnoticed, just a few feet above them several bullets hit the water like miniature lightning bolts zipping down from the surface. They quickly lost their momentum and dropped to the bottom. Something for future archaeologists to ponder over.

When the van had hit the water Barry, standing on the bottom of the dock close to the quayside, had seen the splash outlined against the brighter sky above and then watched it start to sink into the murk in front of him. He leaned forward and started his slow walk toward it dragging the pallet of equipment behind him. The bottom of the dock was a lot firmer than the river bed he had practised on and he found it a lot easier to approach the sinking van.

The van landed silently on the bottom kicking up a small cloud of dirt as it did so. The sides of the wheels touched down first and then the van settled on its right side. As soon as he reached it, Barry released the rope to the pallet and climbed on top, just above the passenger's door. He looked down to see that the guard was still frantically trying to get out and had just managed to push the door up when Barry reached down and slapped a mask on his face and then flushed the water out with a squirt of pressurised air.

Barry held the man firmly, one hand on the mask

and one hand behind his head until the man calmed down. Then he pulled him out the van and launched him towards the surface.

Inside the van the driver had only just managed to release his seat belt. The guard's feet had been pushing him down and the poor man was now desperate and fast running out of oxygen. Barry had been told that getting the face mask onto the driver might be a problem. Doors are surprisingly heavy and this one would need to be held open. To help with this they'd given him two floatation bags and he'd practised tying them to sticks on the river bed and inflating them with the push of a button.

As it happened none of this was necessary. The panic-stricken driver pushed himself up and grabbed at the door frame. Barry, standing on the side of the van, braced himself against the door and slapped the second mask over the man's face before flushing the water out. It took a few seconds but the driver was soon gulping air and calming down.

They were still in that position, with Barry on top of the van and the driver still half inside when Norman arrived. He manoeuvred himself alongside the driver and give him an okay sign. The driver was now unsure if he was being attacked or rescued but the reassurance made him relax even more and Norman was able to pull the straps of the face mask over the back of his head and check the small air cylinder. Barry held the door open and Norman pulled the man out and then pushed him to the surface to join his partner.

On the quayside the guards were shouting frantically at each other. The leader had finally stopped the trigger-happy suits from wasting more ammunition. He was also fearful they'd attract the unwelcome attention of the authorities, if they hadn't already. He looked around to see what else they could do.

Across the way was another dirigible boat bobbing in the water, but it would take too long for the suits to run and commandeer. They would have to run right around the outside of the dock for several hundred metres. To his left, about a hundred and fifty metres away and tied up along the adjacent quay was another, smaller, heavy-duty rubber boat. A RIB, with an outboard motor. He pointed at it and yelled. Three of the guards, including Mr Trigger-Happy, saw the indicated boat and set off for it.

When the guard of the van had first bobbed to the surface the leader's first reaction was to reach for his own gun despite the orders he'd just given. Caution and experience made him pause. The man waved and doggy paddled inexpertly with one hand, the other still holding the mask to his face. Only when he reached the quayside and found a concrete ledge to grab did he take it off and yell to the guard.

Soon after that, the driver bobbed to the surface.

Under the water Colin, Barry and Norman were already using a welding torch to cut away the hinges of the back doors of the van. The torch was surprisingly quick, cutting through the metal like butter and Colin had to do a quick sidestep to avoid the falling metal. Another quick cutting motion and the locking shaft was cut on the right door which fell open. Norman was able to get inside and place straps around the safe. This heavy metal box, only about two feet on each side, now lay on its right side. They were lucky. Adrian had thought it possible it was bolted to the floor, but it wasn't – not for the short journey from the airport to Docklands.

It was easy enough for Norman to wrap the nylon straps around it. Once he gave the okay sign Barry pulled on the ropes and it moved. That was enough.

Barry then gave the okay sign to Norman who broke and released green flares. They bobbed to the surface and started to burn giving off a dense green smoke.

Meanwhile, topside, four other guards from the Range Rover and the two from the remaining van appeared at the leader's side and looked helplessly down into the river.

By now the three suits running for the boat had arrived and they jumped in. One made for the engine while another took the steering wheel at the front. He pressed the engine start button and it immediately roared to life. The third man cast off the boat and it left the quayside turning toward the green smoke that was conveniently signalling the location of the sunken van. Grinning in anticipation Mr Trigger-Happy reloaded his Glock while the other took off his jacket and shoes in anticipation of getting wet.

But the boat lurched, throwing the men forward. The engine died just before it cleared the quayside and got to the open water. The driver frantically punched at the start button and the would-be swimmer grabbed at the engine to see what was wrong. Unknown to the crew, the boat had been tethered from underneath to an anchor and all the fuel in the fuel line had been used up. The petrol tank was empty.

Mr Trigger-Happy screamed in frustration then yelled into the radio microphone in his jacket sleeve. The team leader stamped his feet and swore profusely. He yelled orders at the Range Rover four and they started off for the boat across the quay. It was then that Mam sat up and started the engine. Still dressed as a curvy Rastafarian woman, she opened up the throttle. The boat seemed to dig into the water and the wake from the engine splashed high in the air spraying the quayside behind. Underneath, behind a long line, she was towing the safe and the three men of the Gunnersbury Gang behind her.

Mam's boat kicked up a lot of water but moved slowly. The team leader yelled again into his sleeve mic. He redirected the Range Rover to drive out of the estate and get themselves onto Preston's Road Bridge, but he could tell he was already too late. Mam's boat started to pick up speed and was already approaching the open lock gates. They would not make it in time.

They would have to follow, or at least try, by car. Furthermore, the chances were that the boat would land on the far side of the river – in which case catching them would be impossible. The thought that this could be the end of his career did not help.

He called again to his men and they turned and started running back to the remaining Range Rover parked in the car park. Only now did the team leader, reluctantly, make the call to his superior.

When the four men got back to the black SUV they piled in and strapped themselves up. Even before the four doors were closed the vehicle was moving – but not far. After a few feet the driver realised it didn't feel right. He jumped out. The tyres had been slashed. Furthermore, there was a distinct and growing smell of petrol from a ruptured black can that had been placed under a rear tyre.

Fearing a bomb, all four left the vehicle with great speed and backed away some fifty yards waiting for the bang. After a few minutes, when nothing happened, the driver cautiously approached the vehicle and peered at the can. Apart from the petrol there seemed to be nothing else there.

The three guards scanned the area looking for the perpetrator. They figured there was a chance that the attackers were amateurs and were still watching the car. The men were under orders not to openly display their weapons as that might cause a diplomatic incident. Nevertheless, they kept their hands in their jackets making it clear they were in *no* mood to be diplomatic.

The driver lay on the ground and examined the car's underside. There was a small box with a discreet flashing red LED, just a few centimetres on each side. This wasn't Hollywood, so what kind of idiot advertises a bomb by putting a flashing light on it? He spoke into his sleeve mic to the team leader. Was the remaining van in the car park also booby trapped?

He reached for the device then stopped short. What looked like a wire, or piece of string, went from the 'bomb' to the floor pan. Was this a double bluff? If he grabbed the bomb and pulled, would the string trigger the detonator? Then again, why was it all so obvious?

He gave up and called out to a colleague, an ex-military type who knew about IEDs, and he retired to a safe distance.

All this faffing about was costing them precious time. Two of the guards started running for the bridge on their own initiative, even knowing they'd be too late. Better to do something than stand and watch the criminals get away with their precious cargo.

The experienced IED man lay on the ground beside the Range Rover and looked at the device. They could call the police and ask for the Bomb Squad, but they would have lost everything by the time they arrived. Besides, the ensuing questioning and examination of CCTV would create a situation that would be difficult to explain. They'd rather not disclose the nature of their business, and especially the fact that the guards were illegally armed.

The man under the Range Rover cautiously felt the string. It was slack, and a gentle tug pulled it free from the floor pan. Carefully he felt round the small box. It wasn't large enough to blow up the vehicle, but if it did contain explosive it would be enough to blow his hand off. The box was stuck on with a pink sticky substance that smelt strongly of strawberry. He hadn't come across that one before. Was it a contact poison? He hesitated. Did the box have a motion detector in it? He reached into his jacket and extracted a small hand mirror, a metal one usually used for seeing around corners in a firefight. His smartphone provided torchlight.

The team leader had run to the car park and now looked at the man under the car. The gang had already got away with the safe; he would need the Range Rover ready as quickly as possible. He ordered another man to check under the other van's body to see if there was a bomb there too.

Caffee had been watching them from afar via the reflection in an office window. As soon as she saw the man crawl under the Range Rover she walked away, unable to stop grinning. It was amazing how dangerous a small black box with a flashing LED appeared to be.

What she didn't know was that the man was not so much worried about the bomb. He was more terrified of the pink sticky substance holding it on.

32
Getaway

Meanwhile, Helen had not been dawdling. She had ripped off her trouser suit before dressing in a more practical denim top, jeans and boots. She pulled on a red wig and took a little time to ensure that it fitted okay using a mirror gaffer taped to the side of the van. After the last job, and her experience with the frizz, she had reluctantly agreed to cut it short to facilitate a wig. Part of her hated the idea of losing her femininity. Caffee had always been one step ahead of her of course, and it did make sense. So now her hair was a similar short, pixie hairstyle.

However, a few nights previously she'd seen a film where a bewigged woman had assassinated a rather handsome hunk. So, in another way, she rather fancied the new image. It also had the benefit of distancing her from her past.

Bolted into the centre of the van's floor was a high-powered winch. She released the brake and pulled the cable out of the back door and tossed it over the wall by the river. She didn't have to wait long before she could hear Mam's boat labouring towards her across the water. It would soon be clear of the lock and rounding the corner into view.

She returned to the van, gathered up the rope ladders and staggered to the wall, dropping them over the top too. As the boat rounded the corner, she could see Mam waving wildly, bobble hat and woolly scarf still in place. She was grinning so much her white teeth stood out against the dark makeup and her bobble was frantically bobbling in the wind like a Tesco bag trapped on the tailfin of a Jumbo jet.

Helen thought she looked more like a clown than a Rastafarian, but at least it would make identification of the driver that little bit more difficult.

Helen manhandled a metal 'A' frame under the winch rope as Mam passed her, sidling toward the wharf at an angle. When Mam reached what she thought was the right distance she looked back and waved. Helen again gave her the thumbs up and Mam untied the tow rope and attached it to a lifebelt. She propped a mannequin dressed as Mam behind the wheel (stuffed with several pillows – much to Mam's annoyance) and placed her bobble hat on top with a gentle pat on the head. She removed her multi-coloured jacket, set the throttle to one-third and then threw the lifebelt into the water, closely following it herself with doggy-style splash.

In front of Helen three heads bobbed to the surface and gave her an okay sign. She skipped with joy. Barry and Colin headed for the rope ladders and climbed up the wall. Norman swam towards Mam. As they reached the top they stopped and waited; Helen offered them each a mug of warm soup from a pre-prepared flask. The pair looked cold and drained as they removed their hoods and passed them to Helen before taking the mugs.

"How did it go?" Pleased that everyone was accounted for, Helen was still concerned that something as complicated as this was unlikely to have gone without some sort of hitch.

"Like a fucking dream," croaked Colin, shivering

with the cold and grasping the mug tightly for all the heat he could extract from it. "Fucking cold though. Bloody loud under that boat too. It was weird being dragged along like that." He shivered.

Helen looked at Barry.

"I did not see any fishes," he said, disappointed and shaking with cold. "Do we wait for Mam now?"

"Yes, Barry, then you get out and get dry."

"Oh good. I am cold." He sipped at his soup.

When Mam reached the bottom of the ladder all three helped her up and over the wall before jumping off it and shedding their wetsuits. Mam waited, her own soup in hand, while they were dried and dressed inside the van before taking her turn.

Helen went back to the wall and checked on the dirigible as it chugged away downstream. The tide had just turned and the boat was starting to pick up a little more speed as it was swept away. With any luck it would end up in Silvertown amongst the barges.

She returned to the road and checked up and down. No one was there. She called Caffee.

"'ello," she called out in her best French accent.

"'Ooze this?"

"It is Aye."

"Oo?"

"Ze pooppees are dryin' and ze moos is een ze trap."

"Wot?"

Helen sighed and repeated the message.

"Oh, okay – I geddit. Sorry, I forgot. Is it all okay,

then?"

"All eez as eet should be."

"Fanks, Erfah' Kit."

"Mata. I am Mata Hari!"

"Oh, yeh. Sorry, Helen."

"That's okay, Caff. 'ow eez eet at your end?"

"Fucking aced it! The wankers... I mean, the piglets are squealing."

"Yay!" Helen punched the air and nearly dropped the mobile. "Zee you zoon."

"Yup. Catchya on the flipper."

All good so far, she thought. Amazing.

The men were now slowly hoisting the safe out of the river. Colin sat on the wall. Just before it broke the surface below them and took a blanket with a slit cut in one side. He slid it onto the rope and let it slide down to the safe. As a disguise it wasn't actually necessary as the safe had dug into the mud and streaks of muck stuck all over it.

They slowly hoisted it up into the air. As it arrived at the top Barry reached up with a pole and supported it. It was then a matter of manhandling the package into the back of the van and packing up.

A tug chugged by, but the crew gave the gang only a cursory glance. To them it simply looked like landlubbers recovering something from the mud.

From Blue Bridge two of the guards had jumped down onto the riverside and ran to the end. From there they watched the dirigible being driven, rather stiffly, by the Rastafarian far away into the distance. They made a call for further instructions.

"I hope no one is watching," said Mam.

"The city only watches those whom it wants to watch," quoted Norman as he rubbed himself dry.

Colin put on a pair of glasses and a wig then jumped in the driver seat before edging the van back into the narrow Coldharbour lane.

"Keep low and hide your faces, we are being filmed."

Mam was shocked. "They *are* watching? Are they after us already?"

"Nah! Not yet. If they go to the police, which they might not, they'll have to work through a lot of video footage and trace a lot of vehicles before they realise this one's got false plates. There's probably a few others around too, anyway. We're in the clear... pretty much. Just don't make it easy for 'em though, okay?"

Mam's elation at the boat ride faded as she started to worry about DNA again. She cuddled up to Barry, more for her own comfort than to help warm him up – which he needed anyway.

The back of the van was loud, crowded and uncomfortable with the equipment, four people, wet wetsuits and other equipment stacked at the back. There was a pungent smell coming from the mud on the safe. Mam had tried cleaning it with tissues but there was still a pool of smelly murky water in the back.

The safe in the centre was braced between their feet and all around were the inevitable mismatched pillows and cushions which Mam had thoughtfully provided and for which they were all very thankful.

They had to keep the cushions away from the river mud. It was a strain to talk over the sound of the engine through the thin metals walls so they stayed quiet.

As the van drove north, stopping and starting at the traffic lights, Helen moved along the floor dragging some pillows and then snuggled up to Norman. For a moment he felt awkward, embarrassed, even wary, but she seemed pretty relaxed and she even lifted his arm and put it around her shoulder. For Norman it was a welcome surprise. He thought for a moment about the rumours of her past. Then he remembered that he had one of his own. What would she think of *his* past? Would the girl be just as judgemental of him as he of her?

But in the end, what did it really matter? Two people making contact in their short lives, sharing an experience, an adventure, however briefly and taking comfort in each other's presence. The future could hold anything, including more tragedy. He held her close. In the back of his mind he wondered, was he becoming a father figure to her? Did she have a father? An older brother, perhaps? He would be content with that. He didn't realise it, not consciously, but he kissed the top of her head.

Mam watched, but said nothing. Her face didn't change expression, but inwardly, she smiled.

Their first stop was to be outside London in a quiet country lane where they'd ditch the number plates, pull the fake stickers off the van's side panels, ditch the batteries to the phones and the SIM cards, and Norman would then drive them back to Epping. Colin remained in the front, not eager to sit amongst the wet gear in the back.

Once in Epping, they parked in a side street and waited for Caffee who had taken the Central Line from London. They weren't kept waiting too long before she phoned and they agreed to pick her up at the end of Station Road.

When she arrived, she handed Colin a copy of her checklist then jumped in the back, made a sarcastic comment about the pong, and then embraced Helen. As they drove up through Epping High Street and on towards Harlow Colin glanced back. He couldn't help notice how the girls managed to chat despite all the noise.

Helen caught his glance and they swapped smiles.

As the van left Epping, Colin's mind wandered. He considered the possibility of acquiring the odd piece of jewellery from the safe. A bonus, he thought dryly. A single piece might be worth hundreds, if not thousands of pounds. It seemed funny to him that one small piece of shaped metal could be worth a second-hand car. Or even two or three. On the other hand, he didn't fancy being hunted by those monochrome goons with guns, or losing a nostril to one of Caffee's nail files.

And he didn't want to let Helen down.

He went back to reading the checklist and checking the details of the plan. Later he broke the silence and discussed the next few phases with Norman. They hadn't had the time to rehearse and discuss this part of the plan, unlike the Esher job where everything had been talked through several times beforehand.

Norman was impressed, but said nothing. This

layabout youth sitting beside him was now talking and thinking ahead like a pro. The young man was a little more mature now that he had been on, what would now be, his second 'op'.

The next phase was the securing of the van in Harlow. The safe would be deposited in the warehouse. The phase immediately after that was the retrieval of Adrian, but that part wasn't planned at all and was awfully vague.

As they drove through Harlow Colin glanced back at Helen again, but this time she didn't notice. She was still chatting to Caffee. He shook his head, what on earth could they find to talk about so much?

Then he recalled the image of that sun-soaked beach, coconut trees, her in a white bikini clutching at his muscular arm and looking up at him. As his imagination worked at shrinking the size of her bikini, he felt the need to cross his legs.

33
Retrieving Adrian

The gang entered the hospital through the main doors and shuffled up to the receptionist's window. Several visitors, already registered with the staff, were seated in the waiting area. Only one person was ahead of them in the queue at the window and it didn't take long for them to obtain a number.

"Hiya." Caffee, champing hard on her aromatic strawberry gum, smiled her most winning smile at the receptionist.

The woman looked up from her computer screen and frowned. In that split second bolts of distrust and visceral hatred flashed invisibly in the air. Had a gnat mindlessly buzzed between the two it would have exploded. The phrase 'Shields up, Mr Spock,' crossed Colin's mind. Nevertheless, Caffee's broad grin and the rhythm of her champing remained steely constant.

"How can I help you?" from between clenched teeth.

"We're looking for 'im." Caffee thrust a picture of Adrian under the woman's nose. The woman reeled back from the proffered photo, her eyes widening but never leaving Caffee's, before she took the photo between the tips of her fingers and then peered at it from arms length.

"What is his name?"

"He doesn't know." Caffee remembered that he had agreed not to reveal his identity.

"Excuse me?"

"Granted. Could happen to anyone."

"Pardon?"

"We didn't hear a thing, gel. Don't be embarrassed, even the Queen did it – so I've been told."

"Sorry... Did what?"

"Fart."

"I didn't... I meant... *Really*!"

One nil, thought Caffee. Her grin broadened and the champing sped up a little.

"Doesn't matter. Dew you know where we can retrieve this loveable little scamp?"

There was a short frigid pause as the battle lines were redrawn. Ms Jobsworth Blue-Hair (as Caffee later christened her) did a tactical withdrawal and took refuge behind her defensive wall of red tape.

"I *need* to know his name for the release form."

"But you don't coz he don't. If you called his name, he won't come running out like a pet dog, but he might go running round and round in squercles like a demented dachshund on speed – unless you left a window open. Then you'd have a real problem. He came in early this morning and we'd like to take him home, now. Please. Thank you."

"I'm sorry, young lady, I need to know his name, and yours. I also need to know your address and you must provide me with proof of your relationship, your identity, and your occupancy. It is a legal requirement. We cannot just release people to anyone, don't you know?"

"Oh good. You do have him, then. We're getting

somewhere."

Two nil.

Her eyes narrowed. "That is not what I said, young lady! This is not a lost property office. You cannot just come in here and claim a patient because you happen to have a picture of them. We have a duty of care to perform, so I must ask you for more information." She shuffled a few papers, realised there was no appropriate form at hand and grabbed a blank notepad and pen. "Now then. What is your relationship with this man?"

"Wotchya wonna know that for?"

"I need to know."

"Well... it's personal, like." Caffee shuffled awkwardly on her feet. "We ain't fuckin' or anything. It ain't like that. I did fink about it once, probably coz I was horny and he was the only dick available... save for this old coot standing behind me but as you can see this one's all grey and wrinkly. Besides, he ain't my type really – you know, what with his dippy ways 'n all. Personally, I like a more beefy bod, like a builder or a fireman. One with visible muscles. I like a bit o' meat on my men. Jason Statham would do nicely. Yeh? But wot *he* wants is..."

"That is *not* what I meant. I *meant*, how are you two *related*?"

"Oh... Oh, yeh... Well... We're his family."

The woman blinked. "I see, and how are you *related* exactly?"

"He ain't got any *related* family exactly – except us. Not that we know of, anyway. Just let us see him and he'll confirm that all is kosher and that we're his family."

"I cannot do that, young lady. Not without proper authorisation. I need to know who you are and what relationship you are to him before I can pass on your request to the appropriate authority."

It had been a long day. Caffee lost it.

"Fuckin' 'ell! You're holding him prisoner, aintchya! Let him go!"

She went to reach through the window aiming at the woman's throat but at this point Mam stepped in and pulled her back. "Please, please. You will have to excuse the young lady, here. She is *so* upset. They are very close, you know?"

But the woman's temper was up. "Are *you* with this little tramp?" and pointed to Caffee with her black ballpoint pen.

Caffee's mouth dropped open.

"Yes... Well... No. She is *not* a tramp. We are *not* tramps! We all live in a house. We have a *real* house to live in."

"Really? Then keep this one under control. I've called for security and they're on their way. Any more lip from her, or you, and I'll call the police."

"But lady, we are only here to collect a member of our family..."

"Don't you 'But lady' with me. And anyway, how am I to believe that a black woman like you is supposed to be related to this young man? I need documentation."

It really *had* been a long day. Mam's normally placid temperament evaporated in that instant, not so much because of what the woman said, but more because of the attitude.

"Black? BLACK? How DARE you! I am *NOT* black!" She grabbed the pen from between the startled woman's fingers and held it to her arm. "Am I the same colour as this pen? No! I am *not*. I am *NOT* black. I am brown. Dark brown. A darker shade of the same colour as you." She threw the pen at the wall behind the receptionist and wagged a finger in her face. "And don't you *dare* tell me you're a *white* woman. Paper is white. Under that muck you paste on your face you are simply a paler version of me!"

The receptionist's expression could now be described as very pale, possibly even white, visible even through her thick makeup.

Three nil. Own goal. Caffee was enjoying this. Robust, buxom, well-built Mam had compared herself to the skinny weasel behind the desk. This could be good. She started champing at her chewing gum again but she knew that if she kept her grin this wide her jaw would soon start to ache.

"I did not mean... I did not say... What I meant was... I cannot simply release anyone under our care without the correct authorisation."

"And the colour of my skin is important for this, is it? Why is my colour so important before I can see a member of my *own* family? Whereabouts on the forms does it ask you for my colour?"

"Madam, you must admit that..."

"Madam? You are calling me a *madam*, now?"

Two beefy-looking security guards in black uniforms arrived.

"Everything all right, Pauline?"

Uh, oh. Enemy reinforcements. Caffee frowned and stepped back to watch the battle unfold.

Unconsciously, her left hand started to finger one of her plastic bangles on her wrist. Should a battle ensue, a broken plastic bangle could leave a permanent scar, and with a little skill, even pop an eyeball. Caffee had plenty of practice with broken plastic bangles.

Security! The look of relief on the receptionist's face was clear – until Norman interjected. "Apparently, this receptionist – Pauline, is it? – just insulted this lady here."

"I did not!" she almost screamed.

"I heard you," piped up Helen. "You called her a black tramp, and a madam."

"I... What? I did not... But she is bla... *she's* the tra... What I *meant* was... Oh, dear..."

"Apparently, black women are tramps and whores and are therefore not allowed to see members of their own family," offered Norman, straight-faced and trying his hardest to look like a witness just trying to be helpful.

The receptionist stood and, hands shaking with frustration, pointed through the window at Norman. He looked back at her with his most innocent expression. She went to say something, thought better of it, and beckoned one of the security guards away from the desk for a private discussion in a back room.

Four nil. Our own reinforcements to the rescue! Enemy in retreat.

Caffee scanned the waiting room and called out to everyone. "We've got to stand up to these racist bigots, yeh?"

Most had not been paying attention to the

dialogue until Mam's outburst. They nodded in agreement. Someone murmured, "Disgraceful". Caffee was happy. She had just recruited a second line of reserves and coloured any witnesses' opinion of the event.

"Are you people all together?" the remaining security guard enquired.

"I am but a casual witness as to what appears to be a gross injustice," boomed Norman.

Helen shook her head and stepped behind Barry, who hadn't a clue as to what was happening.

"Please, wait here." The remaining security guard stepped back, took his hand radio from his belt and spoke quietly into it.

Caffee sidled up to Norman, "Fanks."

"What good is a smooth tongue without sharp teeth?" he whispered, feeling somewhat smug. "But we should be wary of the law. They have long arms and incisive questions."

Caffee glanced about. "Where's Colin?"

No one had noticed the scruff's disappearance.

Colin entered the short corridor that led to Milton Ward – this was the ward they reckoned Adrian would be sent to first. He tried his best to make his furtive glances appear casual. He sorely missed the protection of his hoodie but putting it up here would only make matters worse. Instead, he held a handkerchief to his face. This would obscure any direct view of his face. He passed the office and the toilets and stopped outside an ante-room and listened at the door.

"So where do you live?" asked a young female voice.

Colin recognised the voice of the male. "In my hard head of bony bone, but with stereo soul windows to see I see you see I see. See? I got stereo ears too, to hear I hear here and here two too. They're just below my hairy hair although hair is not hairy unless its frizzy – whizzy, wheee! Helen says her hair is hairy frizzy at the ends which is the first bit born, you know? Not like an owl's though, mine are the same height. Look, see? They all lay sometimes on a mattress, fluffy fluff, in a box of hard bricks, knocky knock, in a lot of boxes of bricks, losty lost, in a place where we all speak and listen but few talk and hear but all in the same language, chatty chat. My ears had breakfast once. Coldy cold, brrrrrr. Naughty Caffee. I can feel all parts too, but it's not said to be stereo but it is, I think. Hot, warm, cold, soft, sharp. Ouchy ouch. I can close my eyes and watch the pictures I want. In my boney dome of bone all alone. That's where I live."

Bingo! First time.

"I see... You lost your box of bricks, did you?"

"Yessy yes, but we're going to lose it again. Oh, no! But we're going to get another. Oh, yes! We have plans, I hope they'll work, and if the tan man in tan can, we can. Will he? Should we trust or will he bust? Busty Mam makes softy soft cakes, not like Margaret, her cakes could make bricks to make boxes to live in too. I tried to nibble but my teeth hurty, ouchy ouch. Mam thinks her rock cake is made with real granite. Caffee thinks she made it from real grans."

"I see... Who is Margaret? Is she your mother?
292

Sister, perhaps?"

Colin sniggered to himself. The thought of the Scottish battleship steaming into the room and laying waste to the poor nurse rather appealed to him. But he needed a plan, so he thought for a moment.

Adrian held his head in both hands and looked down at the floor. "Mummy, mummy? No, no, no. Mummy gone. Mummy mum, now. Daddy mum, too. I don't know. I want my mummy. She's not gone, perhaps, perhaps Daddy too, but in my memory all gone. All goney gone. I don't know if they don't know. All red acted and redacted. All my past has gone very fast and I can't seem to see behind the waking and the shaking of the taking. Naughty doctors, naughty, naughty, and faulty. Norman to the rescue! He grabby grabbed and they talky talked and shouted. They got it wrong and I got it long, needles pricky prick and hurty hurt under the white lights. Lights hurt world spinny spins but they pay me now. Not right. Not right."

"I see. So, Margaret is *not* your mother?"

Colin put away his handkerchief, knocked on the door and poked his head round. "Hello. I see you've found him."

The nurse looked up. "Hello. Who are you?"

"My name's Colin – I'm from social. That's Adrian. He's a little weird, isn't he?"

"Yes. Yes, I've been trying to communicate with him." She glanced at the young man who was already distracted with a magazine. She tried whispering, "He's not very coherent, is he?"

"No. I'm here to pick him up and return him to...

uhm... Norman House. The paperwork is being done at reception. Do you mind if I join you?"

"No. No. Come on in. Do you understand him? What do you know about him?"

"Head case. He's a complete head case. A nutter. Omelette froth."

"You mean head trauma?"

"Yeh. That's it."

"What's 'omelette froth'?"

Colin shrugged. "I don't know. Latin, I think. Ask a doctor."

She grinned. "So, his name is Adrian?"

"Yeh. Hiya Ade. Recognise me?"

"Hi Colin. 'lo Colin. High, low. Up and down. Colin is in." He grinned, looked at the ceiling and poked his tongue back into his mouth.

"He knows you."

"Yeh. Yeh. We go way back."

"I've never heard of Norman House. Where is that? And where is your ID badge?"

"Oh, um, down the road a bit. Epping. It's in Epping. Other side, like. I like your shoes."

She glanced at her scuffed working shoes and frowned.

"Want some trainers? I know where I can get some. Cheap, like."

She stiffened. "Would you mind coming with me to reception. We can sort this out there." She stood, placing a hand on Adrian's shoulder. "You stay right here. Don't move. Look at the magazines. I'll look for some bricks for you, alright?"

"Bricks!" he replied. "Lots here. All around. Big box of bricks this. Biggy big. Always in brick boxes we are. Boxes with wrecked angles. Boring without tunnels."

"I'll see what I can do." She patted him on his head and together she and Colin left the room and walked down to the ward's reception desk. Another nurse appeared carrying some sheets. The two acknowledged each other.

Colin was thinking furiously. His plan, which frankly wasn't even half-baked, was already going awry. How was he going to get Adrian out?

"Tell me more about Adrian."

"Not much to say really. I'm not a doctor or anything like that." A touch of honesty should win her over, he thought. Wrongly.

"I gathered that. So, you work at Norman House? What as? Can I see your identification? Don't you have a badge? They should have given you one."

Fuck! Colin fumbled in his pocket and his wallet fell out. He bent over to retrieve it and struck his head on the wooden reception desk with a loud whack. He had made sure it was the desk because, from bitter experience, he knew that this ruse didn't work half as well if he struck his head against a brick wall.

"Ow! Ow, ow, ow, ow." He held his head and squeezed his eyes shut. In fact, it did hurt, but a little self-inflicted pain had often got him out of a jam.

She knelt down. "Are you alright? Are you hurt?"

"Owwwww..." Colin gathered his wallet and made a point of stumbling to the floor. "Owwww. I need the bathroom. Where's the bathroom?" He opened his, now watery, eyes.

"Let me take a look."

Fucking nurses, always trying to care for the injured. "No, no. It's alright. Just show me the bathroom."

"Down here. There's a toilet just here." She helped him up and led him towards the toilet.

Out of the corner of his eye Colin noticed Adrian leave the ante room, do a pirouette and head away into the ward toward the beds.

"Thanks," he grumbled. "You check with reception. They'll tell you about me."

He staggered into the bathroom, ran the tap then cautiously peered out the door. The nurse had returned to the office desk and was dialling the phone.

Colin sneaked out the bathroom and followed Adrian into the ward proper. At the far end was another door leading to a staircase, but Adrian was nowhere to be seen. He ran to the doors, pushed through them and listened. Did he go up or down? He glanced behind and saw the nurse. She'd put the phone down and was striding after him. She must have seen him enter the ward.

Going up was not an option. Too many times he'd escaped from awkward situations by instinctively running upstairs – only to discover that his assailants were nearly always fitter than him and that the top only ever led to a dead end.

He ran down, jumping several steps at a time confident the nurse would not be as quick. A couple of floors down he stopped and waited, listening for the sounds of pursuit. Clearly Adrian hadn't gone down the stairs, the idiot *must* have gone up.

The nurse got to the top of the stairs in time to hear the echoes of Colin's rapid descent. She turned and ran back to the far end of the ward to check on Adrian. When she realised he wasn't there, she ran back to the desk to call security.

Adrian's actual route was a little more 'pirouetty' – if there is such a word. He managed to follow the wall into the ward proper, where the beds were. He promptly turned left and reached the far end of a group of six beds. He grabbed a curtain and spun round pulling it around him, surprising the occupant of the bed to which the curtain belonged. It was then that Colin had strode past.

Adrian stopped, thought for a while and then spun in the other direction but overdid it and managed to wrap himself in the curtain in the other direction. At this point the nurse ran past. The man in the bed offered to help but Adrian managed to untangle himself, thanked the ceiling, considered using the window as an exit and then wandered off.

At the centre of the ward, he spun around again and saw the doors at the far end. He struck out and managed to reach them, pirouetting only twice en route and, remarkably, not knocking anything over.

Colin had cautiously re-climbed the staircase again, listening for any pursuit. When he reached the doors to the ward, he was greeted by Adrian waving at him through the small window. Colin snatched the door open, grabbed Adrian by the scruff of the neck and started downstairs.

Colin flipped open his mobile and speed-dialled Norman.

Meanwhile, at reception the first security guard emerged from the back room with the receptionist.

"Can I take your names?" at which point his radio bleeped and he listened to a dispatcher's nasal voice. He grunted an answer and then called to his partner.

"Hey Rod, look after this lot, will you? Take their details. I'll send for backup. I'm needed up in Milton." He turned to Pauline, "Sorry, love. Must dash. Hold the fort here and I'll be back as soon as I can."

He strode off towards the staircase and Pauline's face fell. The other guard, clearly a junior, looked a little nonplussed but stepped up to take over. Norman excused himself, broke away from the group to speak to Colin on the phone.

"Where are you?"

"I got him. We got to leg it. Where are you?"

Caffee decided to muddle the situation at reception. "I fink we got off to a wrong start, don't you?"

The security guard glanced at Pauline questioningly. She gave a short nod, but her expression could still terrify a Doberman at fifty yards. It was clear the woman was now trying to recall where she could discreetly obtain a hammer, duct tape, and spade.

"I fink we misunderstood what the people's 'ealth service is really about."

Emboldened by the apparent collapse of Caffee's aggressive stance, her expression softened ever so slightly and she pounced at the chance to retake control.

"I need to know *who* you are and what relationship you have with our patient before I can pass on your request to the appropriate authority. However, I think we can..."

"See? it's all about the fuckin' paperwork and not about the fuckin' people!"

The guard quickly stepped between the two. "Now, now. Let's calm down, shall we? We're not here to make things difficult for anyone."

Norman whispered into Barry's ear then grabbed Helen by the arm and nodded towards the main door. A wink and a smile made it clear they should depart. And quickly.

The guard noticed them leaving. "Where are they going?"

"Their father called. I think they're going to meet him."

The guard frowned. Something felt wrong.

Caffee continued. "In order to see my bruv you need to see some proof of identity. Is that it?"

"I need to know who you are and what your relationship is with our patient before..."

"Yeh, yeh, yeh. I got that." She faced Mam. "'ere, Mam, what proof of my identity do you 'ave in your bag at the mo'? Coz I got none."

"I... I don't know."

"Take a look inside and see." She winked.

Mam slowly walked across to a table unsure of Caffee's plan and started rummaging around inside her bag, knowing full well there was nothing, apart from fingerprints and copious DNA, to identify her, let alone Caffee.

"I *was* going to suggest that, if you are happy to be accompanied by Rod here, we can arrange for you to see... the patient."

Rod nodded. It seemed a good compromise, but he was sure that security guards had other, more important jobs to do than escorting visitors to patients.

Mam withdrew a beaded necklace, a mobile phone, and a hairbrush and placed them on the table.

"Let's see wot Mam's got."

Rod had to venture the question. "Is she your... are you related to the... this lady?"

Mam extracted a pen, bracelet, brush, a pocket diary, large comb, a new pack of tissues and several used ones.

Caffee grinned. "You can see the family resemblance, yeh?"

Rod shook his head. "No. Not really."

Mam's burrowing deeper in her bag revealed a box of plasters, another pen, a small box of safety pins, a toothbrush, a nearly empty toilet roll, toothpaste, several coins and a purse.

Mam stopped and looked at Caffee. "Do I have to empty *all* my bag onto the table, girl?"

"No, Mam. Put it all back." Caffee turned to Rod. "I tell you what. Me and Mam'll get our identity papers for Miss Gestapo here, and we'll return all kosher-like to retrieve me bruvver. Is that okay?"

She winked but not waiting for an answer she

bustled Mam away towards the door.

She called back over her shoulder, "See you later, hunky!"

Rod stuck his chest out and turned to Pauline. "Well, that seems settled then, doesn't it?"

"No! We *still* don't know who they are or who that young man is." She returned to the desk to see to the growing queue of new arrivals. A beeper beeped. A doctor was ready to see someone. Now she would have to call for assistance.

She sat down, took a breath, then snatched at the phone.

34
Prey Got Away

Terry had almost given up. He had placed the cameras in a few strategic places along the street and it had enabled him to locate the house with the mini-skirted girl and his prize, the brunette in the anorak.

And now he had a good idea of what the other occupants of the house looked like.

Terry had been working on various ways to kidnap the brunette when they loaded up a truck and disappeared overnight. It was a disaster. Were they onto him? He doubted it but he needed to be sure.

He walked up and down the street a few times hoping to get an indication of occupancy but there was nothing. Later, on the Sunday evening, he took his gun and broke in through the back door, but the property was empty. He searched for a while but found no clues as to where they'd gone. He even checked the rubbish bins looking for ticket stubs, foreign travel brochures or any other clues but again, there was nothing.

There was an old, used pregnancy test kit at the bottom of one of the bin bags. So, he concluded, somebody *was* bonking someone and he idly wondered if they were all at it. He started imagining who did what with whom and how often before he remembered where he was and what he was supposed to be doing.

Once he had the girl, she'd be at his mercy, he realised. Maybe he could have some fun before he handed her over? This thought made him even more determined to get the bitch. It wasn't often an opportunity like this came along.

Terry left just as quietly as he had arrived. He didn't want to report that he'd lost her, but there seemed no other option, at least for the moment. It didn't look like they were coming back.

"I don't think it's a foreign gang. They're a local group from down here. There's three women and four men." Terry was talking on a disposable phone to his employer.

"Only four? Doesn't really make a difference, does it. What else you got?"

"They packed up and left all of a sudden. I figured they changed house."

"You lost them?"

"I got their van's number and the number of a truck they used. Get a trace on these for me, would you?" He read out the registration numbers. "I'm going to hang around a day or two and see if they come back."

"Okay, but I want that bitch and the bastards that murdered John. And I want her NOW! You understand? Like yesterday. I ain't paying for you to have a jolly in London. You understand me? When I get you the trace on those vehicles, you pick that bitch up so I can question her. Okay?"

"Okay. Straightaway. As soon as I find them. You have my word."

35
The Date

Adrian was keen to listen to the events of the day. No one realised this as he rarely made eye contact and tended to hover while the gang chatted amongst themselves. He didn't get the complete story, but he got lots of bits as they told and retold their exploits. However, this suited Adrian fine. He probably couldn't have coped with a single coherent story in any case.

The next morning, they took their time getting up and seeing to breakfast. In the background they all dreaded the upcoming encounter with Malik. Was he going to cheat on them? Would this be the end of the gang? Despite the success of the previous day's work, they were starting to feel tense. None of them trusted the smug man in Armani and his muscle-bound goons.

During breakfast Mam snapped at Barry several times. She didn't mean to and usually apologised after. Barry though, took Mam's comments without any fuss.

Helen was exceptionally bright and breezy.

Colin entered the living room with a plate of toast and a coffee. He kicked the door closed behind him but Caffee was too preoccupied to comment on that.

"Helen's perky," he observed.

"Yup. She's going to meet that fella later."

"What fella?"

"The artist."

"What artist?"

"She met some guy that works for the BBC. He wants to draw her, apparently."

"Oh." Colin's face fell. He put the toast and coffee down on the table and looked out the window. "Where's Norman?"

"Mister Busybody left earlier to get a tool or something. I dunno. He said he'll be back after lunch and for you to continue bolting the tyres to the frame."

Colin swore under his breath and stormed out the house, his toast and coffee untouched.

It was about four o'clock when Norman and Colin returned to the house. Colin had in fact been working at the warehouse when Norman returned from his trip and picked him up. The older man thought it would be a good idea if they all went out for a meal and maybe the cinema later.

Colin tried questioning Norman on where he'd been but he'd evaded the questions saying that it had been a necessary job. Colin wanted to push him further but, feeling a little down after the previous day's adrenalin highs and Helen's absence, he just let it go.

An hour later the six of them were in the living room finishing a cup of tea and discussing the best place to have holidays when Helen stormed through the front door. She threw her coat at the hall wall before stamping up the stairs.

Caffee called out after her. "You alright, gel?"

Helen paused halfway up the stairs as Caffee emerged from the front room.

She turned, her expression blank. "He stood me up," she hissed, then turned and resumed her stamping ascent, followed shortly after by the sound of a door slam.

Caffee thought for a moment then looked back at Norman.

"I don't fink Helen fancies the pictures tonight."

"Give it a short while and I shall have a quiet word with her."

"Yeh. Watch yer step, though. There's a kitchen knife in her room."

Norman nodded. He expected it.

Colin was distracted with the TV, concerned about Chelsea's performance during the last match, but also secretly pleased at Helen's disappointment.

36
The Handover

"Shush." Colin was listening on a mobile phone. "Helen says there are two big black cars, Range Rovers most likely, with black windows. One of them has a... what? A cute pink doggy on the dashboard? Fuck, Helen! Anyway, he's coming."

Helen, dressed as a nurse and pushing Adrian in a wheelchair, was casually walking along the road. Adrian was playing with a plastic spider.

In the warehouse everyone was at their stations. Mam sat nervously behind the safe in the middle of the floor, illuminated by the only spotlight in the depressing building. She shivered. She didn't like the cold or the smell of damp and stale oil. The entire place was gloomy, filthy, and also stank of new paint. There were shallow puddles of dirty water in the concrete floor. She wondered how people could ever work in such a place.

Caffee and Norman sat in chairs at opposite ends of an even darker place. There was no floor there. They were looking down on illuminated Mam about twenty feet below. Both gripped the arms of their chairs which were bolted to metal walls. Caffee wondered what would happen if she suddenly got the urge to pee and valiantly suppressed a giggle.

The two cars approached the entrance to the premises and slowed. The second vehicle stopped outside and two black-suited men jumped out and started to check the perimeter. Two remained inside but alert. The first vehicle slowly entered through the gate and then did a u-turn, ready for a quick getaway. Four men got out, three black suits and the man himself, Malik. This time he was dressed in a light blue designer suit.

There was a quick exchange of words and Malik, accompanied by one of his bodyguards, entered the warehouse carrying a briefcase.

In the centre sat Mam feeling both cold and a little sweaty. She withdrew a brightly coloured handkerchief, dabbed at her face and beckoned Malik toward her. He approached slowly, trying to scan the inside, but then the unopened safe caught his eye. His bodyguard remained by the door, squinting into the darkness, wary, with one hand ready to reach inside his jacket.

When Malik stood before the safe the spotlight snapped off and all went dark. There was a split second of silence before a rumbling crescendo and Caffee screaming "Wheeeeeeee…"

A loud 'barrumph' terminated the rumble. Dust and dirt flew into the air and a yellow light came on. Malik blinked. He was trapped inside a twenty-foot shipping container that had dropped from the ceiling. The bottom had been removed and the edges had been covered with old tyres to soften the landing. Through the dust, behind Mam, he saw Caffee who was sitting akimbo on a chair bolted to the far end of the box. Her bottom was on the edge of the seat and her legs had been thrown up and apart from the harsh landing. She was still giggling.

"Wow! Wot a fuckin' trip." She sat upright. "Ade is a fuckin hoot, I reckon. Hurts yer bum, though." She stood up, wobbled slightly and rubbed her derriere in the manner of a race-weary jockey. She coughed from the dust. "Sorry about the dramatics, Manic. We don't have guns you see, and we want to talk to you, proper like. One to one, sort of. Yeh?"

Malik coughed too, retrieved a handkerchief and dabbed at his eyes. "My men will not appreciate this."

"Tell 'em to stop worrying." Caffee pointed to a microphone. "They can hear everything going on, so you can call for help if you need to. Tell 'em to hold their horses."

"A metal container is not bulletproof. You understand?" he warned.

"No." Norman's quiet whisper, from millimetres behind his ear, made him visibly jump. "But bullets fired through sheet metal do not travel straight. There's a good chance they'll hit you. Especially the ricochets. Tell your men to stand down and wait. You are *not* in danger. You *will* be released."

"This box is for our protection. Not to fuck you over," stated Caffee.

Malik thought for a moment, grinned wryly and shook his head. He spoke some Russian loud and clear for his man outside.

A few seconds later the light in the container dimmed twice then came on a little brighter.

"Good," sighed Caffee. "Sorry 'bout your suit, Manic. It'll need dry cleanin' after this. We did water down most of the dust. You should have seen the rehearsals. Fuckin' 'ell! We were *all* covered in shit." She grinned cheekily. "Which is why we working classes wear cheap clothes. Dry cleaning is expensive for us plebs, yeh?" Hand on hip, she started champing on her chewing gum.

"Quite." Malik, a little angry at the dirt, went to brush at his Armani then thought better of it. He didn't want to rub anything corrosive into the expensive material.

"Luv yer cufflinks. Real gold, yeh?" She squinted closer to their captive. "An' a matchin' tie pin, too. Very posh."

Malik glanced at his shirtsleeves.

"No wonder you surround yerself with muscley morons. You're a self-painted target, aintchya? What with your Rolex, an' all." She shook her head. "But it must make all those social-climbing bints wet their pants at the sight of ya.

"Soooo... Enough of the social crap. Let's get down to business. This here is the safe with the stuff still inside. We didn't open it coz there didn't seem to be a point. Consider it a well-wrapped Christmas pressie. Besides, you've probably got the combination anyway. Yeh?"

Malik noted the scratch marks on various parts of the safe, but it seemed to be still intact. He nodded slowly. "I am pleased you have not opened the safe."

"Good. Like I said before, we did our bit. Now it's your turn to resipro... repriso... do likewise. Yeh?"

"Indeed." Malik placed the briefcase on top of the safe, released the catches and spun it around. Caffee opened it. Inside were several folders of paperwork. Some were thicker than others.

"What the fuck's this, Manic?"

"You have two options. I have the five hundred thousand pounds ready to give to you. I also have this package which, I am sure, we could all agree is a much better option. Far more so than just the money."

"What is it?"

"I have had seven new identities created, one for each of you. Birth certificates, driving licences, paper qualifications, job references and other documentation. If you agree, I shall arrange to obtain legitimate passports as well. Also, there are some notes on your new lives, just to make it all...

authentic. That alone is worth quite a few thousand."
He extracted a blue folder. "Here are the legal papers
to a property in Richmond, just off the green. A
lovely spot, close to the High Street and within
walking distance to the railway. Each of you has an
equal share in a trust that owns part of the property.
The property is worth well over three million. About
two-thirds of a million of it is shared amongst you.
The balance is owned by a company of mine."

"And why should we trust you or your lawyers?"

"Because I want to employ you. That last job was
cleverly done. If you took the cash, you'd get less
than one hundred thousand each. How would you
spend it?"

"Fuckin' monster mate! Wiv fousands of pounds
we'll manage. Yeh?"

"But not for long. And at the end of it all, once it
has been spent, you will have nothing. Do you think
you'll be able to buy a house of your own with that
money? Do you really think that a building society
would believe a homeless person suddenly inherits
enough to put a deposit on a house? And then they'll
start asking awkward questions. You will attract the
attention of the authorities. They always give
wealthy citizens the benefit of the doubt, but never
people with your backgrounds."

"Yeh. Plebes. What do you think, Norm?"

"If money be the food of life, play on. Give me
excess of it, until, surfeiting, the appetite may sicken
– but it would never die."

"Fuck, Norm! You're as helpful as Adrian at a
knicker sale! Mam?"

"It will be Christmas soon, girl. I would like a

home for Christmas. A proper home. Not a squat. Money is at the root of evil. Is this real now? A real house in Richmond? For us all?"

"Probably. Norm? And proper this time, yeh?"

"I am not sure. A new start, money in property, a place to stay. I am sorely tempted by the house in Richmond. Furthermore, there is a good theatre nearby. It will be Christmas soon, and colder. I am thinking a nice house... a fireplace..."

Malik touched the briefcase. "You must understand that Richmond is a very wealthy location. House prices are rising fast. Rising house prices could earn each of you well over ten thousand pounds per year – without any of you even having to lift a finger."

"Fuck! No wonder the rich in Richmond are so fucking... rich."

"Indeed. This is your chance to get on the property ladder to wealth. Real wealth, this time."

"What do you fink, Colin?"

A voice came through a speaker. "Cash."

Malik responded. "Think carefully, Colin. What sort of car would you afford with your share? A nice car, no doubt. But how long before the wheels are missing, or perhaps the car is stolen from you? In Richmond, if you work for me, you'll be able to park a Lamborghini on the street and not worry. You will also have your own room in a very exclusive property. Which would you prefer? Which is the more impressive to girls?"

In the silence one could sense the cogs of Colin's mind racing, and the cogs of his – only *slightly* less intelligent – penile organ racing faster still.

313

"Barry?"

"I would like a home." Barry's deep voice was unmistakable through the speaker.

Caffee nodded. "Helen?"

Colin spoke on the phone to Helen who was still making her way back to the warehouse. "She says to go with what everyone else wants. But a real home sounds nice."

"I'll speak for Ade otherwise we'll be here all night. If we go for this house in Richmond, will we be able to sell it?"

"Yes. You can sell at any time. Spring is the best time to sell. If you sold straight away, you'd probably achieve just under two hundred thousand per share, but then of course, you would have nowhere to stay and you may well have to account for the money."

"How many bedrooms has it got?"

"It has six bedrooms. Two en-suite and an additional two bathrooms. It has a small swimming pool and several reception rooms. We could adapt a spare room as another bedroom."

"Fuck. It sounds like a bleeding hotel. Are you serious? Seriously?"

"I like sweets," offered Barry.

"Lord be praised," whispered Mam.

"Swimming pool?" enquired Norm.

"Frankly, it's not that large. The pool, that is. The jacuzzi is broken but we can get that repaired. There's also a small games room as well. The house only has a small frontage onto the park, but the premises are surprisingly deep. I would have thought Colin would enjoy asking his girl friends around to have a swim... in their bikinis."

The word 'jacuzzi' had turbo charged Colin's imagination, and thereby paralysed his brain. However, his other bits were still working and picked up on the bikini word. "Let's take a look at that house first. Can we change our mind later?"

"Let me propose this. You people take this briefcase. In here you will find the keys." He jangled a large set of door keys. "Take a look at the premises and if you all decide to stay then you can move in with your new identities and we will discuss your next job. The paperwork is unsigned, but if you find a lawyer, he'll be able to check the fidelity of the deal. If, however, you decide to take the money then I shall arrange that, but it is an all-or-none proposition. If you choose Richmond, you will be working for me."

"Wot about the safe?"

"Keep it until you decide. I shall give you a week. Is that enough time?"

They all murmured their assent.

"Good. And here is a mobile phone. My number is on the speed dial. Call me if you have any questions, but please do not use it for any other purpose. Remember to look after the safe. And please, next time, no more abandoned warehouses. Now, may I enquire as to how I can leave this... man trap?" He placed a phone on top of the case.

"It ain't abandoned. We had to hire this place for a fucking month. Can we pass on the invoice to you?"

Malik paused, then sighed. "Oh, very well. But please, no more... 'dramatics'."

"And no more gunned-up goons when you come visiting. Yeh? Makes us nervous."

He nodded. "I am getting that message," he whispered wryly.

Caffee walked to the rear of the container and pushed open a door. The warehouse lights were already on and Malik stepped through.

Colin and Barry watched from a small office in the roof. They saw him leave the warehouse and approach the Range Rover. One of his bodyguards started to pat the dust off Malik's Armani. Malik batted his arms away and for a couple of seconds the two were amused by the sight of Malik and his bodyguard batting at each other like mad March hares. Then Malik's face dropped as he realised he had to sit on the Rover's immaculate leather seats.

"Cup of tea anyone?" asked Mam from the floor below, relieved it was all over.

"STAND STILL!"

From the shadows emerged a man dressed in a dirty raincoat. In his hand was a gun with a silencer. Caffee, Mam, and Norman slowly turned to face the new threat.

This had *not* been planned for.

37
The Hunter, The Fool

"Where are the others?"

"What?"

"The others! Where are they?"

Caffee shrugged as she tried to figure out if he was serious, or just some wally with a water pistol.

"Where is the other one? The brunette. Where is she?"

"Who are you?"

"The man with a fucking gun, bitch! *Where's* the other girl?"

"Who?"

"Don't fuck with me. I've got a gun! Where is she?"

"What other gel?"

"Don't you *fuck* with me, bitch! I'll shoot your fucking face. Move closer together, all of you."

Caffee glanced across at Norman who took a step away and slightly towards the gunman. Caffee followed suit.

Barry had climbed down the ladder from the upstairs office and now paused unnoticed in the shadows behind the man. He was puzzled at the scene before him. Was this part of Adrian's plan he'd forgotten about?

"I said *closer*. Move closer together, you morons! I've got a gun here. It's real. I'll shoot the black woman's face off if you don't do as I say. Now move together! Closer! Get closer!" Terry was not feeling as in control of the situation as he should. He waved the gun from side to side trying to cover both Caffee and Norman.

Norman spoke gently. "I do not know who you are, but this is not a TV show. This is real life. Just because you have a gun, does not mean we'll do what you say."

Terry took a step back and pointed the weapon at Norman. "Yeh? Oh *really*? You stand fucking still, or I'll pop you, grandad. Don't you believe me? You'll do as I fucking say or I'll fucking shoot you!"

Caffee took a step closer.

Barry stepped closer.

"Oh, yes." Norman nodded. "Yes, I believe you. But your gun is a small calibre weapon. A two-two, is it not? Not very powerful and that silencer looks homemade. It's big for such a small weapon. I think that, in order to kill someone, you'll need to be quite close and fire maybe... what? Three or four times? To make sure? You cannot guarantee a stopping-shot with that weapon. Not at this range." Norman glanced around. "And you are all alone, too? Tut, tut. You really *are* an amateur, aren't you?"

"Move closer together or I'll fucking shoot the black woman!" He held the gun up and sighted it at Mam, who stood wide-eyed and frozen to the spot.

In one deft movement Caffee flicked an ankle and a clog spun up in the air almost level with her face. In one fluid motion she snatched it out of the air and threw it hard at Terry's head. He almost managed to avoid it. It struck the outside of his right eye splitting the skin and knocking his head back a few inches.

That spurred Barry to take the final few steps. One hand grabbed the man's left wrist, the other grabbed his right forearm and he pulled them down hard. The gun went off with a crack. A spark and puff of dust kicked up from the floor narrowly missing Mam. It was followed a second later by the sound of the spent bullet pinging off something metallic and tumbling to the ground.

"Do not threaten Mam!" stated Barry.

The man raised a foot and stamped back against a shin, bringing a tear to Barry's eye but he did not even flinch, and the man's arms remained locked in Barry's vice-like grip. He tried again but Barry stood like a rock, pinning the man's arms.

Norman walked up to the gunman and looked into his eyes. "Thank God for TV."

Colin emerged from the same shadow as Barry. In one hand he held Caffee's clog while he nursed a bruise on his forehead. He walked over to Caffee and handed it to her before assisting Mam who was visibly shaking, clutching at her chest and groping for the chair in shock.

The gunman made a lunge then swung his foot up toward Norman's crotch. Norman deftly backstepped, grabbed the back of the man's ankle and lifted it even higher.

"Thank you," he responded. He removed the shoe and sock before examining the foot a little. "Are you ticklish?" But he let the foot fall. "You really should trim those toenails. And the other one?" He beckoned for the man to try to kick him with the other foot.

"*Fuck off*!" Fear and desperation were evident in

Terry's face.

Caffee, happy that Mam hadn't been hit, and now re-armed with both clogs, clumped toward the trio. "Aren't you going to get his gun from this prick?"

Norman shook his head. "No reason to, my dear. This fool thinks it makes him dangerous while at the same time Barry keeps it held safely pointing at the floor. Are you alright, Barry?"

Barry nodded, a tear in his eye. "He was going to hurt Mam."

"Yes," nodded Norman. "Thank you, Barry. You saved us from this nasty man." He turned to the would-be gunman. "You *are* a naughty man, aren't you?"

Terry snarled and tried to spit at Norman.

Caffee gently pushed Norman to one side.

"What are you going to do?" asked Norman.

"One to his bollocks, one to his sorry plexus, and one to rearrange his snotter!" She drew back a leg, but paused when Norman placed a hand on her shoulder.

"Not yet, my dear. Not if he tells us why he wants the brunette."

"What? Who? Helen?"

Norman sighed.

"What the fuck do you want with Helen? You mother-fucking..."

Norman stopped her again. "Not yet, Caffee. Not yet."

Terry noticed the size of Caffee's clogs and re-evaluated his position.

"It wasn't me. She's wanted for questioning by my employer. For that murder. I was supposed to convince her to go back." Terry glanced at them. Which one of these had held Hughes down while they thrust a hook into his back? It must be the older man or, more likely, the muscle standing behind him pinning his arms in place.

"...with an unlicensed gun? Unlikely, I think."

"Well, maybe that was a mistake. I admit it. My boss wanted me to ask her a few questions, that's all. I thought you might object." If he could convince this gang that he was only interested in her, then maybe they'd let him off with a warning. "I'm only doing my job. Just a few questions and I'll be gone."

"...and you said you'll blow Mam's face off? With a two-two? Just to ask a few questions? You didn't think to ask politely first?"

"Oh, come on. You can see my position, can't you? There's a lot of you against just me. You can see it from my point of view, can't you? I wasn't really going to shoot the woman."

"Of course. Which is why you came visiting us with a gun. To *not* use it on us. Why should I disbelieve you? I'm sure Mam feels most re-assured with your... assurances."

Terry sensed his appeals to reason weren't working. "Fuck it! Let me go or my boss will come down here and rip your fucking arms off. He's not one to be messed with. He'll kill the lot of you if he has to. He's like that. He's a fucking maniac. You don't kill one of his boys without him taking retribution. Believe me. He'll fucking mess you up *real* bad. You go back to Doncaster and you're dead meat. All of you! Let me go and I'll tell him you're going somewhere else. He'll leave you alone if you leave Doncaster alone. It's your only chance. I can tell him that."

"A fucking maniac from Doncaster? Thank you. You've just told us why we *shouldn't* let you go. Caffee?"

Norman took a step back and Caffee swung her leg three times. The second time Norman thought he heard a cracking sound. The final time they all heard the crunching sound. Even from where he stood, the sound made Colin feel queasy. Norman took out a handkerchief and retrieved the gun from the man's, now limp, hand and suggested Barry let him fall. He did. Terry curled up into a foetal position on the floor, struggling to breathe and his head in a puddle of blood pouring from his misshapen nose.

"See to Mam." Norman smiled at Barry.

Barry limped away.

Norman leant over the prone body and rifled the man's pockets, searching all parts of his body. Once or twice his probing fingers caused the man to shout incoherently in pain. He pocketed keys, a mobile phone, money, and several other items including some printed photos and a hotel room keycard. The man started making a keening noise, his eyes closed, still struggling to calm his breathing.

Norman rose, handed the pictures to Caffee and casually walked back to the safe, lifted the mobile phone left by Malik and flipped it open.

"Ah, hello, Malik. It's Norman... Yes. It is rather soon, isn't it? I was wondering, in all good faith, you understand, if you could return here and help us tidy up some unexpected mess. We have had a visitor who wanted to spoil our party... Yes. A most unpleasant man. I don't know what he heard. Yes, he did see you, and everyone in fact. I was wondering if perhaps you have need of some... *body* that would be useful to take the blame for, well, for anything you have in mind really... No. He's not one of us. I think he was an echo from someone's past. Are you coming back here? Oh, excellent! I shall wait here for you. However, this time, contrary to what we said before, please *do* bring along your charming friends. See you soon. Cheerio, then."

Norman cut the call and looked at Colin. "You see what I mean about guns? So uncivilised. This rudeness is a sauce to his poor wit, which gives us men stomach to digest his words with better appetite."

Colin nodded, not really listening, only understanding that Caffee's moves had been really impressive for such a small girl. Norman also noted that the young man was shaking a little.

"I need you to help me. Now, let's find the duct tape and plastic sheets. Bin bags might do. I should hate to upset Malik by making his cars even *more* dirty. It's only polite, after all."

"Is he dead?"

"Good Lord, no! We aren't killers. Not exactly." He pondered a moment on the statement. "Most of us. He's just suffering a little... discomfort. Not so sick as he is troubled with Caffee's quick-coming fancies that shall keep him from rest."

Colin looked at Terry's face, eyes squeezed shut, the misshapen mess for a nose and the man's laboured breathing. "He threatened to kill us... he had a gun..."

"Yes. Stupid, wasn't he? In so *many* ways. All it took was that one misjudged act."

Barry, still limping, departed with Mam and Caffee. They left in the van, picking up Helen and Adrian on the way back to the house.

Ignoring his cries of agony, the two remaining men taped the man's wrists and legs and then wrapped him in plastic. Finally, they bound the entire package with duct tape and made sure he had a hole to breathe through. Then they waited for Malik to return.

Malik's expression stayed blank during the retelling of the account. Norman handed a plastic shopping bag containing the gun to one of the bodyguards.

"Colin, can you give the gentlemen a hand with the package?"

"What? The gunman?"

"Yes. Help them with it into one of the Rovers, would you?"

Norman held up a finger and whispered to Malik, "One moment..." and went to the back of the warehouse and came back with another plastic bag. He handed it over to Malik.

Malik peeked inside. It contained a bloody cloth and a kitchen knife.

"A little misdirection if you leave it with that gentleman's body." Malik raised an eyebrow. "It'll tie up another loose end for us." Norman winked.

Malik's entourage departed with the man safely

packed in the boot of a Range Rover.

Norman watched them depart.

"The gunman had a car near here, Colin. Put on some gloves and park it in a side road, would you? Check the boot then leave the keys in it for the locals to enjoy. I fancy a walk home. It should clear my head some." He handed Colin the car keys. "Try not to get caught. That would be awkward." He grinned and Colin nodded. The walk would do him good, and there was Terry's hotel room to investigate too. He would rather do that without Colin there. What he found, if anything, might tell him a little more about Helen.

Inside the Range Rover, the man in the dusty blue Armani made a call and pressed the scramble button.

"Hello, Faisal? It's Jamal. Peace be with you and your family. How is your mother this day?"

He watched the scenery pass the car's tinted rear window as he listened to the phone.

"I am so sorry to hear that, Faisal. But I am calling because I have some good news. I have identified suitable scapegoats for the robbery. A gang who fit the profile quite nicely. Yes... And my new team have just acquired a suitable source of information. I have it in my possession as we speak. These new employees of mine are most diligent, are they not?"

- "It is a simple plan. I propose to send some of my men, two teams perhaps, to a town called Doncaster. They will masquerade as criminals from Eastern Europe. I shall instruct them to eliminate the Doncaster gangsters and, let us say, 'rescue' the heirlooms intact from their criminal clutches. The authorities will never need to be involved, for them it will appear just like another gang war. As for us, we shall be seen as heroes, shall we not?"

- "Yes Faisal, and the wedding will still be cancelled? Excellent. And the insurance?"

- "Well, I am sure we can wait a few months, can we not? The heirlooms are still in a safe place. I have seen them. I shall be returning them to you in about a week. Is this to your liking?"

- "I am so glad to be of service. We shall speak further on this matter soon. With peace, my friend."

He hung up, pleased with himself. Some loose ends were being tied up quite neatly. Very neatly, in fact. Then he pondered on the bloodstained cloth and the kitchen knife. Something else had happened of which he was unaware, but the older man had clearly taken care of it. He instinctively trusted the older man. He knew he shouldn't, not after reading his file, but he considered himself a good judge of character and this ex-officer had stuck by his colleague. Even to the point of sacrificing his life.

He looked down at his shoes and noticed the dirt and dust from the warehouse. In Russian he instructed the driver to have both the Range Rovers thoroughly cleaned and made a mental note to dress down the next time he visited this filthy gang of kafir.

Deal with dirt, and one gets dirty, he thought wryly.

38
The Richmond Ruffians

Mam was allowed the privilege of entering the house first. She opened the large ornate door and stepped over the threshold and wiped her feet on the old doormat. It was almost as if the house demanded it, but in a polite sort of way. The floorboards creaked reassuringly, and she could sense a pleasant scent, or perhaps an aura, which she found comforting. Thick carpets helped to deaden the sounds of the street behind, and the house felt warm. She looked around and immediately fell in love with the Georgian, or at least Georgian-ish, decor. More important to her was that everything was clean, unbroken, and most of it seemed to match. She opened the door to the front reception room and took in the fireplace, carpets, and settee.

To think that she might be spending Christmas here with Barry, Norman, and the others brought a tear to her eye.

And it didn't need vacuuming... yet.

Norman followed and was most happy at the sight. A large oil painting of Victorian gentleman wearing a monocle hung by the stairs and he made a note to try and find out who the good fellow was. A short walk to the second reception/dining room where he opened the door. The first thing he noticed was the wine rack. He refrained from inspecting the bottles and scanned the decor, the chairs, and the large dining table.

He frowned. Adrian must *never* be allowed to demonstrate his safe-melting concoctions in here.

Colin was next through the front door. As soon as Norman entered the dining room, he made a beeline through the hall, the kitchen, and out towards the back.

Helen went straight upstairs, unsure of who would be able to claim which bedroom. She wasn't overly concerned which one was to be hers, but she wanted to make sure that, wherever she was, it was suitable.

A cursory glance in every room satisfied her. They were all well decorated. Each had a different colour combination and, at least in her eyes, were all tastefully done. One particular room on the top floor took her fancy. The bed was made of old wood and seemed wider than a single but not as wide as a double. Cozy, she thought, and made her mind up. This was to be hers.

Barry, still limping, followed Mam into the living room and found the TV remote. He sat in one of the two upholstered chairs with wings. The room was warm. He smiled at Mam. He was happy.

Caffee led Adrian in and stopped just inside the front door. She glanced around.

"Cor! Posh, innit!" She peeked in the living room and squidged her nose. "Mam. You don't fink this is gonna be a bit too posh for us, do yuh?"

Mam shook her head. "No, girl. Not at all. Did you wipe your shoes?"

Caffee nodded. Living here was going to mean

adding a few new house rules. She stepped back to the hall and wiped her feet.

Adrian was already happy with the house. To show it he danced his crazy rain dance on the doormat with Caffee. They laughed a bit before she guided him up the stairs to find him a room.

On the way upstairs he stopped and pointed at an ornate clock on the wall.

"Clock!" he exclaimed.

"Tick tock!" replied Caffee, and they both giggled.

For a full fifteen minutes they all (except for Adrian) wandered the house, poking their noses into cupboards and opening and closing drawers. The question as to whether they should stay or not was never asked. They didn't need to.

At the end of the fifteen minutes, they had all decided which of the six bedrooms belonged to which of the family. The larger rooms were given to the nominal parents, Mam and Norman. Helen got the room she wanted. Barry's room was beside Mam's.

Only Colin was omitted from the list, but they decided he could sleep in one of the basement rooms, near the games room. They were sure he'd prefer that and when it was discussed later, he assured them he did. The idea of being apart from the others appealed to him, it would give him a little more freedom. Bedding and other stuff would have to be arranged but they still had a few thousand in the kitty.

Adrian's room was the smallest one on the top floor – even so, it had its own chair and wardrobe. It had the smallest window (for safety reasons) but he was delighted. The wallpaper was a complex pattern of vines and flowers. This pattern almost matched his duvet. He was entranced and started plotting the detail immediately, completely oblivious to Caffee's questions as to whether he wanted to see the rest of the house. She left him in peace and clumped around from room to room.

By the end of the week there were only a few days remaining until Christmas. The safe was collected from the warehouse by one of Malik's Range Rover teams of monochrome men. None of them spoke English so Caffee's sarcasm went unnoticed – much to her frustration. They opened it and confirmed the contents against photographs and a list before they departed.

None of the Gunnersbury Gang ever did see what was inside.

They had moved into the house that same evening. Arriving late in the old van the rest of the family decided on a takeaway Indian from the local restaurant. Finally, Norman got to inspect the wine rack, the contents of which he fully approved.

After dinner each member was allocated a thousand pounds from the kitty. The idea was that they could go shopping and buy whatever they wanted in the morning while Norman and Colin oversaw the locksmith and alarm company change the security setup. They weren't taking any chances of losing this Christmas in a real home.

Norman, who had always looked after Adrian's financial interests, promised to deposit Adrian's share into Adrian's savings account at the first opportunity.

It was approaching eleven in the evening. The family were all sitting in chairs or on settees around the crackling fire in the living room. Caffee had managed to get one bean bag, the cleanest, into the room but she could already sense Mam's disapproval. It didn't match the decor. She'd have to take it upstairs when she went to bed.

The Indian meal had been excellent. They were happy. With any luck they'd keep the roof over their heads during the coming winter nights. Although... when the money from the Esher job ran out who knew what would happen? Until then...

At the evening's end Helen took Adrian upstairs followed by Barry and Mam. Colin, Norman, and Caffee remained downstairs.

"Ain't life crazy," she mused.

"What fates impose, that men must needs abide. My boots cannot resist both wind and tide."

Caffee glanced at Norman's feet.

"You need new socks," she observed. One was maroon, the other navy blue. A big toe was peeping out of one, and the heels of both were worn through.

"Indeed. I shall spend my allowance on such practicalities."

"It's funny, aint it? A few weeks back we was living in some old biddy's place scrounging for work. Then we robbed a bank, nicked some jewels, and now we're here in a posh house employed by a foreigner to do fuck knows what."

"Tax free, no doubt. One of the many benefits of

such a corporate enterprise."

"But we make a good team, yeh?"

"Indeed."

"Except we're crooks though. Funny that. I never fort I'd ever rob a bleeding bank."

"Political – a word meaning many tickles. Many ticklish ironies. The government says that we're all in this together, pretending to be on our team. But in truth they're on one team, and we're on our own."

"Yeh." Caffee nodded, not understanding. This was becoming too deep for her. She was tired. "I'm off to bed." She got up and hoisted her bean bag over a shoulder.

"And I shall follow you, oh sweet mistress of sleep. Lead on!" Norman rose and followed her out the living room door.

"'Ere watch it, you old perve! You're going to your own room. Unnerstand?"

Norman sighed. "Of course. Of course. That's what I meant. Lead on."

"No, no, no, no, no, no, no. You go first, gitface! You just wanna see up my skirt, dontchya? Aye? You dirty old letch."

"Caffee dear, when you sprawl on that bean bag, we can *all* see up your skirt. It is most disconcert..."

"You dirty ol' git...!"

Colin fancied he could almost hear Caffee's cheeky grin. He listened to the two bickering as they closed the door. He couldn't help but smile.

"I did not mean..." protested Norman.

"You're a worse perve than Colin... 'Ere! What you pushin' in front of me for? Ladies go first, dog breff..."

"And where pray, *is* this lady you speak of?"

Colin continued to listen as their voices faded.

"Wassat? Wotchew mean... 'Ere! Stop following me so close, you wrinkly old scrote. You're looking at my bum again, aintchya?"

"Oh, Dear Lord, save this poor soul."

"Wot you got your 'ands over yer eyes for? I ain't that bad, am I?"

"You just said..."

"I know wot I fuckin' said, Mister Wrinkly. But you don't have to *insult* a gel too."

Colin had recorded a football match earlier. Finally, it was time he could watch it in peace. He grabbed the remote and pressed play, turning up the TV a little but keeping the sound very low.

At about half time, while he was watching the adverts, Helen poked her head around the door.

"Hi," she smiled sheepishly.

"Hi."

She paused feeling a little uncertain, then came into the lounge. Colin did a double take. She was wearing a top which only just reached down to the top of her thighs, and he couldn't *quite* tell if there was anything underneath.

"Mind if I sit?"

Colin, now befuddled, could only shake his head. She sat on his lap, put an arm around his shoulders and kissed him full on the lips. After a few seconds of utter paralysis, he returned her kiss.

After a while they broke apart, both slightly

breathless. She whispered, "Do you want to come upstairs to my room?"

It took nearly three seconds before he realised, he had actually heard her correctly. He could only nod then cautionary flashbacks caused him to hesitate. It was to be *her* room, not his. With a real bed, not a sleeping bag on a wooden floor. This time there was no hot tea for him to spill, no pets to tread on, no leering lads with lager cans egging her on – and she wasn't trussed up in a bulletproof leotard either. This *might* be a prank – but probably not. He could catch up on the game later. Was this finally the moment? His moment?

She stood, spun on her heel and disappeared out the door in one flowing dance-like movement. He could have sworn he caught a glimpse of... under the...

At first his lower brain took control and he ran out the room to the stairs to follow her. Then his proper brain regained control and he swore, ran back, and replaced his can of beer onto the table. The two brains struggled. He ran out again – only to remember the lights. The third time he remembered the TV, but this time he checked around the room carefully, before closing the door and dashing for the stairs.

He stubbed his toe on the first step, swore and fell forward banging his knee. He grabbed his foot, swore again and looked up. She was there, on the landing, watching him and giggling at his clumsy antics. She spun again – and again he thought he caught a glimpse of...

As far as the lovemaking went, it wasn't exactly an erotic explosion of 'Earth-Shattering Fireworks'. It wasn't even a slow, gentle, and romantic dance through the gates of heaven and back. But it wasn't a total disaster, either. It was something both of them would remember for the rest of their lives – although each would remember the details somewhat differently.

Afterwards, they held each other close for several minutes. His arms wrapped around her and she facing away; their arms and legs intertwined. He felt the warmth of her naked body against his and couldn't believe it. This situation usually occurred in someone else's life, or on TV, or maybe in a daydream he'd concoct when he was alone. This was unreal, not the sort of thing that happened to the likes of him. This was something that had gone *right* for once. He cuddled up to her more tightly, and kissed her on the nape of her neck, not wanting to let the moment pass or to let her go.

But something kept nagging at him.

"That man..." he whispered. "The one we wrapped up and gave to Malik. He was from Doncaster."

She didn't respond.

"He said some nasty things... about you."

"That I chopped off that man's... thingy, and stuck it down his throat?"

Colin eyes snapped open. He realised he was in dangerous water. Any moment she could kick him out of bed, but he needed to know.

"No... not exactly."

She turned onto her back to face him. "It wasn't like that," she explained. "I was walking home when

335

I heard a shout. I walked into the warehouse and I saw this old man with his trousers around his feet... and he was trying to stick... he was going to rape this young boy." She paused.

"I called out and he saw me. The boy wriggled free and disappeared but the man came after me with a knife. I went to run out the door but it had shut, so I climbed up onto these big, really big metal shelves. Silly, really. He started climbing up behind me so I kicked out, again, and again. A hook... a big hook broke free from... I don't know, a bracket or something on the wall. It was on a cable to the ceiling and it swung away. He kept climbing up so I kicked again and some metal sheets came down from just above my head and nearly chopped off his nose.

"I guess they chopped... anyway, he screamed. I remember him screaming but he still kept holding on to the shelf. He was looking right at me. It was horrible."

She paused again before continuing. "While he was staring at me, not moving, the hook swung back and hit him... hard. It pushed him right against the shelves and then it pulled him away. It had stuck itself into his back, you know? I didn't know what to do. I watched him swing for a few times. He had stopped screaming by then... before I climbed down.

"I... I found his... thing on the floor. The metal sheets must have chopped it off. I don't know why, I thought maybe they could sew it back on or something. I went over to hand it to him – he'd stopped swinging and was hanging in the middle of the warehouse, unable to move. I asked him if he wanted it back, but he was rude to me, he called me a... well, he was very rude anyway. So, I put it in his dirty mouth and ran out the other door."

Again, she paused for a moment. Then, "I was scared that the police wouldn't believe me."

"Why not?"

"Not after... Well I had, you know... They weren't happy. I just thought... They might not believe me *this* time. You know what the police are like. Questions, questions..."

"Yeh. Yeh, I know." Colin knew all too well. Those nosy bastards always seemed to know what questions he didn't want them to ask. She looked at him with big eyes and they kissed.

"You do believe me, don't you?"

"Yeh. Of course, I do. It must have been horrible. He deserved it."

She smiled, then nodded.

"Didn't you want to tell... you know, your boyfriend?"

"No. No, Colin. I've only had two boyfriends. But they didn't last long. Neither of them made me laugh. Not like you. So, I dumped them. It was their fault. They deserved it. They didn't make me laugh. You make me laugh, though. Promise me, promise me you'll always make me laugh."

"I promise." He gave her a squeeze and thought again how lucky he was to have landed Helen. She may not be a ten, but she could be a nine, definitely an eight though. Certainly not less. He felt privileged to hold her. Her story sounded plausible too.

Well, he decided, plausible enough. He started to nibble her ear.

"Mmm, Colin?"

"Mmm?"

Her hand snaked under her pillow and she felt the reassuring handle of the kitchen knife.

"Do you know where the nearest dump *is*, around here?"

39
Victim of The Donkey Dicker

The officer from HM Security Service sighed feeling a little out of place. He preferred to stand before the dark mahogany reception desk, complete with a brass bell and visitors' book, with his coat draped over his arm while waiting in the small, but surprisingly plush, reception area of the Royal Navy Support Executive. He was conscious of being watched by at least one video camera and the two men guarding the entrance.

He had never been here before and idly wondered what shenanigans this little agency got up to. Until this morning he'd never even heard of it. He stepped past an old worn Victorian chair towards the window and looked out. The people outside were mainly tourists, probably lost or wandering aimlessly. None of them noticed him behind the glass.

The elder doorman opened the door at the rear with a noticeable 'clunk' as he turned the handle.

"Room one-one-two on the first floor," he called out. "It's signed for Doctor Fitzgerald."

What? No escort? After thanking the man, he made his way out the back and then up to the office. Like Evans before him, he eschewed the lift preferring to run up the stairs two at a time. He was met at the office door by a short, anxious man with dark-rimmed glasses, balding but with thick curly hair around the sides.

"You must be Mister Cleary. Come in. Come in."

"Thank you. You are Doctor Fitzgerald?"

"Yes. Yes, I am. So, what brings The Security Service here? Can I get you a cup of tea?"

The officer entered the office and scanned it, more out of curiosity than, as they liked to call it, 'Situation Awareness'. He hung his coat on a coat hook and saw the interview chair.

"No tea, thank you. May I?"

"Yes. Yes, of course make yourself at home."

Cleary waited until the doctor had sat down behind his desk. "I understand that Lieutenant Commander Evans, the man you reported missing, was attached to you. Was it a temporary assignment?"

"Yes. He was assigned to us. I explained all this when I reported his absence."

"May I ask as to the nature of his duties?" Cleary removed a notepad and pencil from his jacket. The doctor noted he was acting much more like a policeman than an agent.

"He was assisting us in arranging a test programme. He was assigned some of the non-scientific tasks. Arranging deliveries, liaison with members of the public, that sort of thing. I can't offer any more details, I'm afraid. Security. You understand?" Feeling a little smug.

"He was a bit senior to be acting as an errand boy, wasn't he?"

"There was more to it than that. We needed his

experience."

There was a pause before Cleary continued.

"I'm afraid to have to inform you that Lieutenant Commander Evans' body was found this morning. He was found in Epping Forest, south of a town called Harlow. Can you tell me if any of his work has a potential national security issue?"

"That would already be documented, if it was. No. No major secrets here." The doctor removed his glasses and pinched the top of his nose as his mind raced. "As I've already made clear, he was not involved in anything serious. Our more delicate operations are handled by other staff."

"Do you know of any reason why anyone would want him dead?"

"He wasn't party to any classified material, if that's what you're asking."

Cleary sized up the doctor's response. He was nervous, he was thinking hard, but this was a shock to him. It was unexpected. Besides, this department hadn't featured on any security bulletins for years. If there was a security issue someone at a higher pay grade than him would have mentioned it. Nevertheless, he decided to press a little further.

"There's no target agency? Foreign or otherwise, related to his activities?"

"What do you mean?"

"His work. It wasn't a threat to someone? He wasn't investigating anyone?"

"No. No, nothing like that. I can assure you our work here is pretty mundane. I can see no reason why he would have been killed." But inwardly he thought, 'It was Leicester! Ex SBS. A trained killer, and still intent upon defending Adrian Channel. The bastard.'

Fitzgerald needed a reason to deflect this agent's questioning. Too much probing in the wrong direction and all his work would surface to official scrutiny. That could lead to a complete departmental review. His previous treatment of Adrian would be called into question and the entire project would be set back months. If not years. He was at the cutting edge of science. He couldn't let that happen.

"Although…"

Cleary raised an eyebrow.

"I understand his personal life was a little… interesting. He liked the ladies. I don't suppose…?"

Cleary nodded. "Yes, we know. We're looking at that side of things too."

"Oh, good. How was he killed?"

Cleary noted the question. "He was strangled with a garrotte, or wire, several days ago, roughly the same time you notified us of his disappearance. Then his body was transported to the forest, mutilated and then hidden."

"Mutilated?"

"His penis was amputated."

"Oh, dear! That doesn't sound professional, does it? Why would anyone…?"

Cleary extracted some photographs from his jacket and leaned forward, placing them face up in front of the doctor.

"Have you ever seen this man before?"

"No. Never. Who is he?"

"The police think the murder is the work of the 'The Donkey Dicker'. This man here." He tapped the pictures. "That's their unofficial name for the Doncaster Murderer, the one in the news. They found him tortured and drowned in the Thames three days ago. He's been identified as Terence Arthur Burnley from Doncaster. A debt collector, by all accounts. A gang enforcer. There is evidence that he was involved in the death of Lieutenant Commander Evans. Did Evans ever go to Doncaster at all?"

"No." Fitzgerald, surprised, shook his head. "Not as far as I know."

"Was he in debt?"

Fitzgerald shrugged.

Cleary gathered the photos and sat back. "It looks like Lieutenant Commander Evans is the victim of the Doncaster Murderer. Although why he should come down to London and pick on Evans..."

Fitzgerald shrugged again. Inwardly he felt much happier. It seemed like they'd found their scapegoat, and he was not talking.

Norman Leicester was either a very lucky man, or a very clever one. Either way, this wasn't over. He still needed Adrian. He needed that biopsy.

He needed another plan.

40
Pummelled Carrots

It was a cold, black night in Richmond. Outside the police car were the bright lights, silhouetted revellers, and the pitter-patter of the stinging, intermittent rain. The swish-swish of the windscreen wipers seemed to be louder than usual.

"Only on Christmas fucking Eve..." The uniformed driver swore quietly while squinting between the hesitant wipers as he tried to edge the car between the rows of tightly parked cars. He approached the small park while at the same time making sure he avoided the drunks.

His partner in the passenger seat spoke into his shoulder radio. "Tango Two Five on scene, Richmond Common."

The police car felt claustrophobic even though there were only the two officers in the front. It was the high visibility jackets, thick uniforms and caps which seemed to fill up the interior. The rain had paused but the intermittent swish of the wipers, the shushing of the tyres on the rain-soaked road, and the black midnight sky altogether made the vehicle feel even smaller, and damper, than it was.

The tinny voice from the radio replied. "Tango Two Five, look for two males on the green. Reports have them using hammers to attack someone. Approach with extreme caution. Tango One Seven is en route. Please keep us updated."

The driver was cautiously moving the vehicle

forward peering for runners. He drove past some Christmas revellers peering at them closely, but they were not coming from the green. He elected to keep the flashing lights and sirens off as he got closer. He wanted to catch these bastards.

"There they are." He put his foot down and the vehicle accelerated quickly towards the two men.

The passenger spoke into the radio. "Tango Two Five. We see them. When do we get our backup?"

"Tango One Seven will be with you... within five." Christmas Eve was always a busy time for the police, nevertheless the other backup would soon be here.

"There!"

Even before the car had stopped, the passenger had opened the door and was out and running toward the thugs on the green. The driver killed the engine, left the headlights and video camera on and ran after his colleague. Both had seen one of them swinging a hammer up and down. Whoever was underneath must be a bloody pulp by now.

Both officers involuntarily slowed as they approached, their breath steaming in the freezing air and just the faint hint of rain making everything feel clammy and cold. Neither wanted to witness the horror lying ahead of them.

The man swinging the hammer, an older man in his mid-fifties, saw the approaching officers. He stood up, smiling and waved the hammer at them.

"Good evening, officers! Merry Christmas."

The senior constable stopped and put one hand out, the other grasped his pepper spray. "Put that down, please."

"What?"

"The hammer, sir. Slowly. Put it down, on the ground. Now!"

"What? Oh! Of course. Yes, of course." He held the hammer at arm's length and in an exaggerated movement slowly laid it on the muddy common.

The other man, a bloody big Nigerian, thought the officer, was on a pogo-stick, or something that looked similar. He got off and laid it down and walked towards the officers. There was nothing threatening about either of them, but the senior constable kept his hand on the spray, just in case. Something was really strange here.

"Stand still. Stand where you are." The two suspects complied. Both men looked completely relaxed, if a little tired. In the half-light and shadows of the streetlamps he couldn't make out what was on the ground. Had the victim been mashed into something unrecognisable? He took out his torch and switched it on, checking the ground where the older man had been smashing away with the hammer.

"What's that?"

"Carrots, dear boy," the older man offered. "For the deer."

"Carrots?" He squinted. Sure enough, it did look like mashed vegetable matter and a large half-empty pack of... carrots. "Carrots?"

"For the deer."

He flashed the torch in the two men's faces. Both were still relaxed. The Nigerian was grinning from ear to ear but said nothing.

He looked back at the pummelled turf. "Carrots?" he repeated. "May I ask why?"

"For our neighbour."

"You're beating a bag of carrots..." He paused. "...on Richmond Green... at midnight... with a hammer... for your neighbour?" These idiots must be on drugs, he thought. He peered at the older man in the eye. "Please tell me, sir. What did these poor, innocent vegetables do to you to warrant such retribution?"

His partner, standing to one side, sniggered.

The older man laughed. "No. Nothing like that, dear boy. It's all completely innocent, I can assure you. We just needed to make sure Santa had arrived. At Christmas I no more desire a rose, than wish a snow in May's new-fangled shows, but Santa's deer's love of each carrot grows. It's for Christmas, you see?"

The officer flashed the torch at both men again. Then pointed his blank expression at the older man again. "No, sir. I fail to see. Pray, enlighten me." Then he frowned, dismayed that he'd just made a pantomime-style rhyme.

The older man went to approach the officer but stopped when the officer held up his hand again. "From where you're standing, if you don't mind, sir."

"Quite." The older man pointed to one of the houses with lights on. "My name is Norman Winchester Haine Le Burgulian. I live in that wonderful abode over there together with this gentleman, Barry. Barry Mandizvidza."

Barry smiled and waved at the two policemen.

"Our neighbour, who lives in that house next

door, has a delightful young lad of six years. He is *frightfully* intelligent. A wonderful young man. Do you know, he understands the difference between Newtonian and Einsteinian physics already? Remarkable, don't you think?"

The officer didn't know what Newtonian and Einsteinian physics was but was prepared to accept that it must be remarkable. His face remained impassive.

"Hmm. Anyway, he's already ascertained that, just like God, Father Christmas doesn't exist. He's discovered his Christmas presents in his parents' bedroom and he's watched all the cartoons. He has come to the conclusion that if no one can represent Father Christmas in the same way, and if his presents have already been bought by his parents, then dear old Santa Claus must just be a myth. Furthermore, the little tyke pointed out that Santa's sled couldn't possibly land on the roofs here, thus proving it must all be just, well..." Norman shrugged. "...make-believe."

The light was beginning to dawn in the policeman's mind.

"So, as adults, and with full collusion of the child's parents, we reserve the right to screw around the young lad's intellect and manufacture Santa's landing place - here. Right here. In this spot."

The officer breathed out, only now realising he had been holding his breath. He relaxed, nodding slowly.

Norman continued. "Santa's sled, and no less than eight reindeer would take up, what... close to forty feet, you know? The lad will figure that out, I'm sure. So, we have to make the tracks on the common here. Then his parents will explain how Santa magically moves through the houses leaving presents. It did mean we had to re-wrap them but in the end, if we can get the young lad to believe that Santa really *did* land here, well then, that would be *our* Christmas made. Don't you agree?"

The policeman glanced at his partner who shrugged. "And you're beating the crap out of those carrots because...?"

"Reindeer, dear boy. They were fed here. They get very hungry, don't you know? All that flying takes a lot of calories. There's eight of them. Dasher, Dancer, Prancer, Vixen, Blitzen... Cupid, Comet... and the other one I can never remember his bloody name."

"Donna?"

"Indeed. Yes. Her too. Anyway, they all ate. Messy eaters, they are. They're in a hurry, after all. Mashed carrots should be enough to convince the lad, don't you think? Yes?"

"Not Rudolph?"

"Well, yes. We thought about him. But that would make nine of the buggers. Not sure of the size of that lot, forty feet is pretty long enough, you know? Fifty feet or so is starting to get, you know, *really* long. I'm not sure we have the space for them all between these trees. We decided Rudolph would take this year off. Perhaps he's rutting, or something."

"You can't leave out Rudolph. His nose lights up the way."

"Yes. Quite! I suppose so. Well, maybe Rudolph made Donna pregnant. Or something and she's the one at home. In the stable... with baby Jesus. That works, doesn't it? Anyway..." Norman flexed his arm. "I'm getting too old for this. My arm is aching."

"Do deer live in stables?" frowned the policeman. "Never mind." The officer flashed the torch at Barry. "And the pogo stick?"

"Adrian's idea. Quite ingenious, I thought. Show him, Barry."

Barry leant down and picked up the wooden pole and cross bar. The bottom was carved into the shape of a hoofprint.

"By jumping up and down on it we can make hoofprints, you see? They've got to be clustered right though, at the front here. Back there, under the tree you see the plank of wood and two bicycle wheels? Later, we'll run that back and forth to make the imprint of the sled's runners in the ground. Ingenious, yes? That should convince the little tyke."

The officer's hand left the pepper spray. "Have you been drinking, sir?"

"Yes. Of course, I bloody well have. It's Christmas Eve and it's cold, isn't it?"

Not an unreasonable answer under the circumstances, thought the officer. Should I charge this nutcase for being drunk while in charge of a hammer? Don't be silly. He knew the names of Santa's reindeer after all, although 'Donna' didn't sound quite right.

He approached Norman. "Breathe on me," he commanded.

Norman huffed at the policeman. "About four glasses of red," offered the older man. "Well, maybe eight, if I think on it," he confessed. "Or nine..."

The officer stood back. He did catch the strong whiff of wine. It all sounded very plausible. "You realise you are vandalising public property, sir." That felt lame even as he said it.

"Ah, but it *is* Christmas, officer. And a young lad's insanity is at stake."

He nodded and turned to his partner who by now was grinning. "Call it in."

The policeman reached up to his shoulder and pressed the button on his radio. "Tango Two Five."

"Tango Two Five, go ahead."

"We're on scene. No problem here. It's a misunderstanding. Just some locals trying to..." He thought for a moment. "...trying to create Santa's parking spot on the green."

"Tango Two Five, say again?"

"A couple of local residents making a parking spot for Santa's sleigh."

"Tango Two Five... a parking spot for what?"

He turned away and tried to explain the details to the dispatcher.

"Look, I know it's a bit of an indisposition, but I don't suppose you two could give us a quick hand, could you?" Norman asked. "It's cold out here, and the mud is awfully hard. Just a couple of minutes... for the lad...?"

Thirty seconds later the backup arrived.

"Tango One Seven. I'm just arriving on scene at Richmond Gree... what the fff...?" The sergeant couldn't believe his eyes.

"Tango One Seven, say again?"

The sergeant stopped the vehicle and got out. His passenger, a WPC, wasn't far behind. In front of him were his two fellow policemen. One was happily pummelling something on the ground with a hammer while the other was leaping on and off what looked like a pogo stick. Two other men seemed to be measuring the ground with a tape rule some feet behind them.

He pressed the switch on his radio. "Tango One Seven, stand by." He walked over to the small group and stood watching them for a moment with his hands on his hips.

"Not interrupting anything, am I?" he asked.

The constable on the pogo stick fell off and the other only narrowly missed hitting his thumb.

"Ahhh..." replied the constable with the hammer.

"That carrot resisting arrest, is it, Reeves?" He waited two seconds for a response, then... "You don't think you might be using excessive force, do you, Reeves? Even for a... carrot?"

Seven minutes later saw Barry pulling Norman and the four police officers sitting on the plank of wood on tyre-less cycle wheels. The resulting indentation looked pretty convincing. Just like the sort of indentation Santa's sled would make. They were all pleased with their deception.

At seven o'clock the following morning, Christmas Day, the sergeant was now thankfully off shift. He had gone home in time for his breakfast/supper – but mostly to see his two girls, Jess and Jen (aged four and six respectively) open their presents. But just before they opened them all he insisted they, and his wife, got dressed. He gave no explanation but insisted.

Once ready he bustled them into the car and drove them into Richmond. During the trip he explained that during the night he had had the opportunity to help no lesser person than Santa himself. Would his little darlings like to see where?

They stopped beside the green where he led them to see the evidence of Santa's sleigh. It was still dark, but the streetlights provided plenty of illumination.

He shone his torch at the ground. There were the hoofprints and the indents where the 'sleigh' had landed. Nearby a six-year-old boy was already there, dressed in spiderman pyjamas, wellington boots, and a thick anorak. He was pacing the ground measuring distances and looking very thoughtful.

Jen pointed at the mashed carrots. "What are those?"

"What do reindeer eat?"

"Bark," she replied, annoyingly knowledgeable about such things.

"And they like carrots, too." He winked at his wife.

The girls peered closer. "They're carrots!" squealed Jen. "He really *was* here!"

"Look! Hoofprints!"

"He really *was* here! He really *was* here!" Jen started jumping up and down.

"Which one was Rudolph?"

"The one in front on the right. Donna couldn't make it. She's pregnant." He glanced at his wife's questioning expression. "Apparently."

Jen stopped and screwed up her nose. "Who's Donna?"

From the lounge window across the road Norman, glass of wine in hand, stood in his bathrobe watching the little tyke examine the scene. Then the girls and their parents arrived and he smiled as they danced and jigged around in excitement. From a pocket he took out a silver-handled comb and read the inscription. 'For S.E. RN, Love J.L. XX' and wondered if it had ever really meant anything to the original owner. He combed his greying hair with it before returning it carefully to the pocket.

"Whatever deceives men seems to produce a magical enchantment," he whispered quietly. He raised his glass. He was to spend this Christmas in a warm house, with his friends and family.

The family of psychologically damaged bank robbers and jewel thieves.

The family he loved.

The family he'd kill for.

About the Author

Martyn lives in a small, quiet town in the Surrey Hills of England, called Godalming. The town was named after a local Saxon lord when house prices were a lot, lot lower. Martyn is a lightly bearded, 1950s vintage, ex-software development manager. He has written many short stories some of which have been published in the series of anthologies called **Godalming Tales** and **Tales from the Surrey Hills**.

His other main hobby is writing songs with his friend, Gordon Ayshford, and performing them on stage. They are the local duo known as Nightingale Road. They also arrange concerts and exhibitions for charity.

When he gets philosophical, Martyn likes to muse on the fact that we all live together on the crust of an itsy-bitsy ball of molten rock while it whizzes around a deadly nuclear fireball. Yet, despite this fact, few of us have yet to fall off. Sometimes, at night, he looks up into the sky and hopes that there's nothing out there intent on bumping into us. And there's a *lot* of stuff out there.

Meanwhile, oblivious to the fragility of our existence, we are busy poisoning our home and squabbling amongst ourselves for reasons that he completely fails to understand.

Also by Martyn MacDonald Adams

Steaming Up Series (Hardback)

ISBN	Book Title	Year
978-1-7396924-0-7	Michael and the Psycho	2024
978-1-7396924-1-4	Officer and the Killer	2024
978-1-7396924-2-1	Gentleman and his Bodyguard	2024
978-1-7396924-3-8	Prisoner and the Pirate	2024

The Furricious Gang of Godalming (Paperback)

ISBN	Book Title	Year
978-1-7396924-5-2	The Furricious Gang Book 1	2022
978-1-7396924-6-9	The Furricious Gang Book 2	2022
978-1-7396924-7-6	The Furricious Gang Book 3	2022
979-8-3231270-4-7	The Furricious Gang of Godalming*	2024

The collection of stories from Furricious Gang Books 1, 2, and 3

Author's website

https://www.martynadams.info/